Shade

Michelle Traver

For my father:

I still miss you every day.

Chapter 1

He'd missed his check-in. She knew it before her eyes opened in the dark hotel room. Hoping she'd slept through it but certain she hadn't, she held up the cell phone in her gloved hand and thumbed on the display. Every hour for the past four, she'd received a text message that read: "3." This time, she saw no messages.

She slipped off the side of the bed and shouldered a knapsack on her way to the door. The peephole revealed an empty hallway. From memory, she dialed a number into the cell phone, sent a text message that read: "2" and walked out the door.

She listened for disruptions of the airflow in the corridor as she removed and pocketed the memory card from the phone. Once through the stairwell door, rubber-soled boots carried her soundlessly down the concrete steps. One flight down, she opened another door and dropped the body of the phone into a brass trash can.

On the ground floor, she cracked the door and stood listening. The automatic lobby doors slid open, and she edged back. Two men in dark suits and quiet shoes blew in with a gust of air from the street. They hurried across the marble tile towards the reception desk, and her eyes picked out the telltale bulge of holsters beneath their jackets. Slipping out of the stairwell, she padded into the night before the doors closed.

One block down from the hotel, she turned the corner and stepped onto a waiting bus, dropping the memory card into a sewer opening. She had designed three exit strategies prior to checking into the hotel and knew that a bus stopped at this corner every fifteen minutes. Seating herself across from the rear doors, she dug another cell phone out of her knapsack. She accessed her email account and found a response to her text from "jonimitchell@bas.com" that said, "In the clouds." She rolled her eyes at the reference--Bas loved cheesy song lyrics. Since there was nothing more she could do, she shut down the phone and settled back to sleep.

"What do you mean they lost her? How do we know she was even there at all? Did anyone actually see her?"

Seated at the conference room table, Reid Amhers looked up as General Ratcliffe shoved the door open. His section leader, John Clemmons, was ushering the aging bureaucrat into the room. He was a big wide man, and judging from the veins throbbing in the man's forehead, his blood pressure was up. The General's bulk and demeanor added to the oppressive feel of the room.

Clemmons closed the door and delayed to adjust his tie and jacket. Clemmons looked like he might be silently cursing whoever had selected him to escort the blowhard. Reid saw two spots of color on the hollow cheeks of his sallow, acne-scarred, face. His brown eyes were bloodshot, but his black hair was combed to its usual perfection. Clemmons' promotion was recent, and he was still young for the kind of authority he possessed, but one of the perks ought to have been not drawing onerous duties like this one in the middle of the night.

Reid's wakeup call from Clemmons informed him that the General was acting as a liaison between the various military and governmental agencies of the alphabet soup that were involved in the present crisis, and they were to provide a briefing in their most professional manner.

Clemmons stalling tactic seemed to have bought him the time he needed. In his usual calm tone, he said, "No, General, no one ever sees her. She checked into the hotel using one of her known aliases."

"A known alias?" Ratcliffe twigged immediately. "Then she wanted to be found."

"Yes, General," Clemmons said.

As he seated himself, Clemmons made the introductions. "General Ratcliffe, this is Reid Amhers, our resident expert on Shade, and Judy Gunderson from his team. I'll turn the briefing over to them now."

Sitting beside Reid, Judy's leg was swinging under the table. Brunette, small, and plump, she hunched in her chair behind her laptop while she stole peeks at the General through thick glasses.

To his embarrassment, Reid had to shift his braced leg in order to offer his hand. The General froze when he spotted the cane hanging from the back of Reid's chair, revealing the psychology of a man who thought too much of physical strength and was uncomfortable when confronted with what he perceived as weakness.

A former enlisted man himself, Reid's legs had been shattered by an IED planted in his quarters, ending a promising career gathering intelligence in Iraq. His superiors had wasted no time converting him from an active role to passively receiving and sifting data. Since he would never walk unassisted again, he was grateful for the position.

As they shook, Reid noted a decrease in the man's blood pressure, an aversive eye-shift, and judging from the swallow, a nervous moistening in his mouth. It was an odd set of behaviors. Reid continued to study him, noting Judy's flinch as the General gave her the same crushing handclasp. Reid added physical domination to the profile he was assembling in his head.

Addressing Clemmons, the General said, "You called her 'Shade.'"

Reid met Clemmons' harried gaze, and receiving a nod, picked up the conversation. "Yes, General, since we have no idea what her real name is, we call her 'Shade.' It's her trade name. She has a subject identifier, but a long string of letters and numbers doesn't roll off the tongue well."

"And this woman is a thief," the General said, still on the offensive.

Reid felt a surge of proprietorial defensiveness and cleared his throat. "She is an accomplished cat burglar, sir, but not petty items like jewelry or artwork. We call it black bag work—the theft of information or items of importance. But that's only one aspect of the work she does. Her relevance to this briefing is her connection to one of the operatives who's been assisting us. An operative, as you know, who's just gone off the radar and may have been eliminated."

"You're talking about Peter Laurent. He's a former operative." The General put a slight emphasis on the word 'former.' "What's her connection to him?"

"Well, sir, for all intents and purposes, he's her father."

"There's no record of children, or even a wife, in Laurent's file," the General argued.

Clemmons inserted an adroit explanation. "From what we've been able to document, Laurent acquired both her and another child years ago and raised them clandestinely. He instructed both of them in the full extent of his own professional knowledge and also had them trained by other specialists. While it's true that he left active employment some decades ago, he's continued to accept contract work for various concerns, and he's deployed them in support of these activities. As you've been briefed, his services are not openly acknowledged."

"So, we're down to relying on two loose cannons? No one knows who they are or how to bring them in on this. And they were trained by him in God-knows-what. In the meantime, we've got a rising body count across agencies and governments, internationally. Who is the other person?"

Reid said, "Ready, Judy?"

Judy nudged her glasses up the bridge of her nose and then typed a sequence on her keyboard. The flat screen on the wall flashed to life. "This is Basilius Drake, also known as Bas," Judy narrated, accompanying a slideshow of a muscular, blond man, shown in armed encampments and using various weaponry. He was pictured alone and also accompanied by other men, all in combat attire. "Unlike Shade," she said, "we can produce his birth certificate from Stockholm, Sweden. We believe his association with Peter Laurent began after the death of his mother, when he was around age eight. He operates very openly, usually with a team of mercenaries, taking on the sort of combat missions you'd expect from someone who looks the way he does."

Judy paused, and Reid saw a flush on her cheeks. The General hadn't noticed; his attention was fixed on the screen. All the women loved Bas' movie-star good looks, blond hair, ice blue eyes, and six-feet-four of solid muscle.

Judy's leg was swinging double-time under the table. "He's an explosives expert and generally takes on what we call bang-and-burn assignments that require demolitions or a combat-trained, elite team. He's also skilled in hand-to-hand combat-- knives and martial arts—and other arcane arts. And from the skills we know he possesses, we can infer a lot about Shade's abilities."

The General rolled his eyes towards her. "You think Laurent taught a little girl to be a killing machine like this man?"

Reid spoke up. "Actually, sir, I believe out of the two of them, Shade is much more dangerous. She never leaves a witness alive to describe her. Not one photograph of her exists. No one knows her real name. No one has ever matched a fingerprint or a hair found at a scene to her. Her name says it all--she doesn't exist--she's a ghost, a shade. But where Drake is mayhem, Shade is finesse. We believe she's handled countless special operations for Laurent--operations that required precise execution without leaving a trace."

"From cat burglar to assassin," the General said, sounding less certain.

Reid nodded. "That does seem to be her primary role in Laurent's group, sir."

Judy flashed a final, black-and-white, grainy image onto the screen. She explained, "This is the only known photograph of the three of them. It's believed to have been taken at Heathrow airport. The only reason it came into our possession was because Peter Laurent was atypically pictured. Normally, he's very good at escaping notice."

Laurent was half-turned towards the camera in the shot, his face clearly identifiable and wearing an expression of curiosity. He was a nondescript dark-haired man of average height and build, which had made him a very successful covert operative until he had abruptly resigned. On his right side, a child leaned against him within the protective embrace of his arm. The child's head was completely covered by the hood of a jacket. The only visible body parts were a small bare leg, and a hand that clutched at Laurent's shirt. A small blond boy stood on Laurent's left side, his eyes glaring over Laurent's obscuring arm.

"That's a skirt she's wearing. You see?" Reid said, pointing at the screen. "We believe that's got to be her."

The General looked askance at him. "Where did Laurent get these kids?"

Reid cleared his throat again. "We've been able to place him in Stockholm shortly after Drake's mother's death, but we don't know how they came into contact. We believe Laurent acquired Shade about two years earlier. Right before his resignation, Laurent's unit was assigned a mission in the Middle East. The objective was to bring down a white slavery ring. A number of women and children were recovered from a compound there. He didn't list a reason for his resignation, but we know he stayed abroad, and there were rumors that he was traveling with a female child."

"You said Laurent's been working as a contractor since he resigned. What'd he do with the kids while he was on a job?"

"We only have theories based on his movements and known associates, but it appears that they were left with a number of specialists. So, while Laurent was working, the two children were in Japan, Czechoslovakia, Brazil, or wherever, learning martial arts, weaponry, and demolition."

The General's jaw muscle worked. "So where are we now on the situation?"

Clemmons diverted him. "General, Reid and Judy's team is only a small portion of the task force. Their involvement is limited to intelligence pertaining to Drake and Shade's activities. As you've been made aware, we've lost a number of operatives, so this situation is being given the highest priority by several teams."

Reid caught Judy's eye. She was probably hearing the same thing: *in other words, General, this team doesn't have a need-to-know what the other teams are doing.*

"However, we do have the final report on Shade's movements. Reid, please continue."

"What we can tell you, General, is that she allowed herself to be found in a Paris hotel by using a known pseudonym. Agents were sent to the hotel, but as usual, she vanished. The desk clerk reported seeing a woman wearing a long, belted, black leather jacket and boots, with a dark beret covering her hair, leaving right after the agents arrived—it might have been Shade. They searched the hotel room registered to the false identity, but it was virtually undisturbed—the hotel stay was probably just a layover or a decoy activity. They recovered a few hairs, which will be added to the collection of 'might-be-hers,' but until we have something to compare them to, physical evidence is useless. A woman matching the hotel clerk's description was seen boarding a local bus near the hotel. So, it looks like Laurent and Shade were in contact, and when he failed to check in, she rabbited."

Judy added, "Drake was incommunicado when Laurent began this operation. He was engaged in an unrelated assignment, and there's no information to indicate that he was even aware of Laurent's activities."

"We have agents at the Paris airport, but since no one knows what Shade looks like, and the desk clerk's description isn't much to go on, all we can do is watch airline bookings for any of her known identities," Reid said. "And the very latest information we have, sir, is that Drake is now on the move. Whether he's in contact with Shade or not, we don't know. But he's listed on an in-bound flight to New York. And he's very easy to spot."

Judy coughed to cover a laugh.

"Why can't you pick him up at the airport if he's so easy to spot?" the General asked.

Clemmons said, "Drake has no wants or warrants against his legal identity as a Swedish national."

"Who cares? Trump something up."

Reid was relieved to see Clemmons wore an expression of distaste.

"That could be tantamount to a death sentence for whoever was dispatched, and Drake would undoubtedly drop out of sight. Better we let him proceed visibly and simply monitor his movements," Clemmons said.

Shade had transferred buses and taken a taxi the rest of the way to the Paris airport. She had extra time before her flight, so she stopped for a cup of coffee on a crowded concourse and sat watching them go by, and then circle back like confused vultures. They were so obvious it was pathetic. She had reached the point where she could tell what acronym they worked for by their appearance. She dumped the coffee and wove back into the crowd. The next one she spotted was fairly clever. He was wearing a baseball cap, baggy jeans, and a slouchy tan jacket. He kept vanishing and reappearing, but she'd seen his reflection three times in the glass windows of the airport shops.

She strolled into the next restroom. Three generations of French women were gathered around a baby-changing station cooing at a screaming infant. A little girl in pigtails, wearing an Angry Birds backpack, was playing with an automatic faucet at a nearby sink. In a rear corner stall, Shade emptied her knapsack. After turning it inside out, it became a different color. With a few snaps, it turned into shoulder bag. She took off her leather coat. It was now only a jacket thanks to a zipper concealed halfway down its length, but they were obviously looking for women wearing black leather jackets. Rolling it carefully around the mechanisms concealed in its innards, she tucked it into the bag; the jacket was her most valuable possession. She swapped out her clothing, and from a small case, selected colored contact lenses. After adding a dark wig, a bit of padding in her cheeks, and some artful makeup, her reflection looked completely different. As a smartly dressed and coifed brunette businesswoman, she walked past the group gathered around the screaming baby and exited the restroom.

She saw Baseball Cap browsing magazines at a kiosk. He cut his eyes in her direction but remained stationary. She knew he'd go on waiting for the blond in the black leather jacket. She headed for her gate and boarded the flight.

After landing at Heathrow airport, she made her way to baggage claim. She presented a voucher for a lost bag and reclaimed a large rolling case that she'd "lost" on the flight in. She made another detour to a crowded restroom, dug out a different passport from the suitcase, loaded the shoulder bag into the suitcase, and changed into another disguise. A curvy redhead with green eyes exited the ladies room, wheeling a nondescript suitcase behind her. The redhead sauntered to the boarding gate for Washington-Dulles International Airport.

Curtis Dean woke to find a figure tucked up on his nightstand like a gargoyle, watching him sleep. He reached under his pillow for the gun, and she held up her open hands.

"Shade, damn you!" he exclaimed, jamming his glasses onto his face.

"I'm already damned." She sounded indifferent.

He studied her in the light from the window and was surprised once again by how unremarkable she was: oval-shaped face that lent itself well to cosmetic alterations, almond-shaped blue eyes, nose not large but not small, lips not thin but not bee-stung the way women were affecting these days. Her hair looked shorter. It was barely shoulder-length and curling around her face. As with everything else about her, it wasn't blond, but it wasn't brown either—if it was really her hair at all. Her build wasn't delicate but she could make herself look that way. She definitely had more muscles than he did, but that wasn't saying much.

He'd asked her once if he actually knew what she looked like and her answer had been, "I'm not even sure I know anymore."

She slid off the nightstand and clicked on the bedside lamp. And then everything changed. As she became animated and smiled, she also became heartbreakingly beautiful. In the lamplight, her hair shone gold. Her eyes crinkled at the corners and became a luminous blue above rounded cheekbones and a breathtaking smile.

Curtis yanked the ponytail holder out of his shoulder-length hair and finger-combed it before re-tying it. He ran a hand over the stubble on his jaw and wished he'd bothered to shower before bed. Like it mattered. He was a skinny, four-eyed, computer nerd with a face like a ferret; guys like him didn't get girls like her unless they invented a social networking site.

"How did you get in?"

She raised her eyebrows. "Really?"

"I have this whole house wired. If there's a vulnerability, I need to know what it is."

Stepping through the clothes littering his floor, she suggested, "That tree could use pruning."

"What tree?"

"The one outside your neighbor's house. I came across the rooftops."

"Up. You always go up."

"No one ever looks up, and people rarely lock things that are up."

"Whatever. But that tree is on a city-owned easement. That's the problem with inheriting a nineteenth-century row house—the Alexandria Historical Preservation Commission doesn't like changes."

"Good old Colonial Virginia." She tweaked a shirt and jeans off the top of the jumble. "So, the attic would be a problem for them."

"I have a soundproofed, access-controlled vault in my attic that's impenetrable to electronic surveillance, and packed full of servers--the Preservation Commission is the least of my worries."

She tossed the clothes to him. "Less worry, more confidence. Peter promised your mother he'd get you out of prison and keep you out. And now by day you're mild-manneredly using your hacking super-powers for the very agency that locked you up in the first place. But if the Preservation Commission, or anyone else, finds out you're Batman by night for *us*, I'll pay a visit to *their* rooftops."

He kicked the covers off, muttering about motion sensors on the roof. After pulling the t-shirt over his head, he had to locate her in the room again. She'd moved to the doorway and was so still that he had no sense of her. That was another one of her gifts. All those clichés like "moves like a dancer," or "fluid as a cat" only scratched the surface of what she did. She moved like air. It was as if his human radar just washed over her without a ping. The hair on the back of his neck rose.

"Is there coffee up there?" she asked in a tired voice.

He'd finally noticed she was in black from head-to-foot and wearing the leather jacket that meant she was working. "Yes," he said, yanking the jeans on. "If you're here, something's up. Where's your brother?"

From the stairs, she called back, "He's not my brother. But Bas should be entertaining ABC's and 123's at La Guardia by now."

He snickered at her pet name for agencies that were known by their acronyms. He yelled, "So, what is it you need at this ungodly hour?"

From the third floor she called, "Peter missed his check-in. In our last conversation, he said he was in Crete. I need you to give me his last known coordinates so I can go kill the assholes who took him."

He hurried out the door and took the stairs two-at-a-time. She had already keyed into the attic and was typing at one of the workstations when he huffed through the doorway.

"You've got enough electronics in here to launch a small war and monitor it via satellite in real time." She swiveled her chair while she scanned the room.

He shut the door, sealing them inside. "Bas usually handles the small wars."

Her chair swung back towards her monitor. "Last knowns, Curtis."

Wincing, he slid behind another workstation. Over the past few years, he'd watched Peter Laurent's field role decrease as Bas and Shade's had increased. Peter had assumed a handler's role, only taking part in an occasional job. Bas had incorporated his side by hiring ex-military mercenaries to flesh out combat-oriented teams. In the last year, Shade had gone strictly solo—each to their own nature, he guessed. But he suspected there was a reason he hadn't seen Bas and Shade in the same room even once during that year.

"Accessing now." He glanced back to where she'd been and discovered her at his elbow. *Air.* "Looks like…north from Crete?" he said as the map came up. He increased the zoom on the area above the island.

"Northeast," she corrected, leaning over his shoulder.

"He could be anywhere. There are hundreds of islets in that area."

"Then you'd better start making a list of islets. Run the known inhabited ones located in a nautical ten-mile-radius, cross-reference to property records, and give me that list. Maybe a name will jump out."

She slid behind her terminal again and started pulling up yacht charter companies. "Curtis, there's a U.S. Military base on Crete, right?"

Curtis gave her a shocked sidelong glance.

She ignored it.

"Souda Bay, yes. There's also a NATO installation north of that island. Why?"

"Because we're going to need a helicopter."

He guffawed. "You're going to steal a helicopter from a U.S. Military base?"

"Borrow," she corrected.

Bas arrived at the house in broad daylight, tripped all the motion sensors in the alley behind the house, and set off the silent alarm at the kitchen door. He disarmed the system at the security panel after he walked in. Curtis, sitting at the kitchen table surrounded by wires and electrodes, silenced a beeping alarm on a handheld remote. He knew Bas had tripped everything on purpose to get on his good side.

"What's all this?" Bas asked, as if he hadn't already figured it out.

Curtis had forgotten how big the bastard was. Big, and blond, and perfect, with eyes like a Husky dog. He had the cheekbones and the kind of smile that made women faint, and always a cool 'do. Lately, he'd been wearing it long on the top, and short on the sides and back, and he'd do this flippy thing when it got in his eyes. Women loved that shit. If that wasn't enough, then there were the muscles. The guy's pecs were the size of dinner plates. There was no fat on him, so he rippled just standing around. Even his name was perfect. In Swedish, his name translated to "royal dragon." Although, Shade's pet name for him, "California," summed him up better.

Seeing him, and hearing him talk in that big, lazy, bass voice, anyone would think he was maybe not so bright—and that was the mistake he wanted them to make. Shade was sneaky and secretive, but she didn't try to hide it. Bas was sneaky in a psychologically manipulative way—he made everyone like him. Curtis really wanted to dislike the guy, and had been trying to dislike him for years, but he was just too damned laid back and *nice*. But Curtis still felt like the Nerd King whenever he was around.

Trying not to sound sour, Curtis said, "I'm wiring the roof with pressure-sensitive plates."

Bas put on a phony interested expression and slouched, leaning against the kitchen counter. As if he could make himself look smaller.

"I'm guessing Shade got in again?"

"I figure if she keeps it up, I'll eventually have this house so locked down that she'll be the only one of us who can get in."

"You shouldn't let her torque you up," Bas advised. "Is there any coffee?"

Curtis waved at the pot and muttered, "Just like your sister," before finishing the sensor he was wiring.

"She's not my sister." He dug a mug out of a cabinet and filled it with hot coffee.

"One of these days, I'd like to hear the story of what you did to piss her off so badly in Colombia."

Bas gulped the scalding coffee without flinching. "I wouldn't know. I was unconscious for most of it. So, she's gone?"

"What do you think? But she left that envelope for you."

Bas picked up the manila envelope and dumped the contents onto the kitchen counter. He pawed through them, pulling out the map first. He looked at Curtis for an explanation.

"She narrowed it down to those three islets as the most likely choices. Said she had a 'really strong feeling' about the second one."

Bas flinched. He slid the map back into the envelope. "That'll be the one, then." He studied the airline schedule printout. "Looks like I'm off to Dulles. Great. The last airport was crawling with ABC's and 123's. Took a *lot* of detours down I-95 to get rid of all the tails. Maybe I should dig into Shade's cosmo case for a fake nose and a wig. Speaking of which, you got any gizmos for me?"

"Shade loaded up, and she packed that bag for you." Curtis pointed to the bulging, canvas duffel on the floor.

Bas hefted it with ease. "Of course she did. Little miss OCD." He opened the door but lingered in the doorway. "All the old man told me about this job was that he was looking into the disappearance of some colleagues. That wasn't all of it though, was it?"

Curtis said, "He was baiting a trap."

"And he didn't tell Shade the details?"

"No."

"Probably has something to do with her." Without waiting for confirmation, Bas shut the door.

"Or both of you," Curtis muttered.

Chapter 2

As Reid limped through the office doorway, Judy relieved him of his gym bag and popped a hot Starbucks into his hand. She knew he had a hard time managing the cane, the bag, and a coffee, so she routinely picked one up for him.

"To start your day off with a bang, Bas boarded a flight to Greece a few hours ago, and John Clemmons wants to see you in his office ASAP."

"Ooh-rah. Here we go," Reid said and swigged the coffee. "Greece, huh? They're either psychic or they had some kind of locator on Laurent to have figured it out that fast. 'Course, I wouldn't bat an eye if we had to add psychic to the list of Shade's abilities. She's too canny by far."

One of the other team members called out, "Before you ask, Reid, I already ran the flight manifest and didn't find any of Shade's aliases. And yes, we have someone standing by in Greece to tail Bas when the flight arrives."

"I doubt she'd risk the same flight with him. I'm sure they already know we're watching him," Reid said.

Judy asked, "Do you think they're deliberately letting us know where they're going or just running out of time? "

"I can't think of a single reason why they'd want anyone to know what they're up to. They certainly don't want or need our help, so I'm sure it's just the time factor. And that makes both of them that much more volatile. We need to caution our people not to approach them. If we lose track of the two of them, so be it--better that than one of our own ending up dead. We'll be able to pick them back up eventually--with Bas involved things are about to get very noisy."

"The question," Judy said, "is what the powers-that-be want as an outcome."

"Well, let me just go and find that out," Reid said with a grin.

John Clemmons was sitting at his desk with his fingers steepled against his bowed forehead. He remained in this position while Reid levered himself into a chair and positioned his braced leg.

Clemmons' office had no windows, and apparently he disliked fluorescent lighting because Reid noticed that he never turned on the overheads; instead, the room was lit by several lamps. While Clemmons prayed or meditated, Reid's eyes wandered around the room. The furnishings were all standard Government-issue. Clemmons had nothing on the walls, no framed pictures or knick-knacks on the desk, and the executive chair wasn't even real leather. There were two wooden chairs in front of the desk for visitors. On top of a large table to the left of the desk, stacks of papers sat in seemingly random piles. Based on his experience with Clemmons' organized mind, Reid was sure the man knew exactly what was in each stack.

Finally, Clemmons lifted bloodshot, watery eyes to meet Reid's. "Laurent dropped off the grid less than forty-eight hours ago. In less than that time, most of it spent in-flight, Laurent's two protégés have seemingly managed to track him down. Meanwhile, our own highly-trained, covert operatives, who were already in position in Heraklion, not only lost Laurent, but have made no progress towards determining his present whereabouts, or determining how he got to wherever those whereabouts are. I'm inclined to just let the two of them proceed without interference. Laurent is most likely in possession of information we desperately need, and we know he'll check in when, and if, he's recovered."

"I've already passed word to have our people in the field stand down, sir."

Clemmons sighed. "Don't call me 'sir,' Reid. I haven't been at this much longer than you."

"I'm sorry, John. Old habits die hard."

"I'll get enough 'sir-ing' in a few minutes when I have to go meet with the blowhards."

"How is the General, John?"

"I fear for his veins, Reid."

Reid stifled a laugh.

Clemmons put his hands flat on his desk and stood up. "Walk with me—er…"

Ignoring the faux pas, Reid said, "I'll try to keep up."

In the corridor, Clemmons kept his voice low. "Going back to the original problem…" he began, and then sighed again.

Reid anticipated where the conversation was headed but waited the other man out.

Clemmons stopped walking and turned to face him. "Tell me this, Reid. You have a situation in which all of the assets you've employed have not only failed, but have probably been irrevocably lost. You have at your disposal two far superior options. How would you proceed if the decision were up to you?"

"With all due respect, I would never assume that those two are at our disposal at all. And I'm sure we wouldn't want to be associated with anything they do."

"Yes, yes," Clemmons said in a tone of dismissal. "But would it work?"

Reid toyed with the grip on his cane and wondered if he was hearing what he thought he was hearing. "If I understand you, sir, no. It can't be done without Laurent. We can't even observe them without their consent, much less employ them-- there's just no way to open a dialogue."

"Yet their clientele seem to manage?"

Reid accepted the sting with chagrin. "That's a very good point, sir. I'll get to work on that right away."

"Start with Al Brandon. He was Laurent's handler and still passes him work. Maybe he knows how to contact the other two. His agency will cooperate--they're involved as well. Otherwise, a successful recovery of Laurent is our only hope."

"I'd take those odds."

"If he's still alive," Clemmons pointed out.

"If he's not, we can just sit back and rest assured they'll resolve the situation."

Clemmons stared at him blankly for a moment. "My god, you're right. Those two will annihilate whoever's responsible. With that in mind, Laurent being targeted could be the best thing for all of us."

Off the coast of Crete, in the middle of the sun-spangled turquoise waters of the Mediterranean, a small luxury yacht sat at anchor. Spanos sat watching the boat on the central monitor in the control room.

"Spanos, what is that boat off our southwest coast?" his relief guard asked, once he was situated at the monitors.

"Just some Cypriot princess and her boy toy from the looks of it. I ran the yacht registration and it's a vacation day-rental. The chick is a real looker too—built. They had some touchy-feely going, but it looks like boy toy is doing some fishing now—would you fish if you had that sprawled out on the deck?" Spanos shook his head in disbelief. "Hit the zoom and enjoy the show. I gotta get some lunch."

The relief guard was punching up the camera zoom before Spanos was out the door.

Lying on the deck of the boat, Shade squinted at the sun and tugged on the long black wig; it was hot and it itched. Her part of this maneuver was boring. Bas was conducting underwater reconnaissance, but he wasn't even willing to let her take a turn. He'd pointed out that a view of him lying on the deck wouldn't hold the attention of anyone watching from the islet, which was counterproductive to their goal: they wanted them distracted and content.

Earlier that morning, they'd chartered a tourist helicopter and done a fly-over of the most likely locations. Her hunch about the second islet seemed to be proving correct. The convoluted property ownership structure had been the initial tip-off, and once they'd skimmed past and noted recent fortifications to the existing stone structure, surveillance cameras, and armaments, it was clear that something illicit was going on.

She got up and fetched another bottle of water and carried it to the fishing poles. Bas had made a show of baiting hooks and then went over the side of the yacht blocked from view by the cabin. In SCUBA gear, and with the assistance of an underwater Sea Scooter, he was scouring the underwater perimeter of the islet. Essentially just a rock poking up out the Aegean Sea, Bas hoped it had either underwater conduits or a natural cave that would give them access to the interior of the islet.

A handful of structures and outbuildings, including a large square building that had to be the residence, clung to the pinnacle of the rocky islet like barnacles. It was almost bare of vegetation except for some struggling shrubs near the waterline. Most of the perimeter was sheer stone rising out of the water, making it nearly impossible to scale. There was only one docking point, and they knew it would be watched. From behind the tinted windows of the cabin, Shade had been killing time using binoculars to plot out distances between the structures and matching them to the photos they'd taken from the helicopter, but she was finished and growing restless.

She went back to the lounge chair and lay back down. She hated all this inactivity. It was making her waspish. She was worried that she might be wrong, and that they were wasting time and risking Peter's life. She wanted action, progress, results.

Part of her irritation, she decided, was because Bas was usually the impatient one. Normally, he couldn't sit still during the planning stages. He'd just disappear and let someone else do all the work. The same was true once the action started: she was calm and in control while Bas was prone to fits of temper and berserker behavior once the testosterone surged and the bullets started flying. And god help everyone if something didn't get blown up. Try reasoning with him once he was in that mental state. But now he was just calmly affable, almost cheerful, and taking a voluntary role in recon, and it was pissing her off.

After the last job they'd worked together, she'd gone off on her own. He'd almost died on that one. They wouldn't listen to her. They'd plowed mule-headedly into a catastrophe. Well, that train of thought was a fast spiral into the depths of memory hell. Maybe the observers would enjoy a little music and dancing.

When Bas finally climbed out of the water, Shade said, "This stuff is melting off of me as fast as I'm applying it." She had a bottle of suntan lotion filled with a body paint in a darker shade than her own skin tone and was smearing it liberally on herself.

"I don't know why you didn't just spray tan," Bas said as he hauled the equipment out of the water.

"Because then I'm stuck with a deep, dark tan for days until it wears off. That severely limits my camouflage options. Who's gonna buy a dark-skinned redhead?"

"You need to think more creatively. Explore some other cultures. You've never done an Eskimo, for example."

"Even I couldn't pull that one off."

"Oh, I don't know," he said. "Take a quick dip to cool off and ponder it while I finish stowing all this gear. I bet you come up with something." He carried the fishing poles into the cabin.

"Just hurry. If you haven't found anything here, we need to pack it in before they get suspicious."

"I'm sure the sight of you strolling around in that bikini has blanked their brains. It's when we leave they'll get upset."

"Did you find anything useful?" she asked.

"Nope. Nothing. I surveyed the entire perimeter and didn't even find a fissure. That is one solid hunk of rock. Looks like we're gonna have to do it your way and go up."

Shade smiled but said nothing.

"Yeah, well, you just better hope your theory about 'up' holds true."

Later that night, in a borrowed Black Hawk helicopter, Bas piloted them back to the islet. He flew in low over the water while Shade napped in the troop compartment. She woke to his voice in her headset. "Now at altitude. Ready to deploy?"

She slid open the cargo door, swung underneath the helicopter, and strapped into the motorized hang glider. It was secured to the Black Hawk's external cargo hook and shielded by the body of the chopper. She detached the line, fired up the small engine, and announced, "I'm go here."

"See you soon," Bas said.

As the hang glider sailed free, Bas veered off to avoid buffeting the glider in the rotor wash. He would stay well outside the islet's potential radar range and double back from the opposite direction. Since it was located between two well-known military bases, and tourist flights were common as well, a lone helicopter shouldn't arouse concern even if he was spotted. On his return approach, Shade knew it wouldn't matter.

She cut the noisy engine on the glider while she was still a good distance out. In their earlier flyover, they'd observed that all the security cameras mounted on the roof seemed to be pointing down and out. On her approach, she confirmed it before landing. She and Bas had blacked out every reflective bit of the glider's metal frame, and the sails were dark blue, so she was silent and nearly invisible against the night sky as she touched down on the roof. It was a zero-slope roof with a four-foot-high, stone lip around the edge. The building was constructed more like a bunker than a house. She crouched down and waited, listening for any sounds of alarm before releasing her harness.

She noted the time, grabbed the backpack that was clipped to the frame, and chose an open area of the roof where she sprayed a large glowing "X" with a can of luminous spray paint.

There was a small vestibule on the roof with a door that she investigated next. She smiled when she could detect no obvious signs of magnetic locks or wiring around the doorframe. The only thing preventing her entry was a manual door lock that she could pick in a couple of seconds. She'd been prepared to bypass anything she found, but this just saved her time. As she kept saying: people always discounted penetration from above.

At the bottom of the stairwell, an unsecured door led into the upper story of the old house. She checked a few rooms in passing, confirming they were unoccupied bedrooms. The hallway was bisected by a landing and a staircase. She hugged the wall as she approached the open area. At the end of the opposite corridor, she saw light leaking from beneath one door. It was located to the left of a pair of double doors. The double doors should logically be the master stateroom. She filed it away.

She edged one eye past the corner and saw the anticipated surveillance camera high in the corner of the landing, one flight down. Its panning motion was so slow that after it made a pass to the right she had time to slide down the banister and wedge herself into the corner beneath it before it began its return trip. When it had panned back again, she went down the next flight.

At the bottom of the stairs she ducked into the dark archway of what appeared to be a living room. She counted off the seconds as the camera panned and went back out the archway. To the left was the main entrance: a pair of thick, peaked, wooden doors with massive iron pull-rings. A closed door to the right of the entrance showed light below it, and she could hear the muffled sounds of voices. She could also hear the hum of electronics and knew that was likely the security control room. On the left side of the foyer was a bolted door, presumably leading to another staircase down.

She headed straight forward, explored the entire level, dodging two more cameras with ease, and then doubled back to the foyer from the other side. The house was expensively furnished and had fine carpets on the floors, but it was empty. Dust lay thick on everything. She crept past the lit doorframe, eased back the bolt on the other door, and went down the dim staircase.

In the basement, she found a mechanical room and ducked inside. Mildewed wires fed into the area from an external generator. A maze of grime-coated pipes vanished into the walls and ceiling, and an ancient boiler squatted in a cobwebbed corner. From one of the pockets in her jacket, she removed tiny limpets and began sticking them every few feet along her path as she made a complete tour of the basement.

She saved the only lit corridor for last. From a musty cross corridor, she studied the two guards seated at small table across from a closed door, playing cards. One of them was wearing her father's watch. Had they bothered to look up, they would only have seen her neon eyes receding into the darkness.

She retrieved a watch face from inside her jacket and pressed a small button, activating a locator. Bas had the receiver on the chopper, and the signal would tell him that she had found Peter Laurent. Cue hellfire on earth.

Her thrown dagger lodged in the neck of the guard with his back to her. As he fell forward onto the table, she was already behind him, reaching across to slit the throat of the second guard. She retrieved her father's watch, and the thrown knife, cleaning both knives before she stowed them back in her jacket. She checked the time. She heard shouts coming from the guard room upstairs, and booted feet moving on the floor. Bas was running early on his approach. No surprise there.

She grabbed the set of keys off the card table, unlocked, and threw open the door. There was only one person in the room, so she switched on the light. Peter Laurent was seated in a chair, head bowed, both arms shackled to bolts in the wall, and his ankles tied to the legs of the chair. His clothes were filthy, and his shirt was in ribbons, revealing cuts and bruises on his lean muscular torso. The white hair above his sideburns had spread even higher into the short-cropped, dark hair on the crown. She felt a familiar surge of pain that she channeled into rage.

Peter raised his bloodied head and tried to give her a smile with the less damaged half of his face. He'd felt the guards hit the floor and knew by the silence it was Shade.

"You ready to go, dad?"

She'd hidden the distress in her eyes so fast he almost hadn't caught it. She was clad all in black, wearing that lethal jacket she loved, showing her real face, and her hair was slicked back and bound in a tight braid that tucked under her collar. Framed by the doorway, she looked like a teenage girl.

"What took you so long?" he said, his voice hoarse.

She said nothing as she strode towards him and unlocked the manacles, flinging them away. He rubbed his wrists, chafing off some of the grime and dried blood, while she cut the ropes on his ankles.

"Can you walk?" Her voice was devoid of emotion.

"You better hope so, Zyllah." He stiffly pushed himself up.

"Don't call me that." She ducked under his right arm and supported him to the doorway.

"Think you could carry me out of here?"

"If I had to, I could. Let's go. We don't want to keep Bas waiting."

"Don't tell me it's just the two of you?" He turned his piercing blue eyes on her.

"Dad," she chided.

At the doorway he took in the downed guards and the spreading pool of blood. "What happened to your rule about no collateral damage, Zyl?"

"I suspend all rules when my family is attacked. Besides, it won't matter in a few more minutes. Now shut up and move your ass."

His legs were working better by the time they reached the top of the first flight of stairs. She released him and moved ahead, planting limpets along the staircase. Then she tensed and cocked her head, and her hand slid into a pocket. Peter melted back against the wall, out of her way.

When the guard room door flew open, Shade's Bo shuriken throwing star sheared through the neck of the first guard and lodged in the man behind him. The only sound was their bodies hitting the floor. She was into the room, over the bodies, to snap the neck of the third man before he even saw her.

As Peter passed her on his way up the stairs, his critical evaluation found no fault. Shade had one advantage over every adversary: she did not hesitate. While the opponent was processing information and deciding on the risk/value ratio, she was already in motion. He'd seen to it that she was trained from childhood in every form of physical combat, but most particularly by a Japanese woman in a specific style of engagement. This woman had taught her every method to overwhelm a larger opponent, and the most critical factor, the one thing she had untaught the young Shade, was hesitation. Shade excelled at lightning-quick, lethal action because she had no fear of being hurt or killed; she was only afraid of capture.

As she rejoined him midway up the staircase, she hissed, "Move at speed. Left at the top and down the hall to the roof stairs. Do not stop."

An explosion outside concussed the house, shaking the staircase. Shouts and gunfire followed. Peter heard rotor blades chopping the air and what sounded like the explosive hiss of hellfire missiles. Glass windows shattered and the house shook again.

He obeyed as Shade ducked right and ran down the opposite corridor. After a few minutes, he heard a muffled yell and a shot. He had only reached the roof door when she was beside him again, manhandling him through the door. She had to support him up the stairs, and then pulled him into a half-crouch once they were on the roof, keeping her body between him and the roofline. His eyes found the glowing "X," and they both went to the center and squatted down.

The gunfire and explosions continued. Over the rim of the roof, he saw fires burning in the darkness. The chopper sounds seemed to be everywhere at once, echoing over the terrain and distorted by the sea surrounding them. Bas was making a hell of a ruckus. The scream of the rotors increased as the Black Hawk dropped to the rooftop. Shade viciously boosted him into the chopper. She threw herself in as Bas was forced to spin the machine. Bullets raked along the opposite side. Bas spun back and opened fire. Shade was manning a side-mounted machine gun by the time Bas veered away from the roof and started to climb again.

When they were safely away, Shade secured the cargo door. Peter was lying on the medevac litter at the rear of the compartment, and she knelt down beside him. She held out a small, silver cylinder with a button on one end. He took it from her manicured delicate hand and pressed the button.

Shade said, "Boom."

The flames shining on the chopper window climbed into the sky. He heard the detonation afterwards. The Black Hawk barely shuddered as the shockwave reached for them.

"They did *what?*" General Ratcliffe yelled through the phone. Reid, sitting in Clemmons' office again, could hear him from three feet away.

Clemmons maintained his characteristic calm. "Essentially, they blew up a small island."

Squawking issued from Clemmons' handset.

"We believe so, General. We anticipate contact from him soon."

Reid waited as Clemmons wound up the call and replaced the receiver.

Clemmons took a moment for himself, staring at the phone and wearing a smile that had nothing to do with happiness. Finally, he asked, "How did they get a Black Hawk helicopter off a U.S. Military base?"

"In a nutshell? We have no idea."

Clemmons nodded.

"We assume someone looked the other way. But most likely we'll never know. They did it though, and then abandoned it on another islet. We're guessing they took a boat out of the area. The blood in the personnel compartment matches Peter Laurent's blood type. So, he was definitely extracted, but we have no information about what condition he's in."

"Any survivors at the site?"

"None. Greek authorities are combing through the wreckage now and retrieving the bodies. Most of them are too badly burned for anything other than dental identification. That pair have made a very clear statement with this action."

"Where are they now? Do we have any information?"

"We have alerts out for both Laurent and Drake, but they haven't shown up on any flight manifests, and there's been no activity on their passports. We're also checking hospitals and clinics for anyone matching Laurent's description. Depending on his condition, they might be holed up in Greece, or if he's fit, they could be anywhere."

Clemmons was shaking his head. "My god. It took them less than four days to track him, penetrate the location, and remove him. And that's with time zone differences. Where were these two when we were hunting Bin Laden?"

Reid studied the wall behind Clemmons' head.

"So, now we wait. Unless, and until, Laurent makes contact, we're operationally dead in the water--unless we happen to reacquire one of them. But in the best case scenario, we'll finally be getting some answers from Laurent, and we can move forward on the original issue."

"I'll keep you posted, sir."

"All hours. Thank you, Reid."

Chapter 3

Peter Laurent was lying in a king-sized bed pressing his fingers into the sockets of his eyes. He wished he could reach behind them and massage his brain. He was alive, sunlight was streaming into the luxury hotel room, the air was warm and moist, and two of the most dangerous people on the planet were guarding him like precious treasure. He ought to feel relaxed. But despite the fact that he was bolstered by an assortment of pillows, the tape constricting his ribs hurt almost as much as the ribs themselves. Every movement tugged or pulled some wound, and his muscles felt like they were in advanced rigor mortis. All evidence to the contrary, he felt incredibly vulnerable, and the mental confusion was the worst part.

On the table beside the bed was an assortment of clear beverages, pill bottles, and an empty soup bowl. Even as a child, Shade had excelled at nurturing behavior. The pills were probably contributing to his clouded mental state, but she'd read him the riot act about secondary infections and the need to rest so his body could heal.

Beside him on the bed was a laptop and a portable hotspot; the hotel's free wi-fi was out of the question. He knew Curtis had everything heavily encrypted, but he hadn't touched the devices yet. Until he could sort out the puzzle pieces in his head, it was better to stay off the grid.

Shade was somewhere in the three-bedroom suite, but he didn't expect to actually hear her moving around. They had stayed in an old house with squeaky floorboards once when she was still small. On a dare from Bas, she'd driven herself nearly to tears plotting a soundless path through every room.

There was a tap at the door and Shade entered, dressed like a fashion plate, be-wigged and heavily made up. She looked very Sicilian and would be unremarkable on the streets of Rome.

"Need anything?" she asked.

He shook his head and watched her dark brown eyes flick over his features, studying his expression, his bandages, the positioning of the pillows, and finally lock on the empty soup bowl and saucer. He could almost hear her ticking.

"You know," she said as she moved to retrieve the bowl, "you need to stop grinding your mental gears. You can't do anything right now anyway."

"Going somewhere?" he asked.

"A bit of shopping," she said. "When Bas gets back from the gym."

They both heard the suite door open, and the positioning of Shade's hands on the heavy crockery changed. Bas' voice called out a greeting, and the saucer gripped in her right hand did not become an airborne projectile.

She leaned in to kiss him on the cheek before leaving the room. She smelled like flowers.

He heard the two of them speaking in low tones but couldn't hear their words. That was an improvement over the cold war that'd gone on for the past year.

When Bas came in to check on him, he had at least managed to prioritize his thoughts. "Is your sister gone?" he asked.

Bas grabbed a bottled water from the bedside supply, and then flung himself into a chair and stretched out his legs. "Yeah, shopping, she said."

"You believe that, do you?"

"I'm sure she'll buy something, but my guess is she's just doing recon and keeping busy."

"Was she wearing a jacket?" Peter asked.

"Some beige silk thing," Bas said after downing half the water.

"That's the black jacket inside out. She loves reversible stuff. Two-for-one."

Bas nodded and shrugged. "Shopping in Rome can be cutthroat. Maybe she thought Kevlar was a good idea."

"Bas, seriously, is there justification for the level of spooky she's at?"

He studied the water bottle in his hands. "They've been tailing us pretty closely, yeah. At least I get to move around openly. She has to work a little harder."

"That's her choice though."

"She's always been cautious," Bas said.

"You do not need a Kevlar-reinforced jacket, loaded with weapons, to shop in the fashion district of Rome," Peter persisted.

Bas sighed and looked at him like he was stupid. "You're really gonna make me say this to you? She loves you a lot, and they came pretty close to killing you, so you need to look the other way if she's acting overprotective. I know I had a few moments wondering if we were already too late. She's working off her anxiety now. If she starts avoiding you, like she does me, then you'll *really* know how much she cares."

"She's still doing that?" Peter frowned.

Laying on the sarcasm, Bas said, "Of course not, everything is fine." Then he added, "And speaking of avoiding dealing with stuff, why don't you stop obsessing about Shade and figure out the next move?"

Peter said, "And that's the pot calling the kettle black."

Bas' affected the belligerent scowl-and-pout he'd mastered in childhood.

"Shoo," Peter said. "Let me check in with Curtis first."

Bas closed the door on his way out, and Peter painfully dragged over all the equipment and logged in.

Once they'd established a secure connection, Curtis said, "Glad you're okay, but, wow, you're a mess."

He probably looked worse than the laptop's low-quality camera was capturing but he hadn't looked in a mirror to know for sure. "Shade patched me up. I'll be fine. Fill me in."

Curtis was working his way through an open bag of cheese puffs and swigging Diet Coke. It was the middle of the night there, and he looked like the carbohydrates and caffeine were losing their war on sleep.

"Have you checked your email?" Curtis asked.

"No. Why?"

"I was running system maintenance and got the bright idea to check your account to see if the ABC's and 123's had anything to say. There's an email you should see. You need a very high clearance just to know that agency exists. All the email says is 'Seeking Shade.'"

After hearing the acronym, Peter was surprised. "I don't have any contacts there."

Curtis said, "Someone must've been in a sharing mood. I've checked our security and no one's gotten in. I may not be able to stop Shade on physical security, but even she couldn't get past me in the virtual realm."

"Al Brandon is the only point-of-contact who knows that email address, and he wouldn't give it to just anyone. Maybe this is legit." Curtis still looked uncertain, so Peter elaborated. "I've known him too long to ever distrust him. He's family."

"Aren't you suspecting an insider leak right now?" Curtis asked.

"I think that's what they want us to think," Peter mused.

"I cannot begin to fathom the convoluted way your mind works."

"Shade said you pulled up the property records for that rock they stuck me on. Did you finish tracing ownership?"

"It took some doing. And interestingly, it just changed hands a few months ago. But the trail dead-ended. I went from one holding company to another and slammed into the wall de Banques Suisses. Getting through that would take a lot of time, and I'm not sure we want the attention that an attempt on their accounts would bring if I get caught. However, the company on the chain before that has ties to a New York lawyer with a history of illegal arms dealing. That points the finger back to our own turf. And the reason the name caught my eye is because Bas' team has purchased from him in the past."

"That can't be right. The people who put me in this condition weren't American. Shade said the guy in charge spoke Turkish."

"Could've been faking it?" Curtis suggested.

"No, when people are dying they scream in their mother tongue."

Curtis grimaced and put down the bag of cheese puffs. "She just killed him without getting any answers?"

"He was just a lackey, and he pulled a gun on her. I'm satisfied with the outcome. She said the master suite was unoccupied and had been that way for a while. Nobody was ever really there. Even the troop presence there was minimal. It's strange, Curtis."

"So, what do you want to do about this email?"

"Find out everything you can about the sender."

"Or you could just ask."

Peter guffawed and then clutched at his ribs. After a few shallow breaths, he said, "Sure, what the hell?"

"I mean, sometimes you three seem to make things harder than they need to be."

"Professional hazard, I guess," Peter said. "If people went around openly asking questions and admitting stuff, we'd be out of business."

Taking a poke at Curtis, Peter asked, "Are you still re-routing us every five seconds?"

Curtis pulled a face. "Hardly. But often enough," he said. "No one is going to track your location, or mine, from anything you do while you're networked in. But I can't say anything about the other end. Anyone there could be reading anything that's sent from them to you or that comes into their accounts."

"Kidding, Curtis. Okay, I'll get back to you."

As Peter ended the session, Bas turned up lounging in the doorway. The whole doorway.

"Poor Curtis," Peter said. "He probably has nightmares about Shade."

Bas snorted. "Wet dreams, more like."

"Be nice, Basilius. You're a tough act to live up to."

"Somebody's got to set the bar--for the ladies' sake."

"I'm sure the ladies appreciate that."

"Oh, they do. Trust me, they do."

"Could you park your staggering ego somewhere else for a while?"

Grinning, Bas headed back out into the suite.

Peter had already located the email. Hitting reply, he typed:

Your request was sent to the wrong account. Who are you?

Al Brandon had reached out as well. The message from him read:

Word on the street is that you're still alive. Should've known better. Forgive me for doubting, it's my only excuse for the other message you'll have received.

An honorable enemy is an admirer of your softer side and he's less of a team player than he realizes. This could be an opportunity.
Anxious people want information, but you know that.
–Al

There was one more surprising message in his inbox. It hadn't attracted Curtis' attention because it came from a sporadic but known correspondent—but someone who was supposed to be dead. The message was a coded phone number. He reached for a cell phone and dialed.

Twenty minutes later, he was trying to massage his brain again when Shade reappeared. To her credit, she did have bags with her from several expensive shops.

"I picked up some things for you since you're short on wardrobe."

"Where's your brother?" he asked.

"In the living room on his computer. Probably surfing his version of porn."

Peter chuckled carefully. "Guns and ammo?"

"Happiness is a warm gun."

"Tell me, Zyllah, are you holding? I haven't finished puzzling this out and I don't want you taking independent action yet. That's why I haven't given you two all the details. I don't want either of you going off half-cocked."

"Stop calling me that. And yes, I'm holding. I won't take any action until you say so."

"Good."

"But I will take out anything that comes near us."

"Understood. Was there anything?"

"I have a feeling of being watched but I didn't see anything. We should be good here for a few more days, and then you'll be ready to travel. Think you can figure out the next move by then?"

"You might need to go on ahead. There's someone I think you should check out. At least, I want to open a dialogue and see if he has any useful information or might be a conduit for us. And according to Al Brandon, he's got a thing for you."

Peter wasn't sure her look of interest boded well for whoever this person was.

At the end of the work day, Reid's team got word that Bas had been sighted at a hotel in Rome in the company of an older man. It was assumed Shade was with them. Agents at the scene relayed that room service requests listed soups and other sick foods going up to their suite, but they hadn't made any calls or accessed the hotel internet connection.

"Tell everyone to back off," Reid told them. "If Laurent is recuperating, and we do anything to make those two nervous…Well, we don't want to provoke them."

In a prompting tone, Judy suggested, "Or we've confirmed their location and don't want them to disappear again?"

"Sure, that too."

Reid decided to postpone reporting to Clemmons until the following morning. He reasoned that since the email reply he'd received had come from Laurent, he'd surely be briefing his point of contact soon, and that was the information Clemmons really wanted.

To cover all the bases, he'd sent a reply back with his own name, suggesting a face-to-face meeting as the next step. So far, he hadn't received a response.

When Al Brandon pulled into his garage, it was after dark. He'd stopped for Chinese take-out on the way home, calling it a reward for a long, exhausting day. He was nearing retirement, and had no idea what he would do when the time finally came. He and his wife had planned a cross-country RV vacation before she'd lost her battle with cancer.

Their modest, two-story home had been built in the seventies and needed updating. Mary had decorated it with too many damned floral prints, and he was reminded of her every time he walked in the door. It was a mausoleum to a happier time and made him dread coming home each night.

The only constant now was his job. He regretted the years he'd spent traveling for work, all the time they hadn't been able to spend with one another. What did he have to show for all those exploits? He was alone, and likely to remain that way, and younger, more able men were jockeying for his job. Most of his peers had either already retired, and were on permanent vacation at Disneyland with their grandchildren, or they'd been killed in the line of duty.

Now there was a crisis at work because agents were being killed. Intelligence coming in had ground to a halt, and the pressure for answers had everyone panicking and trying to avoid being blamed. In that kind of environment, sooner or later, someone was going to crack and the innocent would be made into scapegoats.

Carrying the take-out bag, he let himself into the house through the garage and spent a stunned moment staring at the alarm system keypad hanging from its wires.

"Sorry," a low female voice said behind him. "It's easily fixed. You might want to look into a better system though."

He felt strangely resigned. He closed his eyes.

"Do I smell Chinese? I'm starved," she said.

"Why don't you tell me what you want? I'd rather not see you."

She let out a delighted laugh. "But, Uncle Al, *everyone* wants to see me."

"Sure, until they understand that their lives are the price for viewing."

She made a vague noise that wasn't disagreement. "You'll be okay. I just want to ask a few questions."

He opened his eyes and turned around. She was wearing a disguise, so she probably wasn't there to kill him. He took a deep breath and told his heart it could slow down.

She noticed his relief and immediately became wary.

"You've forgotten," he concluded. "I thought when you said, 'Uncle Al,' that you must remember."

She waited, and he could tell that she was curious but growing increasingly disturbed, and consequently dangerous.

He walked into the kitchen and set down the bag of food, not looking to see if she followed. He pulled plates and glasses from the cabinets and set them on the kitchen island. "Still nothing?"

"No," she answered in a chilly tone.

She was standing less than two feet away, and he hadn't heard her move or registered her presence.

"I met you once, when you were a child, so I know at least that's not your hair, and your eyes are the wrong color. It was right after Peter recovered you. His idea was to leave you with my wife and me because he knew we wanted children but couldn't have them."

Shade was scrutinizing him as he served up the food. By observing him making truthful statements, his body language, the tone and pitch of his voice, and his inflection, she was developing a standard of comparison against which his other reactions and answers would be judged. He knew she was doing it; he even knew who'd trained her to do it. As a handler of other agents, he hadn't needed to learn to control his facial expressions, and he knew Shade would find him easy to read.

Shade would've found documents in the house listing his age as fifty-four. He spent all his time behind a desk these days, so he knew she'd describe him as a soft heavyset man. His hair had been almost black in his youth, but what was left of it had gone completely gray. If he looked hard in the mirror while shaving, he could still see remnants of the strong jaw and chin that'd made him a handsome man, once. But even his blue eyes had clouded over the years, and the laugh lines had been furrowed over by frown lines. He saw Shade's eyes linger on the telltale broken blood vessels on his nose and cheeks; he drank too much nowadays, too.

Meeting the eyes she'd hidden behind contact lenses, Al picked up his story. "My wife was heartbroken when you refused to let us keep you. But during the time we spent with you, you called me Uncle Al."

She seemed still at a loss. "Was I here?" she asked.

"No, we went to a hotel where he was staying with you in Europe. The plan had been to make it seem as though we adopted you overseas. You were still too traumatized, I guess, and went into hysterics when you thought you'd be separated from Peter."

She looked over her shoulder at the rest of the house as if considering an alternate childhood. "Well," she said, "thank you for wanting me, but I was probably better off growing up where I did."

He remembered Peter's stories of her violent first few years and had to agree that placing her with teachers who'd given her constructive outlets for her anger had been the right decision. She'd been a frightening little girl and had grown into a dangerous but controlled adult.

They carried their plates into the dining room. She sat gracefully, but on guard. He watched her smooth a napkin on her lap, rearrange the silverware into the correct order, and align her plate and water glass before she picked up her fork. Half her face smiled when she caught him watching her. He asked, "Why don't you tell me why you're here?"

Around a mouthful of Szechuan chicken she said, "First, I wanted to make sure my—Peter's trust in you wasn't misplaced."

He heard the hesitation and guessed she'd been about to say: *father*. He and others in his field had speculated about whether she and Bas actually thought of him that way.

"I know he's not going to be pleased to hear you second-guessed him," Al said.

Her expression cycled through surprise, sullenness, and finally amusement. "Stop that," she said. "I'm not a child to be scolded by one of Peter's friends."

"So, tell me your thoughts, Shade."

"It occurred to me that during your years on the job, and especially working with Peter since his retirement, you've gained knowledge of, and access to, quite a few of the operatives who've been compromised. That's opportunity, so I came here looking for motive."

"I agree with you. So, what do you think?"

"I see no signs of complicity. I haven't been able to find any indicators of unexplained affluence—no bank accounts traceable to you with large sums of money. You live modestly, and your life is straightforward, so there doesn't seem to be any potential for blackmail. You have no criminal history, and your last drug-screening was clear. And I can't figure any motive for why you'd double-cross him. But people with major upheaval in their lives can snap and do unexpected things."

He ignored the unspoken implication. "So, now that I'm in the clear, you'll be checking out all the handlers of the other agents?"

"Don't be ridiculous. It's too bad about the others, but I'm only concerned about my team."

"Team," he said. "I'm surprised to hear you use that word. You're viewed as a loner."

"If you're trying to psychoanalyze me, you're wasting our time. It's true I work alone now, but it was a change I made for the right reasons. I have no problem admitting that I love Bas and Peter and view them as my family--more that than my team. Don't confuse what I want other people to believe with what I actually think or feel."

He nodded, satisfied. "You have to admit, with your particular excellence at killing, it's easy to assume you're a sociopathic or psychotic personality."

"Assuming makes an *ass* out of *you* and *me*. I'm not a psychiatrist and neither are you. I simply don't buy into the hypocrisy that humans are any better than any other life form. In fact, I've met quite a few humans who have less value than any other life form--and I'll include potted plants in that analogy." She gave him a wry smile. "That may be shocking or disturbed, but whatever. Besides, I was raised and trained to be what I am-- take it up with Peter."

"The training channeled and refined an aptitude that was already there."

She stared at him inscrutably and then shrugged. "He did actually instill morals in both of us, contrary to what you people probably think. But where killing is concerned, humans are a species of hypocrites. But this isn't the time for a philosophical debate."

Al refused to engage and changed tactics instead. "Do you trust Peter?"

"Generally, yes. But he's made two nearly catastrophic mistakes in the past year. So, this time I decided to check his judgment for myself."

An angry look had flashed across her face, which she immediately blanked. He assumed she was referring to what happened in Colombia a year ago.

She changed the subject. "Tell me about this person you gave Peter's private email address to."

"Ah, Reid Amhers. You'll like him I think. He's made a study of you. Check into his credentials, and then take a look at him. I think you'll see the advantage you can gain."

"You mean use him for information." She seemed to view the idea with suspicion.

"I don't see it that way. Peter and I have worked together for years. I scratch his back, he scratches mine. I don't feel used by him, and in fact I've benefitted more times than I can count from intelligence he's passed to me, not to mention the work he's done for my employer."

"Yes, but he was part of the system, and I..."

Al wondered whether she'd been about to say: *and I don't even have a real name.*

He said, "Peter and I aren't going to live forever, so expanding your network is just good sense."

"My network doesn't need expansion. Besides, government contacts are useful for the kind of work Bas does, but I've never had any interest in political cachet or the double-dealing that usually goes along with those kinds of operations."

He wasn't surprised by her attitude. She'd never been interested in international affairs, they'd conjectured, because she didn't know her own origins. But he finally had an answer to one of his concerns. When she'd disappeared after Colombia, Al had theorized she'd experienced a dissociative fugue episode, but apparently she'd just been branching out on her own. The fact that she'd slipped Peter's control was worrying, but less so than the alternative.

Shade said, "I'll have a look at him, but I guarantee he'll predecease you if I suspect for one minute that this is some kind of setup."

He ignored the threat. "Look into the accident that cost him the use of his leg."

"You think he was a discard."

"Yes, I do, and I don't think he knows his own people may have burned him. I wonder if he'd agree that the information they got was worth it? And they got a bonus—he survived being sold out, and is still plugging away for them."

They cleared their plates from the table, and Shade accepted Al's offer of coffee. In the kitchen, he asked, "I'm sure you checked the house for bugs, so why don't you tell me what happened to Peter and how he is? I won't ask where he is."

"It wouldn't matter anyway. Bas will have moved him by now."

She pulled out a chair and sat down at the kitchen counter. She'd angled the chair so she had a clear view of the doorway. He wondered if it was even a conscious choice anymore.

"Good. So, what did happen?" he asked.

"He walked into a trap. He suspected it, and went in anyway. He was supposed to be meeting a contact about the job, just like all the other specialists who've disappeared."

She focused on him, her eyes skipping around reading his cues, and he knew he'd given it away.

"The contact didn't show up, and his questions apparently got him noticed. They strong-armed him out of a bar in Crete, chucked him on a boat, and transported him to a hunk of rock northeast of the main island. A rock, coincidentally, that was once owned by the United States Government—and may still be."

"That's a pretty steep insinuation." Al poured the coffee for both of them.

"Well, that's the question, isn't it? Is there a leak? Is someone on the inside masterminding this whole thing?"

She shoveled four teaspoons of sugar into her coffee, added creamer, and stirred vigorously. Balancing the teaspoon precisely on the edge of her saucer, she waited for him to take a first sip. He obliged.

"So, we're back to me again?"

"Anyway," she continued, "he gave me only the briefest background info, put me on standby as his lifeline, and went in before I could object. He wanted me to divert attention from his movements. When he missed his check-in, I had to start from scratch tracking him down."

"Which you obviously managed."

"Honestly, it wasn't all that difficult. Which is perplexing in and of itself. They kept him alive because they were trying to get information out of him, but why did they need information? They've demonstrated that they're already plugged in to the network. So, now, tell me what you're hiding."

"I didn't know he hadn't told you," Al said.

"Told me what?"

Her hands had dropped out of sight. He knew what she had in her sleeves and spoke quickly. "My guess is that they were trying to draw you and Bas in by using Peter as bait. A three-for-one deal. But they didn't expect the speed and strength of your response."

"There wasn't enough manpower or armament at that location to have pulled that off, regardless."

Al laughed. "Yes, well, I didn't say they were smart."

She actually preened for a moment before her natural caution surfaced again. "What makes you think this?" she asked.

"Because what he didn't tell you is that he found the same solicitations directed at both you and Bas' through your usual business approaches."

"That jackass."

"Now, now. We all thought he knew what he was doing. We never expected they'd grab him since he only went in as a go-between. They had no reason to suspect he was actually trying to identify them. But we hope they only took him as bait. If we're wrong, they know that we know what the real agenda is--the systematic termination of every contract specialist and intelligence agent across several nations."

She sat back, looking surprised. Peter had obviously been withholding quite a bit of information. But her hands were back in sight.

"I knew the numbers were climbing," she said, "but you're making it sound like some sort of professional genocide. And what's with the 'we'--he was cooperating officially on this?"

"That's a very apt description. And the answer to your question is, of course, *unofficially* officially. So, tell me, how is he?"

Her mind still obviously occupied, she answered, "He has fractured ribs, a concussion, and a whole bevy of other contusions, cuts, and scrapes."

"Thank god it wasn't worse."

"They're all dead though." She sounded satisfied.

"Not quite all of them. Definitely not whoever's behind the whole thing because two more assets have been reported missing."

"Really," she said. "Well, that'll change."

Peter Laurent finally called while Al was sitting in a recliner flipping through old photo albums. He had his feet up, relaxing, and he'd poured himself a drink, hoping to numb himself enough to fall asleep.

"Al," Peter said.

"I had a visitor," Al said.

"Dammit. After I specifically told her to hold off."

"Once I'd gotten past the initial horror of supposing I was about to die, I actually enjoyed her company."

Peter's booming laughter filled his ear. "What's wrong with you?"

"Must've caught it from you," Al replied.

"Seriously though, I'm sorry. She shouldn't have done that."

"Someone is burning people. *I* would've suspected me."

"Still. Was there any destruction?"

"She took out my alarm system, but I'd been meaning to upgrade. But listen, I sort of let the cat out of the bag. She knows they were being targeted. I didn't realize you hadn't told them."

"It was time to tell them anyway. Did she seem to remember you?"

"No, not at all."

"She's really good at forgetting the bad stuff."

"Peter, she excels at concealing herself. I wonder if this is just something else she's concealing. Not from herself, but from you?"

"You're saying a six-year-old child could fool me like that?"

Al thought of names like Dahmer, Bundy, and Gacy and remained silent.

Peter said, "The reason for this call was to tell you about a telephone conversation I had with someone who is definitely not dead."

Al sat up in his chair. "One of the reporteds?"

"Yes. Lying low just like a few others."

"The body count is actually dwindling. What the hell is going on?"

"In this case, he told me he went in, didn't like the smell, and aborted. Then he heard about the other disappearances and went to ground to wait things out. Incidentally, he's been having a really fine vacation, the bastard. Wish I was there."

"Shade said your contact didn't show, and you stuck it out anyway. At what point did this guy bail?"

"Before that. He said he thought he spotted someone. Someone who has a very nasty reputation. And the possibility was enough to turn him right back around again."

"Did he give you a name?"

"Yeah, but I don't really know much about the guy."

"I'll look into it and see what I can turn up," Al said.

"I don't know that we should make any noise about it," Peter warned.

"Ah." Al changed tack. "Maybe we need to ring some more doorbells and see who else is actually hiding out."

"They're all out bird-watching, or at least picking up birds. So much for having friends in this business. You'd think they'd give a bloke a warning before they jack-rabbited."

"I hear you, Peter," Al said, acknowledging the coded words.

"One more thing--when they were beating hell out of me, they kept asking who sent me. I didn't think much of it at the time, mostly because I was more concerned about how I was gonna get the hell out of there, but also because I just assumed they'd figured out about the cooperation I was giving you guys. But now I'm starting to wonder. If they're the ones who targeted my team, why that question?"

"That's not good news," Al said. "What are you thinking?"

"I'm not sure. I'll tell you, concussion aside, this thing's been making my head pound for days. I wish the little miss had left me some stronger painkillers."

"How're the ribs?"

"Not bothering me as much. Probably just bruised rather than cracked."

They trailed off into small talk and then ended the call. Peter had given Al a clear direction for inquiry, so he grabbed his jacket and headed back to the office. He'd heard of an English operative who was a notorious ladies' man, and the term "bird" was British slang for a certain type of girl. The operative's codenames were derived from the British slang words for spy: "bird-watching" and "friends." And his first name happened to be Jack.

Chapter 4

Reid Amhers lived in an older apartment building in Arlington that had only an intercom and a door buzzer for security. Defeating the magnetic lock had been child's play. Shade had let herself into his neat-but-not-anal modernist apartment, familiarized herself with the layout, and finding nothing of concern, she'd spent the rest of the day stalking him.

Reid was an attractive young man. His hair was sandy blond, neatly styled but not over-groomed. He had a symmetrical face, and dimples when he smiled. The smile was bright and engaging, and he used it often. He did not wear contacts or glasses over his cornflower-blue eyes. She had confirmed a gym membership, where he went daily, and regular physical therapy sessions. Despite this, the leg in the brace was atrophied, and his left leg seemed weak as well—possibly due to the time he'd spent in a wheelchair during his recovery. After looking at his medical records, she knew it was a miracle he had legs at all.

She watched him interact politely with everyone he encountered and noticed no few women giving him admiring looks. He ate his lunch outside and read a book while he ate a nutritious, health-conscious meal.

Once he appeared to be in for the night, she combed through his service record and the personal history Curtis had assembled for her. When she was sure he was asleep, she let herself back into his apartment.

He was sprawled on his stomach on the left side of the bed. The only straight limb was the damaged leg. Without the cane and the brace, it was unlikely he'd be able to get out of the bed, much less offer any resistance or pursuit. And according to his military training record, he was no match for her—particularly now.

The rattle from the coffeemaker woke Reid out of a sound sleep. He squinted at the glowing, bedside clock and read 12:30 a.m. When he rolled over, puzzled, she was sitting on the foot of the bed.

He sat bolt upright and flinched backwards so violently that his bare shoulders slammed into the headboard.

"That's so much more gratifying. The last person I visited was just so blasé. It really put me off."

"Shit," he said. "You're her."

"Don't reach for the lamp," she cautioned.

"Um, is the other person still alive?" He swallowed.

"He was when I left. Things happen though."

"Especially when you're around."

"You know, I'm not sure I like how this conversation is going. You're embarrassed about being frightened but insulting me won't make me less scary—in fact, the opposite. Besides, being frightened of me is really quite sensible."

"Uh huh. What are you doing here?" he asked.

"You said you wanted to talk face-to-face."

"Holy hell," he said. "I meant Laurent."

"You asked for Shade."

"Nobody's ever seen you. It's that simple? Ask and you'll show up?"

"Sure. I don't make any promises about how things will turn out though."

"You going to kill me?"

"I haven't decided yet."

He laughed nervously.

She didn't even crack a smile.

"Did I hear the coffeemaker?" he asked, his pulse still racing.

"Coffee is your last request?"

"That is so not funny."

She slid off the corner of the bed and backed towards the doorway, instructing, "You sit there. Don't move towards the light or the phone--I will know. I'll be back with the coffee, a blindfold, and a cigarette."

"Does this pass for humor in your circles?"

He listened to her low chuckle fade away and then glanced at the curtained bedroom window--no light there. His eyes landed on the bedside clock. Its feeble glow was the only illumination in the room. She'd been sitting with her back to the doorway, where a slightly stronger green glow emanated from an emergency light plugged into a hallway outlet. If the power went out, it would automatically shine a brighter light, but now it was only enough to navigate by if he got up in the middle of the night. He considered his gun—that was in a case in the hall closet, so that was useless. Then he realized that he hadn't heard any noises coming from the kitchen.

"Shade?" he called out. He felt strange calling her by name.

"Yes?" She was standing in the doorway.

She was dressed entirely in black: in a leather jacket and matte fabric pants that seemed to have a lot of patterns stitched on them. Her build was slim, and she seemed to be medium height. Her hair was long and straight, falling well below her shoulders, and silvery blond. The rest was impossible to make out clearly in the darkness.

Holding two mugs of coffee, she sat back down on the corner of the bed and held out a mug at arm's length, making him reach for it. He hadn't felt the mattress move under her weight.

He reached for the mug, and his fingers brushed— fabric? And he realized that she was wearing some kind of thin, flesh-colored gloves. The boys in the lab would be upset when they found out that none of the entire collection of prints on file could be hers.

"Ah," she said, noticing his reaction. "The gloves. They make these for people with various skin conditions who don't want to be obvious about the fact they're wearing gloves. I find them quite useful and they really do wear like a second skin." Her voice had become mellifluous like a TV commercial.

Add "smartass" to her file. Right under "scary."

"What did you want to talk about, Reid?"

"Oh. Uh, I was asked to try to establish contact with you or with Bas when Laurent went missing—wait, how did you know I take cream and sugar?"

"Really?" she asked.

"You've been…watching me?" He winced when he realized how hypocritical he sounded.

She ignored the question. "But Peter is no longer missing. He answered you, and you still suggested a meeting. By the way, I don't believe in poisoning people," she said. "It's cowardly. So, the coffee is safe." She took a big swig of her own.

He'd forgotten he was holding it. He sipped it and tried to recover his train of thought. "So, like I told you, I thought I'd be meeting with Laurent. It seemed like a good idea to follow through, and my supervisor is anxious for any information he might have."

"He sent me along since it's our understanding you're in charge of the segment of this that involves…me. So, then, presumably, there's someone else on Bas?"

"Um, no, I'm the team lead. The person covering Bas is under me, actually. And if you could get her an autographed eight-by-ten glossy of him, she'd probably die of ecstasy."

From the way her silhouetted cheeks rounded, she seemed to be smiling.

He mentally cringed. He was sitting in the dark in his boxer shorts with a professional killer at the foot of his bed, and he was cracking lame jokes. What the hell was the matter with him?

"I could probably do that," she said. "But let's move along. How much have they told you about what's going on? Or do you just think you're monitoring illicit behaviors of persons of interest?"

He was sure she could tell by his reaction that that was exactly what he used to think. But he got a grip on himself. "Field agents are being killed by persons unknown."

"What's interesting is that it didn't start out that way."

Reid was trying to focus, but he couldn't see her and it kept distracting him. The green glow was enough light for her to read his facial expressions, but he could only see the outline of a dark shape in front of him. She was also unnaturally still, and he wondered if that was why he couldn't get a sense of her physical presence. He was completely unnerved. It was like having a big black cat drop in for a visit: might be friendly, might not.

She was still speaking. "At first it was just private operators who were going down. So, it's interesting that all of a sudden the organized intelligence community became so interested that they started sending in the legitimate people—so to speak."

"I guess I hadn't thought about it that way."

"Well, we like to think of ourselves as a cut above. So, why send in the B-team after the A-team?"

He had to concede her point.

"Then the stink started about international intelligence agents being targeted, perpetuating the situation as they dumped more and more resources into the mix."

"Okay, I guess that's where I was pulled in."

"And now some of the earliest casualties have resurfaced."

"What do you mean?"

"They're not dead."

"How do you know this?"

"Peter has made contact."

"Does my side know this?"

"I don't know, Reid. I was hoping you might be able to tell me. But maybe someone does know and they're keeping it to themselves. In which case, poking around might not be a good idea. How much poking are you in a position to do without being noticed?"

"If you're asking me to spy on my own government…"

She sat silently, studying him. Then she seemed to make up her mind. "Do you know what a discard is?"

He shook his head.

"It's when your own agency lets you be blown up in your apartment, suffering permanent disabling damage, in order to protect more valuable agents. Sometimes, the more valuable agent gives up the information on purpose in order to give themselves credibility as a double-agent."

She waited, as if she was expecting him to say something. He wanted to deny what she was implying, but he was too stunned.

"It would be absolutely legitimate in light of your present duties for you to look into the ownership of the island where Peter was being held, if you haven't already. We've reached a blockade we can't get past. You won't be able to do it either, but you have access to people who could. The problem is your roof is rotten somewhere, and you might bring it down on your own head if you're not careful who you talk to."

Reid watched her slide off the bed again and move towards the door. Damn the leg, he couldn't get up even if she'd let him. "Tell me this--who are the good guys?"

"In my experience there aren't any. Whether someone is good or bad varies from moment to moment as they make the millions of decisions that get each of us through our day."

"That's pretty cynical."

"You say cynicism, I say realism. But don't call me a cynic when this entire nation is popping anti-depressants just to cope."

"Touche," he said.

As she faded out of the room, he called, "Wait! Shade, tell me just one more thing, my curiosity's killing me."

She didn't answer but she reappeared in the doorway.

"Please, tell me how you manage to remain unrecognizable. I mean this thing you're doing right now doesn't work in broad daylight, and a wig doesn't change the features of your face."

"Wow, you don't ask much, do you?" she said, edging back out. "But since it won't make any difference, I will tell you. I spent a considerable amount of time studying with some very talented, Hollywood, makeup artists. They're dead now. Natural causes, not...me." Her voice was growing fainter as she made her way down the hallway. "So, don't bother looking for them. Anyway, you'd be amazed what I can do with some tape, cotton balls, and pancake makeup. And nowadays, with advances in latex prosthetics, I could walk up to you wearing Mrs. Doubtfire's face and you'd never believe it wasn't real."

He heard the front door opening as she called out, "You think on things. I'll be in touch, Reid."

She let herself out of the apartment and walked down the empty hallway towards the stairwell door. The elevator chimed as she approached, releasing two dark-haired men wearing navy windbreakers, dress shirts, jeans, and sneakers. One of them was holding a lit cigarette. Odd. Problem number one.

They stood studying the directional signs, trying to find the apartment number they wanted, and then turned in her direction. They saw her at approximately the same time she smelled the aroma of the smoke. It brought back a recent memory of a man who had screamed in Turkish; it was the same brand of European cigarettes. Problem number two.

Their disinterested expressions changed to surprise and quickly became calculating as they studied her in turn. Problem number three.

She was already in motion. Everything had slowed down for them: the woman approaching, their decisions to reach for the guns under their jackets, the smoker dropping his cigarette. But it had sped up for Shade. She had already made the shrugging motion that released the ten-inch, spring-loaded blades concealed in the forearms of her jacket. Her fingers curled around the grips as they slid into her palms.

She thrust both blades at the juncture of neck and chin while the two men were still fumbling for their weapons. The thick blades, resembling short swords rather than knives, sheered easily through their tracheas and severed their spinal cords at the base of their skulls. She shoved the men backwards, and they slid off the blades onto the carpet, making very little sound.

Shade crouched between the bodies, listening, and then wiped the blades before retracting them with another shrug of her shoulders. She checked their coat pockets but found no identification credentials. They were not law enforcement, then. Each had American currency in their trouser pockets. The smoker had a pack of Turkish cigarettes, and a brass Zippo lighter. Neither of them had car keys or a hotel room key. One of them had a slip of paper bearing a handwritten telephone number with an American area code. They both had silenced, low-caliber, semi-automatics holstered under their coats. She studied their faces, disgusted with their sloppiness.

She walked back to Reid's apartment door, popped the lock again, and let herself back in. His bedroom light was on, and she heard the ripping noise of Velcro straps as he attached his leg brace.

"Reid," she called.

"You're back?"

He turned off the light, and she moved into the bedroom doorway.

"I just killed two assassins in the hallway."

"What?" he exclaimed.

"No one knows I'm here. They were looking for your apartment. They were here to kill you."

"What? Why would anyone want to kill me?"

"You've spent about a year rehabbing from your injury, right? What did you do before that? Wasn't it intelligence work in the field?"

He let out a sharp exhalation.

"I guess they didn't hear about the job change and you're still on their list," she said.

He pushed himself up from the bed, balancing on the good leg, and pulled on a t-shirt.

"You can't live here anymore. And don't drive your own car until someone checks it. Do you understand? Do you know who to call to take care of this?

"Yes," he said. "I think so."

"Then you need to pack a bag and go now. When those two don't report back, whoever sent them may try again, and thanks to me, they'll figure you're a hard target and up the ante."

"There're really two dead men in my hallway?"

She said, "I'll wait downstairs until you're safely away. You won't see me unless there's a problem."

He grabbed the cane and began hobbling around the bedroom, opening drawers and throwing clothes into a pile on the bed. "You're like a natural disaster. Everyone who comes near you dies."

"You're still alive."

"Damn. Thank you, Shade," he called. But she was already gone.

Chapter 5

She stopped just inside the rear building exit and covered her pale hair with a beret from a jacket pocket. She doubted the two men would have taken a cab to Reid's building, it would have been memorable and stupid, and she already knew there was no public bus line servicing the neighborhood. Since neither of the men had carried keys, she expected to find a third person waiting in a car.

She'd entered through the same door earlier and knew there were two overgrown bushes on either side of the door, and that the light above the door was only lit by one bulb. But she would still be clearly visible from the waist up to anyone in the parking lot. The parking lot itself had not been well-illuminated.

After she'd stepped outside, she made a show of searching her pockets while she scanned the parking lot. A few yards away, she saw cigarette smoke drifting upward from a parked car. A swarthy, dark-haired man sat in the driver's seat of a gray sedan. The engine was off, and the window was open.

"Honestly," she muttered. "If you're gonna make it that easy…" She tugged off the beret, fixed a smile on her face, and sashayed towards the car. She let the breeze sweep her platinum hair across her face obscuring his view of her.

At the car, she extended her hand and mimed flicking a lighter. "Hey, do you have a light?"

The guy grinned and bobbed his head. A couple of his yellowed teeth were missing, and his nose looked like it had been broken a few times. He needed a shave and smelled like he'd skipped showering too.

As he turned towards the center console, her hand continued forward, grabbed him by the collar, and slammed his head into the frame of the door, knocking him cold.

She opened the car door, dragged him out onto the pavement, and patted him down. She pocketed his gun and a keycard that was still in the paper folder listing the hotel's name, address, and a room number. From her jacket, she pulled two zip-ties and trussed his wrists and ankles.

She searched the front and back of the car, checked under the seats, and folded down the visors, but found nothing.

Getting Swarthy into the trunk took some time. He outweighed her and was heavy in a soft, doughy way that was hard to grip. Once she had him folded and positioned so that the trunk would latch, she caught movement on her left with her peripheral vision.

Out of the corner of her eye, she saw Reid standing outside the building between the two bushes. He had a large gym bag slung over one shoulder and was leaning on the cane. His mouth was open.

"What?" she called out to him, keeping her face turned away. "This one is still alive."

He shook his head but couldn't seem to make a sound.

"I am a very bad person, and I do very bad things," she said, slamming the trunk.

She slid into the drivers' seat, started up the engine, and chirped the tires backing the car out. A dark sedan with fat tires and government tags pulled into the parking lot from the other side. If they'd seen the plates of the vehicle she was driving, she was sitting in a ticking time bomb.

Out on the main road, she pulled up the GPS on her phone and entered the hotel address. Fifteen minutes later she parked the car down the street from the hotel.

When she got out of the car, Swarthy started thrashing around and making thumping noises. She popped the trunk and knocked him cold again.

She kept her head down as she walked back to the hotel. It was a seedy no-frills flophouse. She scanned the area as she walked. Vehicular traffic in the area was light but steady. Around the corner were a variety of other businesses, lighting a bright boulevard. She saw one desk clerk through the lobby window. His attention was focused on a corner-mounted television behind the desk, and he was eating a candy bar. There were no patrons in the tiny lobby. She threaded her way through parked cars to a side entrance. Letting her hair hide her face, she keyed in, and then took the stairs two-at-a-time to the third floor.

She wrinkled her nose after she'd entered the room. The three men were slobs and the room reeked of stale sweat, feet, and tobacco. Empty coffee cups and takeout containers filled the trash cans. She made a whirlwind search of the room, dumping duffel bags, searching clothing pockets, and gathering up scraps of paper and receipts, including three passports and a manila envelope. She shoved everything that looked remotely useful into one bag and went out the door fifteen minutes later. She would have Curtis check the registration on the room, but doubted it would provide any information.

She exited the hotel through the same door she'd entered, but had to make an abrupt turn in the opposite direction when she spotted a police cruiser and an ambulance parked alongside the car. The uniformed officer had his back to her and was talking into the car radio. The trunk was open, and it was empty. Either she hadn't been quick enough, and Swarthy had woken up again, or Reid's counterparts were exceptionally efficient. As she walked away, another cruiser turned the corner and passed her en route to the scene.

A few blocks away she spotted a Metro bus shelter and ducked into it. She dialed Reid's cell phone and said, "Dirty trick. I needed to question that guy."

"It wasn't me. You saw my ride. They saw the plate."

"You better tell me what he says, or I won't tell you what I got from the room."

"He won't be saying much of anything. He's dead."

"Hey, he was alive when I left him."

"Yeah, he was alive when the cop opened the trunk, too. But after he put the guy in the cruiser, he went into convulsions and was dead a few minutes later. "

"Idiot must've cut my zip ties. Unless the guy was epileptic, he swallowed an l-pill rather than be questioned."

"Every conversation I have with you is surreal in the most horrific way."

"Meh. And I was starting to sort of like you. But hey, at least you didn't say 'Kafka.'" She turned the phone off, yanked the battery, and then climbed the steps of the Metro bus that had just rolled up to the curb.

"Curtis, wake up," Shade called as she climbed the attic staircase. She heard thrashing and a thump as he fell out of bed.

"How do you keep getting in?" he yelled.

There was a crash, probably the lamp going over, and some muffled cursing.

Shade had sorted through the debris she'd removed from the hotel room during the bus ride. The contents of the manila envelope had to be dealt with right away. She was feeding the pages into a scanner when Curtis finally showed up, cradling a liter bottle of Diet Mountain Dew and an armload of junk food, staples of computer geeks everywhere. He looked like he'd been caught in a small tornado. His glasses were askew, his clothes were rumpled, and his multi-directional hair was defying gravity.

"Athletic dreams?" Shade asked.

He shot her an irritated look and thumped into a chair, cracking open the soda. "New wig, I see. What's all this?"

"It appears to be a hit list. Five names and addresses, all agents, all located in this commuting area. Photo of each of them. They almost got one of them tonight, only I got them first."

"Holy shit."

"Now, the only question that remains is whether there's a B-team. Or a C, even. And whether the hit tonight was the first one, or the last."

"That's three questions." Curtis was still acting peevish as he sorted through the papers. "Passports?"

"Yes, can you run them? And also the registration on the hotel room and this license plate number?" She'd finished with the scanner and was typing on one of the computer terminals.

"What's this handwritten phone number?"

"It's evidence of gross incompetence. At least I hope so. We definitely want to know who that belongs to. And can we reach our two idiots yet? I don't care what time it is wherever they are."

"What are you doing?" he asked.

"Emailing this list to Peter's government contacts. They need to take steps to protect these people if they're not already dead."

They had to do a little technology leapfrog to get from Bas' cell phone to Peter's laptop and into a web conference session between all four of them.

After Shade had given Peter and Bas the highlights, Peter said, "Busy girl. And also a visit to Al Brandon, I'm told. We'll get to that later. I thought I told you not to stir anything up?"

"What, like I'm a magnet that drew the assassins to his apartment? They had his name on a list. What was I supposed to do?"

Bas wisecracked, "Yeah, but you still have to admit that tit-for-tat your body count is probably higher than my whole team. We're talking epic proportions here."

"I seriously doubt that, but even if it were true it's only because your team doesn't stick around to count the crispy critters after you torch the place. How many people were on that island? I'm nowhere near your quota for *this week*. So, you shut up."

Shade zeroed in on Curtis. He was eating Doritos one after another, right out of the bag. They were so intensely red they had to be radioactive. He wore a grin from ear to ear and was jiving his head. At least someone was entertained. "You keep eating those, you're gonna shit red for a week, Curtis."

"Don't pick on me. I'm on *your* side."

On the screen, Bas clutched at his big chest dramatically and dropped out of view. Peter shot him a look over his shoulder and then rolled his eyes.

"So what did you think of this Reid Amhers guy?" Peter asked.

"He's green. He's dangerously green."

"I thought he had a combat record?"

"Military," she corrected. "He was overseas, but we're talking about combat by its looser definition. The impression I'm getting is that he thinks his job is fun, but he isn't liking the reality of what he's gotten himself into. He seemed a little freaked out."

From somewhere off-screen, Bas called, "Nancy-boy!"

"Shade, you still freak Curtis out and he's known you for years. Do you ever wonder if you might be the problem?" Peter asked.

"You raised me, so pot-kettle." She scowled at Curtis, but he just shrugged and kept eating. He'd moved on to the next food group: chocolate.

Peter suggested, "Give the guy a little time, he's in over his head at work, his C.O. sold him out and got him blown up. Today he had a crazy lady stalking him and showing up in his bed, someone tried to kill him, and there are two dead guys in his hallway."

"Whatever, that's a slow day at the office for us. And I wasn't *in* his bed."

"That might actually have helped."

"He's a little too white bread for my tastes, thanks."

"Nancy-boy!" Bas called out again.

"And he's 'green.' Duly noted," Peter said. "But he's still alive, so you must've liked him."

Shade made a noncommittal noise. "He's likeable, and seems bright, but he'd need a lot of mentoring."

"Train 'em up the way you want 'em. Worked for me."

"Really? Did it? That's why you keep bitching at Bas and I, right? Can we move along now? I'm sleep-deprived and you know how punchy I get when I don't get my beauty rest."

"Yes, sweetheart."

Bas, back on screen, quipped, "'Punchy?' More like stabby."

Peter made a quick movement that was blurred by the image resolution, and there was the sound of an impact. He smiled happily into the camera at Shade.

She sniggered.

"Your aim sucks, old man," Bas called.

"Shut up! Don't you two understand that laughing and bruised ribs don't mix?"

"Moving along... Okay, so, these guys were incredibly sloppy. Turkish passports, Curtis is still looking them up, but my guess is garden-variety hired guns. The car was reported stolen from Florida--we all know that won't lead anywhere. The hotel was a walk-in, cash down. Nothing useful there. I emailed the list of names to your contacts, dad. Their agencies can pass the word along to get the remaining three people protected. One name on the list is already down. A Google search on the name led to a newspaper article that lists an accidental drowning in the guy's own swimming pool as the cause of death. His wife found him. Last but not least, there's the phone number from the assassin's pocket."

"A local number?" Peter asked.

"Upstate New York. It belongs to a lawyer whose business partnership has cropped up in association with your recent stay on a certain rock. A Mr. Liam S. Rawlley."

"Oh goody. Finally, a direction."

"Tell Bas he can't blow up the lawyer until after we get all the information we need."

His big blond head filled the screen, eyes shining with mirth, as he leaned in over Peter. "That's so not fair, I let you do all the B&E and sneaking around your little heart desired before I started blowing stuff up on that island. Even when I do what you tell me, you still give me shit. Where's the love?"

"Oh, that reminds me. Bas, some female on Reid's team named Judy is hot for you. Wants an eight-by-ten glossy—autographed."

He narrowed his eyes and disappeared from view.

"Is she cute?" Curtis asked.

Chapter 6

Reid had been escorted directly to headquarters to be debriefed. As summoning calls went out to ruin people's sleep, he'd checked his email. The shit-storm that had erupted in the conference room after he'd shared the contents of Shade's email was still spawning minor dust-ups in departments he'd never even heard of previously.

Once all the need-to-know staff had assembled, they'd made him talk until he was hoarse. During the process, people kept dashing out of the room to deal with cleaning up the aftermath. He was sure the local police would have one less body in their morgue, and one less car in their impound lot. He was equally sure that neither the local police nor any of his neighbors knew anything about the bodies outside his apartment.

Finally, it was just Reid and Clemmons left. Reid had lost track of how many cups of coffee he'd drunk and was sure he looked like hell if Clemmons' appearance was anything to go by. Clemmons had seated himself at the other end of the table at the start of the debriefing, and Reid wondered whether the physical distance had been deliberate, and also whether Clemmons was regretting his meteoric rise through the ranks. After meeting the live version of Shade, he might need to rethink his own career. The sight of the bodies in the hallway, both of them large men, killed almost surgically by a woman who'd made him a cup of coffee, had chilled him to the bone. Collecting interesting minutiae about people who only lived on pieces of paper was one thing. Meeting them in the flesh was sort of like finding out the bogeyman was real.

"She actually showed up at your apartment." Clemmons. said. "How do you know it was really her?"

"Well, technically, I don't know." Reid waited for Clemmons' coffee to kick in.

"Yes, of course," he finally said.

"You did ask me to make contact with her."

"I meant...email. A phone call? Something. Not two murders in a residential apartment building in Arlington. Did she seem deranged?"

"Not particularly deranged, sir, no."

"Forgive me. I'm a little slow-witted tonight because I've been caught off-guard. It doesn't happen often. I can't believe I missed a connection Shade made almost immediately-- it should have occurred to me that your field work could put you in jeopardy. Now, let me rephrase my question. I know you've studied psychology and profiling, what was your impression of her?"

Reid took a deep breath as he gathered his thoughts.

Clemmons said, "No, I didn't mean a technical summation. Just give me five words or less--your gut reaction."

"Ruthless but captivating."

Clemmons studied Reid silently. "Thank you. And if she contacts you again, I want to know immediately."

"Of course, sir."

"You'll have a guard until we're sure the threat has passed, and you'll be assigned temporary housing. Someone downstairs is seeing to that now. Despite the chaos, I'm glad she intervened—I wanted you to know that. Now, go get some sleep."

Reid was more than willing to put his head down right there on the conference table, but Shade's request was still on his mind, along with one other thing.

Instead of going downstairs, Reid went back to his office. Ironically, the skills he'd developed accessing various governmental databases in order to monitor the activities of Shade and others like her made his task easier.

The explosion that had almost killed him had been deemed a random attack, and that explanation had been good enough for him at the time. During his recovery, Reid had been interested in his medical charts and not much else. But now, cross-checking other activities and persons in operation in the same area, at the same time, Reid saw a pattern emerge that supported Shade's theory.

The smattering of General Ratcliffe's name on some of the records was even more disturbing. Reid thought back to his meeting with the General and the odd reactions the man had exhibited towards him. With guilt in mind as the cause, they made more sense.

The disappearance of a man he'd known in the field, and the abrupt classification of that man's file, might mean he was now undercover with the group that had supposedly targeted Reid. Had his own associate knowingly sold him out?

He was still grappling with his emotions when Clemmons appeared in his doorway.

"Still here, Reid? They're looking for you downstairs."

His face must've betrayed his state of mind because Clemmons stepped into the room and closed the door.

"Shade conveyed something more that you didn't mention in the debriefing, didn't she?"

"Did you know about this?" Reid asked. "That I was a—a—discard?"

Clemmons' assumed an understanding expression. "I don't officially know it now. But I admit when I heard about your circumstances, I drew the same conclusion. It's one of the reasons I requested you as a team leader. I felt you'd been undervalued and wanted to make sure you had an opportunity to prove them wrong."

"You felt sorry for me. Well, thank you for that. I appreciate the job."

Clemmons frowned. "It wasn't a question of pity. I don't think a human being should be exploited and then discarded when they've served their purpose. There are a lot of nefarious practices going on in our industry, and I'd like to see them abolished."

Reid studied him, noting the high color in his sallow face, the fervor in his voice, and his forthright body language. He actually believed in what he was saying.

"There's one more thing I need to tell you," Reid said. "I hope I'm making the right decision."

It was common knowledge that one of the reasons Clemmons had risen through the ranks so quickly was due to favors he'd done for others. After Reid relayed what Shade wanted, Clemmons called in a few of those favors, resulting in a domino-effect of other calls.

Clemmons gave Reid a name for the Swiss account in less than twenty-four hours. The problem, as Reid saw it, was getting the information to Shade. He took her warning seriously, and not knowing what communications avenues were being monitored made him leery of all of them. Since he had a bodyguard following him everywhere, and was lodging in a safe-house, even non-official avenues of contact were risky.

He was standing in line at Starbucks considering pre-paid cell phones when he realized that he was staring right at a totally unconnected, untraceable phone sticking out of the bag of the woman in front of him. He checked the location of his guard and found him still waiting outside the door. He lifted the phone, and then sent a text to the number Shade had called from, praying she hadn't ditched the phone. He typed: *Got it. Don't reply,* and then deleted the thread from the phone's history. Dropping the phone on the floor, he said, "Ma'am, you dropped your phone."

What Reid hadn't expected was that Bas would be the one who showed up. Reid and Judy were at a restaurant near their office, waiting on their bill and chatting idly in a room packed with the lunchtime rush, when the big Swede slid into the wooden booth beside Judy. She vibrated like a plucked guitar string.

Reid's guard, who was supposed to be protecting him from deadly assassins like this one, glanced over from his meal at an adjacent booth and started to move, but at his headshake, relaxed. Reid suddenly felt a lot less safe.

Bas hadn't even bothered to look in the guard's direction, just draped himself on the bench seat. Beside his long, muscular frame, Judy looked like a plump little house mouse. She scooted into the far corner and sat ogling Bas while he took up the remaining three-quarters of the seat. She looked like she was memorizing the narrow Nordic nose, high cheekbones, and angular lines of his face.

Bas said, "That guy must be a Secret Service dropout."

"I guess you don't look enough like an assassin to him. Maybe next time you could come in screaming in Arabic and carrying an uzi."

Bas made an affirmative tock noise out of the side of his mouth and winked. He filched a handful of French fries off Judy's plate and popped them into his mouth. His downcast eyes flicked in her direction as he said to Reid, "Shade's in stitches out in the car. Any idea why?"

Judy caught Bas' glance and took a small quick breath, narrowing her eyes at Reid.

"No, none." Reid covered his chagrin with a gulp of iced tea.

"You're done with these, right?" Bas asked Judy. He was gazing into her eyes and flashing a great-white smile, like a shark might give to a seal.

She nodded emphatically, swallowed, and said, "S-sure, help yourself."

Making a show of smoothing his napkin in his lap and hoping Bas noticed, Reid asked, "So, to what do we owe the pleasure?"

Bas' eyes darted towards Reid's lap. He said, "Uh, no reason. We were picking up takeout, and I thought I'd come say hi. Heard about the other night from Shade." He paused almost imperceptibly. "It seemed like a good idea to check on you."

For no reason that he could put his finger on, Reid thought he was picking up enmity in Bas' demeanor. It was gone in a flash.

Bas took Judy's hand and kissed it. "A pleasure meeting you, Judy." The corners of his mouth twitched as Judy flushed up to her hairline and fluttered her lashes.

As Bas slid out of the booth, Reid extended his own hand. "Take it easy, man."

Bas returned the handshake with a steady grip. After a glance at the guard, and a rueful shake of his head, he ambled away. For a big man, he moved lithely through the crowded restaurant and quickly disappeared from view.

Judy craned her neck out of the booth to watch him go and then sank down in her seat like she'd liquefied. She was still blinking and began patting her napkin against her throat and face. In a breathless voice, she asked, "What was that all about?"

Reid put on what he hoped was a mystified expression. "I have no idea."

"That is one beautiful hunk of man. I just love a man whose thighs are bigger than mine. And he smelled good too."

"If you say so," Reid said. "He does a good job of coming across as a big, dumb, nice guy. Until you remember what he does for a living." Reid knew they'd just been handled. Meeting Shade had actually been frightening, yet as skilled as he was at reading people, Bas seemed like just an average guy.

Judy made an exasperated noise. "Don't you ruin this for me, Reid. Can we go back to the office now? I need to gush about his supremely fine ass, and you're not playing ball with me. Hey, how'd he know my name?"

Reid deftly borrowed Shade's, "Really?"

Bas slid into the passenger seat of the idling car, and Shade pulled away from the curb. Once they were out in traffic, she asked, "Well, what did he have?"

Bas was unfolding the piece of paper Reid had passed to him. "Your boy's not as green as you think. Or you just rattled him the other night. He gave me this note with a very smooth brush pass when I shook his hand. Even took advantage of me distracting his lady friend to dig it out of his pocket and hide it in his lap."

"Lady friend, huh?" Shade craned her neck to examine the sheet of paper taking shape in Bas' hands.

"Yeah, just about peed her pants when I sat down. She totally has the hots for me."

"Aw, maybe we should start a fan club for you. She could be president."

Ignoring her jibe, he studied the sheet of paper. "Ladies and gents, we have—a Russian?"

"Really? Wait, what year is this?" Shade asked.

"Yeah, I thought the Cold War was down to a cool breeze? Vassily Nemrovsky—doesn't ring a bell. Says here he's former KGB. Sitting on a butt-load of money too, according to the banking intel. This is mostly dated information though—stuff about espionage activities from years ago. Looks like our boy gave us an agency fact sheet."

"It's a place to start. If this guy is the owner of record for that island, or even if only ties him in somehow, it might lead to bigger and better things," Shade said.

"What if this is disinformation?" Bas asked. "They could point us at anyone they'd like us to take out. Say this guy is on a list of leftovers--people they meant to get around to knocking off. And here's their opportunity."

"I thought I was supposed to be the paranoid one? We'll check it out, that's all. So you don't think Reid's as green as I do, huh? Why not?"

"He seemed pretty composed to me. But broad daylight and being fully clothed does tend to make people more confident. He's a good-looking guy, Shade, but he can't handle you so knock off the silly game."

"Spoilsport. It was Al Brandon's idea, and Peter seems to like it too."

"They're always trying to pull other people in, but you and I both know better. Don't we."

Clemmons requested a briefing after Reid's lunch encounter. When Reid walked into his office, Clemmons had his hands steepled in front of him again. He looked less stressed than Reid could remember seeing for weeks though and exuded an air of satisfaction.

"Were you able to pass the information to Drake?" he asked.

"Yes, sir."

He nodded and went back to his private ruminations.

"What's our official position now, sir? Are we to keep operations going or…?"

"Good question. The unofficial answer is no. We want to give them as much latitude as they need, since they're essentially doing our work for us."

"It's a sweet deal for us, especially since they're not on the payroll."

"And there won't be any repercussions if their actions are controversial," Clemmons said. "However, the official position is that we're still working on the problem. With that in mind, we'll continue surveillance, but obviously with a lower usage of resources. Everyone can ease off the frenetic pace we've been keeping, at least."

"That'll certainly be good news to my folks."

"I didn't like the policy of continuing to expend our resources when we were being so obviously targeted, so I'm putting a stop to that immediately unless I receive counter orders."

Reid was reminded of what Shade had said about the incongruence of sending in the B-team.

"What is it?" Clemmons asked.

"Just something she said, sir. About that."

"There's more you didn't share?"

"She made some allegations—more like aspersions, I guess--along those lines. It didn't make sense to her, what was going on."

"It never has to me either. I assume she had a theory?"

"She didn't share that with me, sir, but I don't know if that's because she didn't know, or just didn't trust me enough to tell me."

"I'd been thinking of her as a more of a tool in Laurent's hands—a weapon he pointed. But you're the first person to ever speak to her face-to-face and survive to talk about it, and from what you've conveyed, she possesses quite a bit of cognitive ability as well."

"We've always known she was clever," Reid said.

"All predators are clever. They're good at camouflage, stalking, and using stratagem to attract and capture their prey. That doesn't put them on par with…a chess master, say. And that's what we need here."

"Interesting analogy, sir. I was thinking more of a shell game--catch the shyster at sleight of hand. Look here, while it's really going on over there." Reid tried to keep the personal bitterness out of his voice.

Clemmons gave him a measuring look. "You might just have something there."

"Do I keep looking into this Russian, sir?"

"Yes, but do it carefully. Only you. Don't brief the others. If we can feed information to Laurent, we're furthering our own aims as well."

Bas had delivered Peter to Curtis' house in the dead of night. Peter was still recovering, and his ribs were painful, so Curtis had offered to let them stay at his house to minimize his physical activity. Peter dragged himself out of bed at the crack of dawn, appalled by all the creaks and pops his body made as he climbed the attic staircase.

A very rumpled Bas stood in front of the coffeemaker, arms folded across his chest and mindlessly watching it brew. Bas looked like he felt.

"No sleep?" He eased himself into a chair and took the cup of coffee Bas handed to him.

"I helped Curtis for a while, and then my brain wouldn't shut down. I'd forgotten how much I dislike this country." He raked his fingers through his blond forelock and parked his butt on the tabletop.

Peter doubted the country had anything to do with it. He was pretty sure the close quarters they'd all been keeping were more to blame, specifically the close quarters with his sister. "It's a carefree way to live, running around in jungles, always on the go, non-stop adrenaline. But if you don't slow down, it'll eventually catch up with you. Your brain probably has a backlog of things it wants you to deal with, so you may be in for a few sleepless nights. My advice is to face the music."

Bas scowled. "Easier said than done."

Shade breezed into the room wearing a baseball cap over a ponytail, a sweaty sports bra, and yoga pants. She was carrying a half-empty water bottle and working her way through the rest of it.

"Doing a little jogging?" Peter asked.

"No, Curtis loaned me his gym card." She planted a kiss on an un-bruised section of Peter's forehead and then settled into a chair.

Bas sat down across from her and propped his head in one hand. "Oh ho, Curtis joined a gym?"

"Hush, Bas. Don't you dare tease him," Shade said. "He has a hard enough time feeling inadequate around you as it is--as you well know."

"You never give me enough credit. Who do you think gave him workout pointers in the first place?"

"Looking buff, sweetheart," Peter said to change the subject.

"If I have to keep manhandling you two out of sticky situations, I figured I better bulk up. Neither of you is getting any lighter as the years go by."

Peter pinched his flat belly. "Hey, I can still fit into my fatigues from twenty years ago, I'll have you know."

"But I bet your shirts wouldn't fit through the shoulders or arms. My guess is you're on the Bas-workout-program too."

"Where is Curtis? Still in bed?" Peter asked.

"No, he's at work, dad. Remember he has a day job? And we've been keeping him up nights for a while now, so both of you need to go easy on the guy."

Bas scoffed, "The way I hear it, you're the one who keeps showing up in the dead of night scaring the shit out of him. Not to mention foiling his latest attempt to sneak-proof the house."

"I can't help the hours. And frankly, he ought to be thanking me. If I can get in, so can someone else."

"I'm not so sure about that anymore, Zyl," Peter said.

She made a moue with her lips but didn't comment.

Bas said, "Curtis and I burned the midnight oil on our two names. The lawyer in New York was a lot easier, of course. We haven't been able to get much on this Nemrovsky dude yet. He still owns the property in Turkey listed on the fact sheet, so maybe he's still there. His wife is dead but we found a son and a daughter—a Natalya Nemrovsky. She's a looker. Lives in London. The son, Alexei, doesn't seem to have a permanent address. Maybe he still lives with daddy."

"My bet's on Nemrovsky. Wasn't Turkey strategic during the Cold War? Technically an ally but due to their proximity to the USSR they were sort of a mish-mash of loyalties?" Shade asked.

"That was true during World War II as well. That country has had an intriguing history—pun intended," Peter said.

"So, after the collapse of Soviet Russia our guy just relocated next door until things simmered down. A former KGB agent might've considered that a move to a healthier climate," Shade said.

"Turkey's a big place to get lost in," Bas said.

Peter said, "But what's the connection? Why would he all of a sudden start killing operatives?"

"Maybe he had a score to settle," Shade said.

Peter said, "We've got that lawyer, Rawlley, cropping up a couple of times, let's start there. I'm not willing to take any handout at face value right now, regardless of what a nice guy this Reid kid is."

Bas said, "About Rawlley-- I've come across his name before as a source of arms supply. Never had any contact with him myself, but guys on my team have used him. Curtis checked around and he's got a very healthy cash flow situation, but no actual employment of record."

"I thought he was a lawyer?" Shade asked.

Bas answered, "Still has his license, but it was a near thing. Looks like he got political aspirations--big surprise there-- and started rubbing shoulders with the wrong people. He was looking at charges of bribery and extortion and cut a deal with the D.A.'s office. Whoever thought he had a bright future in politics must've come up with another use for him because right after a long vacation overseas, he started running guns. Officially, he's independently wealthy and hobnobbing with other rich and famous S.O.B.s. Unofficially, he's got an extensive client list--including Uncle Sam—that insulates him from any more criminal charges."

"They hire a private contractor to do a job, and when the contractor needs guns, they tell them to go see Rawlley?" Shade asked.

"Pretty much."

"So hiring a hit squad would be right up his alley," Peter said. "The question remains—who solicited it?"

"And whether or not we can find that out, depends on how smart this guy is," Bas said.

"Most humans are inherently stupid, so our odds are good," Shade said.

Peter had rolled up to a terminal and was checking his email between sips of coffee. "Hold that thought. I have a call-me from Al. Gotta go downstairs." He levered himself up and went to make the call from the non-shielded, part of the house.

"He should not be moving around so much," Shade said, worried.

"Try telling him that."

They each grabbed their drinks and followed Peter downstairs to eavesdrop.

"Al, I gotta keep this short, but what've you got for me?" He braced himself against a wall on the bedroom level and took shallow breaths against the pain.

Shade sidled up, looking sternly maternal. Bas slouched against the wall on the bottom step.

"A mutual *friend* has been spotted. And I heard it from another person who isn't dead," Al replied.

"This is starting to stink," Peter said.

"How about dinner at that place Mary hated?"

"They had cheap drinks at happy hour, right? See you there."

Peter clicked off the phone and removed the battery. Studying it absently, he said, "We go through too many cell phones. Curtis needs to work something out, there."

"We should get an encrypted line, especially if you're going to be making calls from here for a while," Shade said. "You shouldn't be running up and down the stairs every few minutes. You need to be resting and healing."

He looked up at the staircase and sighed.

"I'm getting your pain pills." Shade hurried down the hallway before he could protest.

Bas said, "I'd offer to help, but you'd pull a macho routine on me and chew me out."

"Actually, I wouldn't. Ribs are damned painful. But anything you'd do to help would just hurt more. Just walk behind me and make sure my old ass doesn't fall back down the stairs."

Once the flurry of Shade forcing pills down his throat, nagging Bas to bring up a recliner from the first floor, and wedging pillows around him to support his torso had subsided, Peter told them the bad news. "Al just confirmed a suspicion about the involvement of another operative. And also that another one of the private contractors who was reported killed isn't actually dead. There's something going on here, and I don't like it. So, until we know more, I want us to sit tight."

"You're meeting him at five?" Shade asked.

"Yeah. Maybe I'll learn more tonight. But I have to tell you, I don't like the fact that it feels like I, or we, are being set up here. Whether it's a setup to take a fall like the others, or a setup to make us do all the dirty work that the officials don't want to do, I don't know and I don't care. We're not getting paid to solve their problem. I went into this initially because some of the guys who supposedly got hit were friends of mine. And then it looked like my family was being targeted. But now it's starting to look like some kind of shadow op, and I'm not sure we need to play anymore."

Bas said, "These guys kidnapped you, beat the hell out of you, and were going to kill you. You're gonna walk away now?"

Shade added, "We're making progress here. They're not better than us. We can unravel this. We can always back out later if we feel there's a setup in play. You know I'm good for that instinct."

Bas looked away, and Peter shot Shade a sharp glance. "I know, sweetheart, but I will never put you in that position again."

Al's late wife had disliked Indian food. It wasn't one of Peter's favorite cuisines either—curry didn't sit well with him the next day, and he didn't think yogurt belonged on any menu outside of Los Angeles. But Al loved it, and Peter was willing to go along with anything that put a bright spot in the man's day. The other benefit of the restaurant was that there were several small rooms available, separated from the main dining area, so complete privacy was possible.

Peter let Al order food for both of them but drew the line when Al ordered wine. He ordered whiskey, and told the waitress to keep bringing them. Shade would chew him out later for mixing pain meds and alcohol, but Al was one of the few remaining people in the world who spanned most of Peter's life and he was looking forward to the face-time.

Al opened with, "Let's get the business out of the way first."

"Go for it," Peter said.

"I have a positive ID on our boy. And he's still operating under the name 'Jack Friend.'"

"Someone else saw him?"

"One of the missing-presumed-killed. He said he got to the rendezvous point early. Very early. Because he'd heard some weird things were going on in the industry—his words, not mine. So, now, looking back, he thinks he beat Friend to his setup. He told me he saw Friend, clear as day, getting out of a car. Our guy was on a rooftop, waiting to see who came in. He said he didn't know at the time whether Friend had been solicited as well or was the point-of-contact, but he knew the guy has a black reputation and decided to clear the field."

"And that's it?"

"No. And then our guy hears that he's dead, MPK. Himself. So, he decided to go along with it and dug himself a hole to hide and wait it out."

"None of this makes any sense," Peter said.

"What do you know about Friend?" Al asked.

"Just the usual from the rumor mill. I've never met him or come up against him, and I'd kind of like to keep it that way. Like you, I heard he's got a black reputation--he'll kill you as soon as look at you. Dirty piece of work, yada yada. He's English, he's ex-SIS, or not, depending on who you're talking to. He's been around a while, but nobody seems to know much about him because he does not play well with others."

"That's the same story I've heard," Al said. "No one's ever confirmed a handler for him, or even the intel connection. He's ex-military, supposedly, so that'd be a matter of record, but no one seems to be sure what his real name is. I've never bothered to look into it before because I never had a reason to--

England is an ally, and as you said, he's never crossed any of my ops. As for the bad reputation, I heard he's been doing red team work recently—contracting himself out to people who were paying him to penetrate their security to identify vulnerabilities. Frankly, I wouldn't want to be one of those clients and have him walking around knowing my weaknesses if he's as dirty as rumor has it. But that reputation and the loner status are just shades of Shade. You know they call her Medusa, softly, when they're sure she can't hear them, because one look at her will kill you."

Peter made a rude noise. "I am never telling her that."

"You opened the door on Greek mythology with that whole 'Hydra' moniker for your team."

"Yeah, her idea--go after one head, two more come after you."

"There's a Greek island that got a little lesson in its own history, then," Al said.

"My god, these kids. Did I tell you? She handed me this gadget in the chopper and said to push the button. Didn't mention I'd be blowing up the whole damn place. And that's only what Bas hadn't already set on fire, shot missiles at, or otherwise exploded."

"You raised them."

"I keep hearing that from her, but I'm not taking all the heat. I blame that crazy asshole Dominic I left them with out in the desert. He was the one who taught them all this bomb shit. Bas' favorite person in the world? That guy."

"Shade doesn't seem to use explosives very often," Al pointed out.

"That's just because she doesn't like 'collateral damage.' It goes against her personal creed. What these gossipmongers don't understand is that she actually makes an effort to keep the body count low—it goes back to her ideal of precision. If she's planned the job right, she's in and out without anyone the wiser. She's never more pissed off than when she has to kill someone who wasn't supposed to be there. But it's true that she absolutely will not hesitate if someone sees her."

"And she almost always wears a disguise now."

Peter nodded. "She has that down to a science. The only person she can't fool is her brother. They've got that Spidey sense, the two of them. Always know where the other one is."

"It's funny how it all turned out. I mean, there you were with that sweet-faced, little girl that you thought needed a nice home so she could play dollies, and yet out of the two of them, I'd lay odds on her in any maneuver."

"I wanted to train a young man. I didn't see my world as any kind of place for a female. But don't sell Bas short—he's a survivor and very good at what he does," Peter said.

"Oh, I know, but while Shade can and has done his variety of mercenary work, he could never do what she does. Surely you see that, Peter? The mere fact that she's a woman opens approaches and opportunities that a male operative would never have. The fashion and the cosmetics alone make her more easily covert than any man."

Peter made a noncommittal noise.

Al said, "I've always felt that women are under-utilized in the intelligence community. They can be even more ruthless than their male counterparts, blend in to almost any scenery, learn the same weaponry and combat skills--just look at the things Shade's accomplished. She's your greatest achievement, and you don't even realize it."

"She's faster. She's possibly even more skilled than Bas. She's definitely better at blending in. Nature did him a disservice there--he's just too damned big and pretty. Who knew he'd grow the way he did? But you forget that I've watched the two of them drill. In hand-to-hand combat, she can only beat him if she stays out of range—if she's quicker than him and wears him down. Once he gets his hands on her, it's over. She's no weakling, but the fact remains that despite every bit of compensatory training I was able to get for her, she'll most likely lose in unarmed combat against a larger, male opponent."

Al made a dismissive hand gesture. "That's true of a smaller man as well. How often has she been beaten? And by anyone other than Bas?"

"Not yet. But so far, a broad daylight, weaponless, hand-to-hand test hasn't happened."

"I think you're just afraid. It's not that you doubt her, but that you're afraid of how guilty you'll feel if she fails and gets hurt or killed. Can I remind you now of the same thing I just told her? She chose to stay with you."

"Al, she was—we don't even know how old—five? Six? She had no idea what she was choosing. I should have forced her to go with you and Mary."

"After what she did to the Sheik who'd been holding her captive? I think we both know you made the right choice. You've said it yourself--the mindset was there. Who knows how she would have turned out otherwise? And you wouldn't have met Bas either. Rest easier, my friend."

Chapter 7

"What do you think he'll decide?" Bas asked. He was tapping away on the keyboard of his terminal while Shade peered and squinted at the screen of her own.

"I think he'll come home drunk, have a horrible hangover tomorrow, his ribs will be even more sore from laughing and probably falling down, but I expect after he recovers he'll start gnawing on this like a dog with a bone and not be able to let it go. Consequently, I'm doing research to figure out how we can set this up."

"Set what up?"

"Well, have you found offices for the lawyer?"

"No. Great minds think alike. I can't find any property holdings or leases in his name that aren't residential except for this LLC listing overseas, and that's a group." Bas rolled his chair backwards from the worktable and stretched, rubbing his eyes.

"We can have Curtis check his passport activity, but I doubt he's flying over to conduct routine business. My guess is he's doing everything by network. Probably from his highly secure compound in upstate New York. So we need to get in there and find out."

"Highly secure against what?"

Shade said, "People like us. No shit, seriously. I found a society page article on an event Rawlley hosts annually. He invites lots of models, the latest pet pop stars, and a few children of rich people who-think-they're-celebrities-but-aren't, and the photos show mobile patrol vehicles with the Briggs-Hempmeyer logo. They're top of the heap in private security and not opposed to using illegal methods to get the job done." She tapped her screen.

Bas got up to look over her shoulder. "Are you being vague on purpose?"

"No, I'm trying not to insult your intelligence," Shade said, looking up at him. "Why don't you know these things?"

He sat on the edge of her desktop and crossed his arms over his chest. "Because unlike you, I don't make a living sneaking around on rooftops or breaking into people's posh private residences. Someone hires me, I go in, shoot people, blow shit up, and do whatever I was sent to do."

She smiled slyly. "Yes, B-S-U--Blow Shit Up. Also known as B-F-T--Bas' Favorite Thing. By 'illegal' I mean lethal, anti-personnel devices.

Bas grinned. "Sweet. Tell me more about those."

"Grr. Look it up for yourself."

"I was kidding about that part. Got a guy on my team right now, used to work the bomb squad. Stick him in front of something that has wires, he can make it work or not work in a matter of seconds. The guy has kept members of my team from getting killed by anti-personnel measures more times than I can count. I can get him up here if we need him."

She pushed her chair out and started shutting down her workstation. "We won't. It'd be much easier to go there on a day when we don't have to deal with whatever precautions Mr. Rawlley may or may not have in place."

"Let me guess--the day of that event?"

"Bingo."

"And how are we going to get invited?"

"One of my posh private clients, of course." She stood up and faced him.

"And here all this time I thought you were Scary Spice."

"Har har, California. Anyway, tomorrow I'll make a few phone calls." She left him sitting on the table and walked out of the room.

Shade's prediction came true: Peter came in late and drunk. When he tried to make it up the stairs, he fell right back down. Shade rousted Bas to carry him upstairs and prevent a repeat. She grumbled and gave Peter black looks, but he seemed so happy with himself, and she knew he'd forget anything she said to him, so she decided to save it all for his hangover.

Watching him drag into the attic the next morning looking like road kill, she took pity on him. Curtis kept looking back and forth between her and Peter like he was disappointed that a thrashing wasn't going to occur; he'd been woken up too. Bas just looked content.

Shade forced large quantities of water, toast, and pain pills down Peter's throat while they shared information around the room. Once they were all caught up she said, "Okay, I spoke with Javier, and he attended this event last year, so he had some good information about the interior layout and general security," Shade said.

"Who is this guy?" Bas asked.

"He's a fashion designer. Very up-and-coming. Everyone wants his stuff right now."

"A fashion designer hired you? Should I even ask?" Curtis said.

Shade gave him a lofty look. "He hired me to steal something and implicate someone else. Fashion is a cutthroat industry. He was so pleased with my work that he padded my fee."

"Can he get you an invite?" Bas asked.

"Yes, he said he was asked to invite models. I guess they're intended to be party favors or decorations."

"Can he keep his mouth shut?" Bas asked.

"He knows if he doesn't I can burn him badly. So, yes."

"I'm not sure I like the idea of you going in alone," Peter said.

"Why? I do this kind of thing all the time."

"Not in a crowded environment like this with so many variables. Not to mention a large staff of hair-triggered security personnel. We're rushing, here, and it's not a good way to start a job."

"Security will be relaxed for the event. Javier said last year all they did was wand the guests—Curtis, that means handheld metal detectors. There'll be hundreds of drunk and doped partygoers strolling around acting entitled. One person wandering off won't be noticed, and if I'm found in the wrong place, I'm just a dumb model."

"What exactly is the agenda here?" Peter asked.

"We need to get into his records to see if there are any links to either that island or Vassily Nemrovsky. Even if Rawlley's company innocently sold that island to someone, we might be able to find out who that was. In other words, get confirmation that Nemrovsky is or isn't the direction we need to go. And if he's been hiring hit men to target U.S. intelligence personnel, maybe we can find financial records of that."

"Are you thinking there'll be documents lying around?" Curtis asked.

"Of course not. I'm sure I'll have to get into his computer. Email, banking records—there's bound to be dirt somewhere."

"What are you gonna do if you can't hack his computer?" Curtis asked. "I mean, you're competent, but if he's got anything high-tech, you'll need my help. "

"You can walk me through it on an earlink," Shade said.

"Maybe, maybe not, but it'd definitely take twice as long."

"Curtis, you just want to go because of the models, and there's no way I'm taking you with me."

"I think he's right," Peter said. He ticked items off on his fingers. "This is a one shot deal. If you get in there and it goes wrong, we don't get another opportunity. It's gonna take a lot of improvisation. We don't have floor-plans, firm information on hardware, or on personnel. And you said he doesn't mind helping intruders get dead, either."

Bas said, "No way will anyone buy Curtis as her date."

Curtis looked sullen. "I could be the guy that invented Microsoft. Those guys all have arm-candy that's way out of their league."

"Yeah, but you'll be memorable if anyone asks questions later," Bas said.

"I think we all need to go," Peter said.

"Now I have to get four people in?" Shade groused.

"Not four, just Bas and Curtis. I'll be the driver. I'm not physically up to scampering around with you two right now."

"With that in mind," Bas said, "we really need a fifth. Sorry, dad, but if something goes wrong, you're not up to reinforcing us."

"This is getting blown completely out of proportion--it's a one person job," Shade insisted.

"It's not," Peter said. "And I agree with Bas--we need four plus Curtis. I'm not taking any chances. There's too much we don't know about the details, and more to the point, who this guy might be connected to. I'm going with my gut on this."

"You're worried about that guy Al mentioned?" Bas asked.

"Is he that good?" Shade asked.

Peter said, "I don't know. He may be, and that's one of the things that bugs me—we haven't been able to find out much about him."

"Remind you of anyone we know?" Bas pointed out.

Shade darted a pen at Bas' head, which he ducked and ignored.

"He does. And that's a compliment, sweetheart. But I won't risk sending you alone, and that's final."

Bas said, "I'll call one of my guys."

"Not so fast," Shade said. "I want in on the selection of this guy. I want qualifications and a bio before we decide. I'm not going in there with some yahoo who's not going to take orders."

To her surprise, Bas gave her a level look and said, "No problem. "

Ultimately, the idea of Peter driving was vetoed in favor of hiring a car service. Shade pointed out that if anything went wrong on the exit, they weren't leaving a team member exposed that way. If things went well, she said, they got in the hired car and left like all the other guests.

The sprawling estate was surrounded by a ten-foot stone wall, holding old-growth forest at bay. Peter and Ricardo Chavez were ensconced on a ridge that had a clear line-of-sight over the manicured lawns, tennis courts, and a pool and formal gardens at the rear of the house. They were babysitting a Chevy Suburban that was equipped to handle off-road terrain in the event that a backup vehicle was required.

Shade had selected Chavez out of Bas' current ten-man team after reviewing their dossiers and listening to character references supplied by Bas. He had seconded the choice. Chavez was a former Marine, an excellent marksman, and in Bas' experience was cool under fire. And most important to Shade: he followed orders to the letter.

Peter found the kid friendly and easygoing, willing to talk or shut up as the circumstances required. He was in peak physical condition, useful muscle but not bulky, and he handled himself well. He was a good-looking young man with lazy Latin-lover eyes that made him a favorite with the ladies, according to Bas. His hair and eyes were the color of honey, and his skin was tanned to a dark, caramel color. From the photo in his dossier, Shade had dubbed him 'El Dorado,' the golden.

Chavez and Peter were laying belly-down in the dirt. Peter watched him set up a sniper rifle and high-powered scope with clear competence.

"Car pulling up now, sir," Chavez said, looking through the scope.

"Dispense with the 'sir,' please, Chavez. Just call me Peter."

"Will do."

Peter brought binoculars up to his eyes and they both watched as a tuxedo-clad Bas exited the limousine and turned to offer his hand to Shade.

Her platinum blond hair was twisted up in some kind of fancy arrangement on top of her head, and as she rose from the car, her bare back seemed to go on for miles. She was wearing a black leotard with a lot of wide, red, satin ribbon looped around her, mimicking a mini-dress. Peter had watched her spend hours stitching a high-tension aircraft wire into the satin ribbon. It was the kind of wire stuntmen used—thin, light, and strong. Her elbow-length gloves were a matching red satin. The thigh-high, black, suede boots with stiletto heels had enough buckles and studs on them to make any metal detector go haywire. She was showing an alarming amount of cleavage.

On Bas' arm, she walked towards the entry with a cat-walk strut, hips swinging. When they stopped, she cocked a hip, looked over her shoulder in their direction, and winked.

Chavez cleared his throat, and both men pulled their eyes away from the eyepieces.

Curtis was sweating like a pig. Bas had forced an amazingly thin Kevlar vest on him, and Shade had added some kind of harness with clips, then buttoned and tied him into a tux. He'd never worn a tux before, and rarely ever wore a tie for the very reason that the thing was throttling him now.

Shade and Bas looked oh-so-perfect, smiling and nodding like visiting royalty. Meanwhile, he had to trail along in their wake pretending to be her personal assistant, sweating and ready to jump out of his skin. Whose idea had this been?

Shade was doing a Zsa Zsa Gabor imitation at the entry, pouting and making sulky eyes at the two security guards, while the metal detector wands shrieked over her boots. Finally, the aggravated apes gave up and just waved her through.

Bas, movie-star smile going full blast, rankled them for a different reason: he was bigger than either of them. Smell the testosterone. But when the wand went off, they passed the jumbo-sized flask in his pocket with only a cursory examination. Curtis knew there was no liquor in that flask.

Curtis handed off his PDA to a guard and passed inspection without incident. He was supposed to be forgettable. Easy enough to do.

The main doors opened into a cavernous foyer with marble floors. Curtis tried not to gawk like a dork. Double doors to the right and left led into crowded great-rooms. A wide, shallow-stepped, red-carpeted staircase ascended from the center like a scarlet tongue. The banisters were carved with scrollwork that matched the crown molding. Towering arched windows set high in the front wall made the house seem open to the night sky. Uniformed wait-staff wove through the glittering guests, who were trying to look haughty and bored while they whispered about every arrival.

Once they were inside, Curtis took his cue from Bas and Shade, and discreetly inserted in-ear communications. They looked just like Bluetooth earpieces and would go unremarked in an environment filled with celebrities and power-types.

"Lots of pretty people." Bas put his arm around Shade's waist.

Smiling, Shade leaned into him and intoned, "Reading *Rolling Stone*, reading *Vogue*."

Curtis eyed them curiously.

"You'll fit right in," Peter's voice said in their ears.

Shade announced that she needed to find the little girls' room and left Curtis with Bas. He watched Bas note her departure time on a pocket watch and realized she wasn't actually going to the bathroom.

"Let's act normal and find drinks," Bas murmured. He set a course through the partygoers and led Curtis into a room that had been cleared for dancing.

"Ten-two on location tracking," Peter said.

Curtis suppressed a giggle.

Bas gave him a stern look and grabbed a couple of glasses of champagne from a waiter's tray. "Knock that back," Bas instructed.

After a few minutes, the women started targeting Bas. Curtis stood slightly to one side and pretended he was busy with his PDA, watching Bas ply the coy smile, baby blues, and the hair flip as he strung them along. When Shade finally turned up at Curtis' side, Bas excused himself and left them heartbroken.

"Nothing on this level, and no surveillance cameras." To Bas, she said, "Think you can get upstairs?"

"Let's see."

Shade babbled something airy about finding a drink and dragged Curtis along on a tour of several rooms. When he finally snagged a glass from a passing waiter, she only pretended to sip at it while keeping them in almost constant motion. He finally realized that her movements corresponded directly with any attempted approach by a male.

They reconnected with Bas at the rear of the foyer. "Second level, more party. Third floor, big question mark. I got up there, but security very firmly turned me back downstairs."

"What's up there?" Shade asked.

"Lots of doors, all shut. Maybe bedrooms. Except I saw cameras. And motion sensors at floor level."

"How many personnel?"

"Three."

Curtis heard music coming from one of the great rooms. It looked like Rawlley had spared no expense on club lighting and ambiance, including a DJ spinning a mix of dance tunes.

Shade's attention tracked in that direction. "Everyone here is either chemically enhanced or staggering drunk." A new song started and she asked, "Is that a Jon Secada song?"

With a conspiratorial smile, Bas said, *"Do You Believe In Us?"*

Shade laughed and let him guide her to the floor.

Peter's voice said, "No showing off!"

They ignored him.

Watching them dance, Curtis was astonished. The other dancers kept moving out of their way with envious looks as Bas partnered Shade through some kind of fast, hot, Latin routine. They stalked each other across the floor with synchronized steps, flicks of heels, and twirls. He rolled her into a gravity-defying, dip inches from the floor, and effortlessly pulled her upright again. Shade even sank into the splits to appreciative gasps from those watching. Maneuvering through the other dancers, they circled the floor with interweaving steps, and suggestive hip movements. They'd managed to steam up the entire room, and Curtis gave another tug at his collar and finished off the drink in his hand.

He was amazed to see Shade displaying herself, but then realized she really was still masked. She was wearing multiple hairpieces, her eyes were taped to a cat-tilt and made smoky with heavy eye shadow, her red lips were artificially plumped, and her cheekbones were exaggerated somehow. All anyone would remember was a beautiful blond dancing with an equally handsome partner.

On the in-ear, he heard Bas say, "Patrick Swayze?"

Shade laughed. "Absolutely no lifts. Things will fall out of my boots."

"And here I thought you'd tucked it all down…somewhere else."

Peter's voice said, "Unbelievable."

The song ended and Bas said, "Time to trade you off. I need some *fresh air.*"

He handed her off to another tuxedoed partner, and she continued holding most of the attention in the room. No one but Curtis noticed Bas slip away.

The new guy was a capable dancer, but he lacked Bas' smooth grace. He kept rolling his heavy shoulders in towards Shade so that the lines of their movements weren't as clean. He was closer to her height, and his features were too rough for him to be one of the model-actor-pop-star-wannabes. Curtis also noticed his hand was too low on her back, and he was holding her too tightly--too tightly for Shade's comfort as well, apparently. She locked her elbows, forcing some distance between them. As the song ended, fanning her face dramatically, Shade pushed away from him and made her way back to Curtis.

Bas' voice said, "Ready."

Taking Curtis' arm, Shade steered him with surprising strength toward the main foyer. She hustled him up the first two flights and slowed as they neared the landing at the bottom of the third.

"Now," she said.

All the lights went out. In the pitch blackness, Curtis felt Shade shove him to one side of the staircase and almost drag him up the remaining flight of stairs. He didn't know how she could see where she was going. Her grip on his arm was the only thing keeping him on his feet. Halfway up, she stopped moving and shoved him against the railing with her body, clamping her hand over his mouth. A pair of footsteps pounded past them down the stairs. Curtis heard shrieks and glass breaking on the lower levels as Shade dragged him up the remaining steps and opened a door, hauling him inside. He was going to have bruises. Two more sets of footsteps thundered by.

She clicked on a tiny penlight, opened the door, and flicked the narrow beam down each side of the hallway. Then she pulled him back out and down the right-hand corridor in a headlong rush to the end. She clicked on the penlight again, and Curtis saw a digital keypad on one side of a door in front of them. It was fail-to-secure.

"We need the power back on to unlock it," Curtis whispered.

And the lights came back on.

"You're on," she murmured to Curtis.

He attached the fake PDA to the keypad, and in a few seconds, he'd deciphered the code. The lock released.

Shade pushed him out of the way and peered inside. Satisfied, she jerked him in and closed the door behind them. "We're in," she announced, searching the room with her eyes. They were in what appeared to be Rawlley's office. Curtis saw a large wooden desk occupying the center of the room. A wall of books lined the left side of the room, and tasteful oil paintings hung on the right-hand wall over a small lamp-table. Two padded leather armchairs sat facing the desk. There were windows hung with heavy brocade drapes on either side of the desk.

Curtis slid into the chair behind the desk. The laptop centered on a leather blotter was state-of-the-art, and he could tell from the warm air movement at his ankles that additional electronics were concealed inside the desk. He extended a USB cable from his device, plugged it into the laptop, and got to work.

Shade continued to prowl the room, holding some device, and eventually focused her attention on the windows. She was giving almost sub-vocal instructions to the rest of their team, but Curtis was too absorbed with his own task to pay attention. He wasn't aware until she spoke that she was looking over his shoulder.

"How's it coming, Curtis?"

"Damn it! Stop doing that! He's got a…it's complicated. You definitely could not have done this, and I'm not sure I can."

"We're running out of time," she said. "It would be logical for someone to check this room after the power failure. They may only check that the door is locked but they may come in. As you can see, there is nowhere to hide here, and we can't both fit under the desk."

"I'm going to Plan B," Curtis said.

"Which is?"

"I've copied some likely stuff via the USB, but most of the files are individually protected and it's not like this guy has helpful filenames like, 'How I Hired Foreign Illegal Assassins.' I'm going to plant an executable that will run in the background and upload the information to our network. I can crunch it there at my leisure, providing he doesn't have the know-how to catch it running."

"Do it," she said.

He had initiated the file transfer when Bas' voice said, "He's coming up. Two babysitters."

Curtis threw a glance at Shade and then went back to what he was doing. She unwound the red ribbon from herself, and out of the corner of his eye, he saw her fishing several metallic objects out of her boots.

"Chavez," she said, "ten-nineteen to rendezvous. Bas, what's your twenty?"

"Foyer. Bottom of the staircase."

"Relocate to the area beneath the landings, just in case."

Curtis finished was he was doing, shut everything down, and then Shade guided him to the window.

"We're going out the window?" he asked after she opened it.

She jammed a metal wedge under the frame, yanked his shirt out of his trousers, and clipped a hook onto the harness he was wearing underneath.

"You are." She heaved him out the window.

He let out a yelp until he realized a line was playing out slowly, lowering him to the ground.

She whispered, "Shh!" from the window.

He touched down, and she chucked the wedge out after him. The line retracted as it came down, eventually hanging from the clip on his harness.

Peter's voice in his ear instructed, "Curtis, if you can easily make the wall without being seen, and can see a place to conceal yourself, move your ass as fast as possible in a direct line to the closest intersect and hunker down for Chavez. If not, stay where you are and he'll come to you."

"I'm moving," Curtis said.

Shade closed the window and melted back against the wall behind the door, pulling a gun out of her boot. The door opened and Rawlley walked in, flanked by two guards. She was just about to slip out the door when she spotted Curtis' tie lying on the desk. So did Rawlley. Shade thought about how much she hated working with other people.

She backed silently out of the room and sprinted down the hallway to the stairs. Yanking off the stiletto shell covering her boots, she was left wearing flat-soled suede. She jumped onto the railing and surfed down.

As she reached the landing, a guard above her yelled, "Hey!" but didn't fire the automatic in his hand.

"Bas, I'll be dropping in."

Footsteps hammered the stairs as she repeated her slide down the next railing. A one-handed vault launched her over the final railing, and she dropped into Bas' arms. He went down, absorbing the impact, and they both rolled and came back up running.

They spotted three guards pushing through the crowd in the foyer. Bas grabbed Shade's arm and ducked left, careening through wait-staff and into the kitchen. He held up the automatic that had been hidden in the fake flask as he charged through, and the kitchen staff jumped aside. Shade dumped the stilettos into a trash can, leaving her holding her gun and the coiled red ribbon. She tailed Bas out a back door. They both spotted guards on their right and bolted left across the lawn.

Bas said, "Looks like we're coming to you too, Chavez."

Peter barked, "Belay that! You've got to draw them off Curtis."

Shade produced one expletive and then saved her breath for running. They both veered right again, racing each other to a formal garden crisscrossed with flagstone paths and a central gazebo.

A glance over her shoulder revealed five guards in pursuit, and she knew the mobile unit would be arriving any minute. They heard the first shot as they reached the path. Bas slowed to put himself between them since he was the only one wearing a bulletproof vest.

Shade saw steps leading down from the path to a sunken garden. She avoided them and dove instead, tucking herself into a somersault and rolling back to her feet at the bottom. Bas did a similar maneuver as she fired three shots to slow their pursuers. They took off running again and headed towards the gazebo, veered around it, vaulted back up the other side of the garden, and lit out through open space for the wall at the back of the property.

They heard the mobile patrol coming in from their right to cut them off.

Peter's first shot with the sniper rifle hit the windshield, causing the driver to swerve. His second shot, a couple of minutes later, hit the left front tire, and the vehicle veered left and slewed across the grass to a halt. Time passed again as Peter refocused the rifle, and then he put three rounds in succession into the driver who'd exited the vehicle and was taking aim at them.

"Fancy, Pop. The tire shot was nice. Don't you dare re-injure those ribs," Shade said, still running.

"Nag. Screw it, I was aiming for the driver," Peter growled.

They heard more shots from the guards behind them, but they were wide and ineffective. They kept to their pace, trusting that Peter would now be re-sighting the rifle on their pursuers.

They were running on open lawn with nothing between them and the wall, but Shade knew there was no way either of them could get over it alone. She was easily keeping ahead of Bas, but that would have to change before they got there. And something had to be done about the guards chasing them, or they'd be sitting ducks once they reached it.

About twenty feet out, she slid to a stop, spun, dropped to one knee, and fired shots cleanly into the chests of the leading two guards. Bas passed her, still running. A third guard slowed down and crouched low behind the downed men. Her next shot went too far to the left, into his shoulder, but it was enough to knock him down. The other two were still too far back to matter. As she disregarded them, Peter hit the nearer one squarely in the back, and the man fell, plowing his face into the grass. She jumped up and sprinted for the wall again.

Bas was squatting in front of the wall, breathing hard. She got up her momentum, leaped onto his thigh and up to his shoulder, and he shot upright launching her into the air. The red ribbon played out behind her, and he caught it with both hands. She somersaulted over the top of the wall, landed, and rolled. She heard another echoing crack from Peter's rifle. On her feet again, she ran back to the wall, reeling in the slack as she went, braced both legs against the wall, and leaned back hard. Bas used the ribbon to scale the wall, bellied over the top, and then flipped down. Shade dropped hard to the dirt as his weight was released from the line.

"Damn, you need to go on a diet." She gathered the ribbon and shoved it into her boot.

He plucked her off the ground and dragged her back into a run without answering. He was not built for speed over distance, and she knew he was saving his breath.

They had almost reached the trees, where it would've been easy to disappear and double back to Peter's location. But they heard another vehicle somewhere nearby, and since the wall was now blocking Peter's view of them, he couldn't provide support.

"We have ongoing pursuit," Shade said.

"Shit," Peter said.

Chavez chimed in. "If you can get to me, Peter, I've got our boy and I'm on your way to their twenty."

"Once we're in those trees, these guys are toast," Bas growled.

The two of them plunged into the underbrush moving fast and loud at first but slowing when cover thickened. Bas lost track of all noise from Shade at that point. Picking a likely tree, he crouched down to wait. He knew Shade had gone up again.

He'd finally caught his breath, slowed his heart rate, and was patiently listening to the first one creep into range. He heard a shot as Shade took him out. The second guy came in from the other side, attracted to the noise, and Bas put a bullet in his chest. Bas had gotten a good look at him, and the guy wasn't wearing a suit jacket and tie like the ones back at the house. He had on a black long-sleeved t-shirt, black cargo pants, and combat boots. Bas crept towards Shade's direction.

When a deadfall became a person and moved, he spotted her covered with leaves and twigs. He knew he'd seen her only because she'd allowed him to do so. He put his back against an adjacent tree. She had dirt smeared on her face and arms to hide their paleness, and she'd nixed the red gloves. She looked ticked as hell that he'd ruined her trap. His highly-visible, white, tuxedo shirt probably wasn't improving her outlook. She jerked a thumb over her shoulder. As he peered behind her, he saw slow movement in multiple locations through the undergrowth.

She gave him a look as if to say, *Can you believe it?*

He agreed that this level of pursuit was excessive. What did that guy have in that house? Or maybe her look meant, *You idiot, you almost walked right into them.*

She signaled him going right and her going left. They moved off.

He had established himself in a spot that gave him a clear line-of-sight on most of their trackers when he heard a loud thump off to his right. Most of them turned, bringing their weapons to bear in that direction. Shade dropped lightly out of a tree off to his left and put bullets in four of them. Bas got three more before the rest took cover, and then he relocated himself.

From the in-ear, accompanied by heavy background noise, Peter said, "Five minutes on your southwest."

Bas fired a round into the guy who thought he'd heard something in Bas' direction and had come over to look. Off to the side, Shade did the same. Her next look definitely said, *Peter and his big mouth.*

He was moving southwest, with no idea where Shade was, when he heard a male yell that was immediately choked off. He suspected high-tension wire was in use as a garrote. She was still behind him.

Their route to rendezvous with Peter would take them along the searchers' back-trail. No telling how many more were still ahead or if more had arrived. As he thought about it, another one popped up. Bas shot him and continued on.

A few minutes later, he heard a burst of machine gun fire from Peter's direction and glass shattering. Over the in-ear, Chavez' voice said, "Clear here, all speed."

Somehow, Shade was at the Suburban before he was. Chavez was watching the woods with an assault rifle held at the ready. Bas and Shade both sprang into the back of the Suburban. In the other SUV, Bas saw one dead guy in the driver's seat and another in the roadway. It was missing some windows, and the tires were punctured for good measure. After Chavez hopped in, Peter spun the tires pulling out.

"Let's hope they don't have a damned chopper when we hit the main road," Peter yelled.

"What a sloppy mess," Shade said in an acid tone.

"Nice little engagement," said Bas.

"Dammit, Curtis. Your tie. Do you know where your goddamned tie is?" Shade yelled.

Curtis' face went pale. "Oh, god. I'm so sorry."

"I hope the file you planted will have time to run. After finding your tie lying on his desk, what do you think he'll do next? Do you suppose he'll get someone to check his computer?"

"Okay, Shade, that's enough," Peter said. Curtis, for future reference, when you're on a job you should consider yourself a separate universe from your surroundings. If it's on you, you don't set it down. It stays on your body or goes in a pocket. It's like camping--what you bring in, you have to take back out."

Chavez, in the front seat, said nothing and kept his eyes fixed forward during the drive. He'd told Bas he'd heard Shade's reputation and had no desire to die.

Slouched back against the seat, Bas said, "Remind me never to do any cross-country races against you, Shade, unless someone's standing by with an oxygen tank." He struggled out of his mangled jacket and draped it over her.

Shade hid her face in his neck and closed her eyes.

They'd dropped Chavez at the New York airport where he'd hopped a flight out. Bas had given him instructions to track down the rest of the team and have them standing by against future need.

Curtis was in the attic trying to process the data he'd received before the connection had been cut and prevent a counter-attack against their network. As Shade had predicted, Rawlley had taken steps.

Bas and Shade had showered, loaded carbs, and then collapsed on a sofa watching TV. They were both out cold. Shade was curled endearingly into a tiny ball with her head on a pillow in Bas' lap. Bas was sprawled with his feet on the coffee table, arm along the back of the couch, head leaning back at a crazy angle. Watching them sleep, Peter was glad they were finally getting along again.

He went up to replenish Curtis' soda supply and found him hunched in front of a monitor with his head in his hands.

"Oh good, you're awake," Curtis said. "Come over here and see if this makes sense to you. I am an IT expert, not an intelligence analyst. I think my head is about to explode."

"Are we still secure here?" Peter asked first.

"Of course we are. They tried me, they hit air. We're temporarily residing in the warm embrace of an agency I'm not going to name. It should scare the hell out of his guy."

"What am I supposed to look at?" Peter asked.

Curtis thrust a wad of printed sheets into his hands and grabbed a soda. "You tell me. This number here is that Swiss account I can't crack and that we were told belongs to Vassily Nemrovsky."

Peter took one of the sodas for himself, spread out the pages, and sat down. After a few minutes he said, "Okay, I see transactions coming into what you've marked as Rawlley's account, but what are these over here?"

"Those are an overseas LLC that Rawlley is in business with. It's a group with multiple shareholders."

"Looks like each transaction to Rawlley has a matching transaction, on the same date, to the LLC," Peter said.

"But the amounts are different. Why is the LLC getting the bigger cut?" Curtis asked.

"It's being divvied among a larger number of people?" Peter suggested.

"Yeah, okay," Curtis said. "But is the amount Rawlley's getting enough to hire foreign mercenaries, get them into the U.S., outfit them with a car and guns---"

"No. So maybe the overseas partners do the hiring, and Rawlley just supplies them with papers and weapons."

"Why though?" Curtis asked. "That's what doesn't make sense. Why would Nemrovsky pay a European group to hire Turkish assassins and export them to an American lawyer? Doesn't that point the finger right back at Nemrovsky?"

"And you claim you're not good at analysis."

"And look here," Curtis continued. "This account right here? You'll see it over and over." He shuffled through the sheets. "Guess who that belongs to? Our boy Nemrovsky."

"So who the hell does that Swiss account belong to?"

"Yeah, you have fun with that. I'm going to bed now before my brains leak out of my ears. Tell Shade if she wakes me up, I will shoot her."

As Curtis stumbled past, Bas said from the doorway, "We are such a bad influence on him."

"What'd I do?" Shade complained sleepily.

Chapter 8

Al Brandon almost jumped out of his skin when Peter Laurent tapped on the passenger window of his car at a stoplight. He unlocked the door, and Peter slid in, still favoring his ribs. Al said, "This is unexpected." The light changed to green and he stepped on the gas pedal.

"You're only being tailed by Bas, if that's of any interest to you," Peter said.

Al glanced in his rear and side-view mirrors and then wondered why he'd bothered. The road was packed with rush hour traffic. "What's up?" he asked.

"We've been fed some bad intel by John Clemmons via Reid Amhers."

Al gave Peter a surprised glance.

"How much do you know about Clemmons?" Peter asked.

Al thought it through. "No, I can't believe it. I checked him out thoroughly. He's a Dudley Do-Right. Straight A's on all his transcripts, never been in trouble in his life, and I even looked for sealed juvie records. He has no military background at all. He got into intelligence work on the merit of his smarts—the guy is a braniac. He started out as a pee-on and worked his way up the ladder fast by being a damned good administrator."

"Maybe too smart. Maybe he made some bad friends. All I know is we asked for information on a Swiss account, he pointed us at a target, and now we have evidence that the account doesn't belong to that target at all."

"Okay, I'll do some more checking. But my gut says he's squeaky clean."

John Clemmons' house was a one-level rambler on a corner of two intersecting, suburban streets. The lot was a generous size for the area, enclosed by a six-foot wooden fence that backed up to a heavily treed common area. A few abandoned bicycles lay in driveways, and one neighbor had a portable basketball hoop weighted down with cinder blocks in the street in front of the house. Shade heard a dog yapping once from several houses down. Parked at the curb across from the common area, she waited until neighbors began turning on lights inside their homes, cut through the woods, and went over Clemmons' fence. There were no dog feces in the yard, so she wondered about the fence. Maybe Clemmons just valued his privacy.

The interior of the house was furnished in a utilitarian style. Clemmons obviously preferred function over form. His home was clean and tidy, sparsely decorated, and it was obvious that a bachelor lived there. She saw no signs of undue affluence; the home and his belongings were strictly middle income.

She had searched through his personal papers and was in his den hacking his computer when she heard someone trying to open the front door. Someone who wasn't using a key. In the ceiling of the hallway outside the office, she remembered seeing an attic access panel. She slipped out of the room, lifted the panel, and swung herself up. She was sliding the panel back in place as two sets of heavy footsteps entered the house. She sent a text message to Bas and then got comfortable.

It was about thirty minutes later when she heard the automatic garage door opening. Presumably, this was Clemmons coming home.

When John Clemmons let himself in through the garage, he was surprised to find total darkness. He usually had a lamp on a timer for this very reason. The damned bulb must've burned out. As he walked towards the lamp, two large shapes rose out of the darkness near the sofa. One of them clicked on a lamp.

They were both pointing guns at him. Clemmons froze. The two men were dressed in charcoal-gray suits. Their brown hair was worn in conservative cuts, and their faces were unremarkable. They were both large men, and the shorter of the two had his jacket open, revealing a flabby gut.

"Mr. Clemmons, I'm very sorry about this," the taller one said. "But you're about to have a little accident."

Clemmons heard a rending sound, and plaster dust settled onto the two men's heads. While they were still looking around in confusion, Clemmons looked up at the ceiling. Two sharp blades sliced through the drywall, followed by a sharp cracking sound. A section of the ceiling crashed onto the men's upturned faces.

A figure clad all in black dropped silently through the hole, both blades slashing out at the two men. The taller man skipped backwards, but Clemmons saw a line of red across his chest through his sliced jacket. His gun flew under the coffee table, and as he dove after it, the black-clad figure kicked out, driving him head-first into the table. Glass and wood splintered. The man didn't get up.

The second man was clutching his arm, blood seeping between his fingers from the slash that had disarmed him. He launched himself at the person in black, who slid aside. The beret came off as he narrowly missed her, spilling out braided, gold hair. Clemmons realized it was Shade. As the man flew past, her backwards kick connected soundly with his skull, and he slammed into the floor. As Shade whirled to pursue him, Clemmons saw green and black camouflage paint marring her face. She was devoid of all expression, her flat eyes focused on her opponent.

Clemmons shivered.

The taller man had regained his feet and tried to grab her from behind. She stomped hard on his instep, elbowed him in the gut, and then spun, bringing the wicked blades to bear. The man reared backwards and fell, landing face up on the floor. She had scored him a second time, on his ride side, as he fell. She held her ground, seeming to anticipate that he would roll to attempt to knock her feet out from under her. She leaped lightly over him as he did so and dropped to a crouch as the shorter man attacked again. As he attempted a flying tackle, she simply stepped away, slashing him with a blade as he passed. Her motion had brought her closer to Clemmons.

"You might want to think about going out the front door," she said over her shoulder.

The taller man, his shirt soaked in blood, came up with a gun pointed at Clemmons.

Shade launched herself at Clemmons. He felt her body jerk when the shot hit her in the back. They both went down, and she let the momentum carry her into a roll and came back up in a crouch.

Clemmons scrabbled across the floor to hide behind a chair.

The second man charged right into Shade's crouch. Her leg lashed out, knocking his feet out from under him, and she rose up with both blades as he fell onto them. His weight flattened her to the floor.

Clemmons heard a loud crunch, the front doorframe splintered around the lock, and the door flew open and slammed into the wall. Basilius Drake came through like a charging lion. The tall man fired another shot, hitting Bas solidly in the gut of his bulletproof vest. Bas' didn't even flinch as he hurtled forward and leapt over Shade. Bas' left hand swatted the man's gun aside before he could fire again, and his right fist plowed into the man's face, snapping his head back and launching him to the floor. Still moving forward, Bas kicked the gun out of his hand and then picked it up at a safe distance, shoving it into the back of his jeans.

Shade let out a guttural exclamation and heaved the shorter man off of her. She arched her back off the floor and began tearing at the blood-soaked zipper of her jacket, almost writhing. Clemmons crawled towards her thinking she was hurt.

Bas said, "Don't go near her." He strode towards her and knelt to help her loosen the jacket. "Anything broken?"

"No," she gasped. "But it felt like it after he shot me." She sat up and slid a hand under the back of the jacket. It came out blood-free.

Bas grimaced at Clemmons as he loosened his vest, explaining, "Kevlar stops the bullet, but the backface pressure and soft tissue damage is almost worse." And to Shade: "Now what were you gonna do about the second guy when you were pinned down by a corpse?"

She held up her hand and showed him a metal object with sharp edges.

Bas raised his eyebrows and nodded. "That would've done it."

"He's getting up, do you know?"

The taller man was dragging himself slowly to his knees, shaking his head.

Bas walked over and clubbed the man over the head with a fist. He bent over and examined him, yanked him up by his hair, and banged his head against the floor. Twice.

"He's bleeding a lot." Bas looked over his shoulder at Shade. "Do we want to keep him alive for questioning?"

With shaking hands, Clemmons dug his cell phone out of his coat pocket. "I'll make a call."

"What took you so long?" Shade asked Bas.

"There was another guy outside in a car," Bas explained, looking around the room.

"What'd you do with him?"

"He's in his trunk."

"Alive?"

"Yep."

"Then we don't need this one."

Clemmons shot her a horrified look and rattled off the codes to get assistance at his home.

Shade shrugged and let Bas pull her to her feet. She extracted some zip ties from a pocket and handed them to him. She began systematically searching the dead man but came away empty-handed. "Damn," she said. "Ruined a jacket for nothing."

Clemmons ended the call. "What is—what are—what is that jacket?"

She gave him a steady look. "It's something a gentleman in Japan designed for me. I'd consider it repayment if the information doesn't end up in one of your files. The blades are made of a special blend of carbon-fiber-reinforced-polymer. Hard as shit and will pass most metal detectors. It's Kevlar-lined, and I can add hard-trauma plates. And it's got lots of pockets for other things I might need."

Across the room, Bas snorted.

"But why didn't you just shoot them?" Guns he knew about, her ballet-like proficiency with two evil-looking blades had been macabre.

"Gunfire tends to make neighbors call the police. We like to avoid interaction with the police whenever possible. It gets innocent police killed."

"Which is why we'll be going now," Bas said. He finished trussing the unconscious man and made a quick search of pockets but also came up with nothing.

"Oh, by the way," Shade said. "I was here snooping, but you appear to be innocent. Congratulations."

"Innocent of what?"

"That Swiss account doesn't belong to Vassily Nemrovsky," Bas said.

"What?"

"You'll probably want to be careful tracking down where your request for information went awry," Shade said. Pointing to the two men lying on his living room floor, she added, "These guys were in a different league from the ones sent to Reid's apartment."

Clemmons frowned, trying to process what she was telling him.

"We'll be in touch with Reid," Shade said. Grabbing her beret off the floor, she went out the back door, and Bas went out what was left of the front.

Sitting in her car, Shade wiped the camouflage paint off her face and texted Bas: *Nice vest, btw. R U worried about getting shot again?*

Bas answered: *No, but I knew U would be.*

Shade texted: *They never say thank U. I'm letting the next one die.*

Bas texted back: *No one in this country has any manners.*

Shade replied: *Wait, what country were U born in again?*

Bas banged the phone on the dashboard once and then tossed it on the passenger seat.

Chapter 9

Reid was still on lockdown and told Judy that dining with a bodyguard was embarrassing, so she and another analyst, Patrice, went out at lunchtime to pick up takeout for everyone.

They were each carrying a brown shopping bag filled with takeout containers as they dawdled along, perusing shop windows, and enjoying the sunny day. On the crowded sidewalk ahead of them, Basilius Drake stepped out of an entryway. The two women stopped in their tracks and watched him stroll through the crowd towards them. He was wearing a pair of faded loose-fitting jeans, and a light blue t-shirt that looked painted on. He eyed them both from under a forelock of blond hair that had fallen forward over one side of his face. He had a rolling, open-kneed amble with a little bounce at the end of his stride. His hands were tucked into his pockets, hiking the jeans up through the crotch.

Judy felt Patrice clutch her arm as they stared.

Flicking his hair off his forehead, Bas pulled one hand out of a pocket and offered a folded envelope to Judy between two fingers. She stared into his sky blue eyes for a few seconds before recovering the presence of mind to take the envelope from his hand.

"Could you give that to your boss, please, Judy?" He gave her a winning smile, nodded his head, and continued past them.

Both women revolved on the spot and watched him until he turned a corner.

Judy sighed, "My god he has the most perfect ass."

Patrice took in a breath, but nothing came out.

"And that walk," Judy said. "You just know he's hung with a walk like that."

Patrice murmured, "I think I counted every one of his abs. The size of him. He's just so…big. Oh, Judy, I could eat a five course meal off that man's chest."

"I wouldn't kick him out of bed, that's for sure."

"I'm not sure I can go home to my husband tonight," Patrice said. "Where's the car? I need to sit down."

They were still discussing him at the level of detail and lewdness typical of female-only conversations when they got back to the office. Reid, overhearing them, made a face. Judy handed the envelope to him, and said only, "Bas," by way of explanation. Patrice bustled towards their female coworkers and began whispering excitedly.

Judy waited while Reid opened the envelope and pulled out a single sheet of paper. It read:

If you have any information for Peter Laurent, make a reservation for dinner at Curry Mantra. Bring your boss.

Reid put the note his pocket and headed for Clemmons' office.

Reid and Clemmons walked into the private room at Curry Mantra to find Al Brandon and Peter Laurent already seated at the table. After all the introductions had been made, Clemmons said, "First, please convey my thanks to Shade for saving my life. I was so overwhelmed that night that I forgot to say anything."

"I'm wired." Peter pointed at a cell phone on the table. "So, you just did it yourself."

"How is she? Is she all right?" Reid asked.

"Sure, she's tough."

Listening at the other end of the conference call, Bas made a soft disgruntled noise. Shade grinned. When Curtis eyed them inquiringly, Bas lifted the back of Shade's shirt to display the round purple and black bruise that would have been a bullet hole if not for her jacket. Then he lifted his own shirt to display a matching bruise on his stomach. He affected a hurt look and mouthed, "Where's the love?"

Peter asked, "Any luck identifying your three thugs?"

"The two live ones aren't talking, of course. But their prints were on file. A few old, petty crimes, and a few wants for questioning referencing an ongoing investigation," Clemmons said.

"That just means this is the first time they've gotten caught at this kind of work. Shade said they were more skilled than the last batch."

Reid winced at the reminder.

Clemmons managed to look stoic.

Al said to Clemmons, "As you already know, you weren't on the list of names she found. That doesn't mean there aren't other assassins working on this, but since you were never active in the field, my guess is that someone doesn't want you sniffing around that bank account."

Clemmons nodded. "I agree. And I'm looking into that very carefully."

Peter added, "It can't be a coincidence that you were targeted right after we busted up Rawlley's party. They knew we'd tell you that account didn't belong to Nemrovsky. So, someone doesn't want you taking it any further."

"Be that as it may..." Clemmons looked Peter in the eye.

They heard a tap at the door, and a smiling dark-haired waitress wrapped in a green and gold sari shuffled in to take their orders.

"About the list," Clemmons said after the waitress left. "I researched the other deceased agent. He was recently retired from active service, and his death was officially ruled a suicide. The details weren't provided by the press because the family wanted it hushed, but his medical history included a depressive disorder. Perhaps it was merely expedient to make it look like a suicide, but there were no indications of foul play whatsoever."

Al said, "And the other names on the list are all alive and well and in protective custody."

"That doesn't mean they wouldn't have been hit if Shade hadn't taken those guys out," Peter said.

"True. But the consistent theme is that all the other names on the list are low-ranking personnel," Clemmons said. "I'm sorry, Reid."

Reid shrugged. "It's true. I am low-ranking."

Clemmons said, "You misunderstand. Out of all of them, you're actually the highest-value target, simply because of where you work."

"Why import a team of foreign assassins to take out such little fish?" Peter asked.

"There haven't been any other attempts either. Everyone has been keeping a tight watch on their people—both active and inactive," Al said.

"You don't think Reid was the only real target?" Peter asked.

"Precisely," said Clemmons.

"Why?" Reid asked, appalled.

Peter glanced down at the phone lying on the table. "That doesn't make sense. Why take out someone whose only involvement is knowledge of Shade?"

Al suggested, "Unless they were just supposed to rough him up."

"But why?" Peter asked. "There's no way anyone could've known she'd be there, much less that she'd stop that attack."

"Maybe this was another attempt to draw her in?" Al speculated.

The waitress sidled through the door again, balancing a tray of drinks, and hesitated when she saw the silent frowning men. She glanced around uncertainly, deposited the drinks, and bustled back out the door.

Clemmons said, "Al, I'm glad you're here. I don't have anything concrete yet, but I did get a tip that may have some bearing on the attempt on my life, and I'd value your insight."

"Sure, about what?"

Clemmons asked, "How involved is George Ratcliffe with your agency's activities?"

Reid twitched beside Clemmons.

Al's eyes grew distant as he thought about it. "That could be a possibility."

"Isn't he the one liaising between different agencies?" Peter asked.

"Yes. So, it would be easy for him to manipulate things, or just feed them to someone else," Al said.

"Do you know who delegated him?" Clemmons asked.

"No, I can't say I ever heard."

"Our Director informed me about his role, but I never actually learned how he'd been chosen for the position, or by whom," Clemmons said.

"Maybe he just liaised with the wrong person," Peter suggested.

Al said, "You just jogged my memory, Peter—'liaison.' I remember reading something recently about Ratcliffe--about a wedding. It was his daughter, or maybe his son, to some Congressman's daughter or son. Harrison. That's it."

Clemmons straightened. "Congressman Richard Harrison? The guard assigned to Reid worked on his security detail when Harrison was receiving death threats. I checked the man's service record and remember being impressed by a personal recommendation from Harrison."

Peter said, "Where's the guard now?"

"Out at the bar," Reid said.

"Why was Harrison getting death threats?" Peter asked.

"I can't recall exactly, but I want to say that it was just some unbalanced person who disagreed with his political views," Clemmons answered.

Bas' voice spoke from Peter's cell phone. "Richard Harrison and Liam Rawlley went to law school together and are still pals. Harrison's family is old money and contributed to Rawlley's political campaign before it tanked. I read all that when I was researching Rawlley."

Al said, "It'd be interesting to check whether he is, or ever was, a member of that LLC group of Rawlley's."

Bas said, "He's not showing up. But that doesn't mean he was never a member, or that he's not a silent partner."

"That gives me a place to start, at least," Clemmons said. "Needless to say, I'm very upset about having been used to transmit false intelligence. My network of contacts has always been reliable until now."

"When was the guard assigned to Reid?" Al asked.

"The night of the attack, actually," Reid answered. Turning to Clemmons, he added, "You did tell the General I was an expert on Shade. Maybe that's why I was targeted? It gave them a reason to assign this guy to watch me and relay information about her activities. And another thing, when I was researching what happened to me in Iraq, I came across his name a few times. But it could be a coincidence."

Clemmons was back in his praying pose.

"What is that saying?" Al mused. "Coincidence is the word we use when we can't see the levers and pulleys."

"I'm not a fan of coincidences in our line of work," Peter said. "And we have several of them now."

"I'm going to pursue this," Clemmons said, sounding agitated.

"Good luck taking on a Congressman," Al said.

Peter frowned. "Regardless of who it is, someone in our government is pointing us at Nemrovsky. I'd like to know why but it appears the only way I'll get an answer is by doing what they want us to do--visit Nemrovsky. What I don't understand, is why they've wasted all this time making us dig up the information when they could have just sent us, or someone, at the guy. If they did, and he reacted by killing operatives defensively, then who just targeted you two and those other agents? Who started this whole ball rolling? Someone's made it look like it was this Russian. But if it was him and those were his people on the island, why did they think I'd been sent by someone else? If it isn't him, then someone is trying hard to make him into a scapegoat. And on a tangential note, I'd like to be getting paid for this shit."

"I'm actually working on that," Al said.

Clemmons flushed and said to Al, "Maybe we can establish an interagency agreement."

Chapter 10

Peter found the three of them in the vault when he got home. Bas was lounging at a workstation, his long legs stretched out under the table, halfheartedly killing things in a computer game. As usual, Curtis was eating--some kind of dip and potato chips--and squinting at his monitor. Peter's eyes passed right over Shade at first and then found her reclined in his own chair, her socked feet propped up on the footstool, reading a book.

Without looking up, Shade said, "Curtis found something."

Curtis whipped his head around, startled.

Bas scooted back from the table and stretched out to his full length, reaching over his head behind him. "What was that black ops guy's name—the one spotted by one of your not-dead friends?"

"He goes by Jack Friend. Why?"

Bas flung out a hand in Curtis' direction, inviting him to speak.

"Okay, so I planted that malware script on Rawlley's computer," Curtis said as a lead-in.

"Yep," said Peter.

"It was designed to get the newest files first and start working backwards. But of course, they shut me down." He glanced nervously at Shade, who was still reading her book. "Since we weren't really sure what we were looking for, I had it pull his calendar, address book, and anything related to finances. I had only looked at the finance stuff until a little while ago."

Peter corralled a chair and sat down next to Bas.

"In his calendar, he had an appointment listed on the day of that event with the notation 'Friend.' It was scheduled a couple of hours before the party started."

"Nothing else, just that name?" Peter asked.

"No, there was a number entered beside the name. So, I cross-referenced that to his financial files, and it's a billing code for Nemrovsky."

"Jack Friend is working for Nemrovsky? That's not good news." Peter gave Shade a thoughtful look.

Feeling his gaze, Shade looked up. "I thought you said he was ex-SIS? No way is anyone in SIS better than us." She looked at Bas for support.

"I don't even know that for sure, sweetheart," Peter said. "Neither Al nor I were able to find out much about the guy."

"So, tomorrow we do more research," Bas said, resigned.

The next morning, Curtis and Bas were sitting at workstations, electronically pursuing Jack Friend. Bas had pulled up Friend's Interpol fact sheet, but there weren't many facts on it. The other databases he'd searched had given him nothing. Peter's voice had been background noise as he ran through his contact list on the phone, but Bas realized he hadn't heard him for a while.

Looking over at Curtis, Bas watched him eating his way through a package of Oreos. He methodically ate each cookie across the three rows before progressing to the next cookie in a row. Sometimes there was milk involved, and sometimes there wasn't. He never pulled the cookies apart and ate the cream filling first though. Gauging his own mood, he knew he was getting punchy. "I need to get up and walk around," he announced.

Curtis mumbled something through a mouthful of Oreo.

Peter was in the kitchen assembly-lining sandwiches when Bas wandered in. He grunted and handed Bas a plate stacked with sandwiches.

Bas peeled back the bread on the top sandwich and examined the contents.

"Where's your sister?" Peter asked.

"I think she's at the gym," Bas said, setting the plate down and opening the refrigerator.

Peter paused, holding a mayonnaise-coated knife in mid-air. "Is she spending a lot of time at the gym lately, or is it just me?"

"It's just you." Bas rummaged in the refrigerator and pulled out a bag of mixed, raw vegetables. "She works out every day. Have you taken a good look at her lately? She's pretty ripped. She doesn't get big, but she's all muscle."

Peter stared at the ceiling, as if trying to recall the last time he'd really looked at her. "Yeah, I remember thinking she looked pretty buff." He shrugged and dug into the mayonnaise jar again. "She's always around the periphery, but I never really see her—it's like she's always just out of my line of sight."

"Uh huh," Bas said in a neutral tone. He dumped a load of vegetables into a blender, added an egg and some milk, and let it rip. From a cabinet he pulled out a grocery bag containing powdered supplements and began shoveling in a spoon of this and a scoop of that and then turned on the blender again.

"You're gonna drink that?" Peter yelled over the noise.

With a single bite, Bas halved a sandwich. Killing the power on the blender, he poured some of the concoction into a glass, and then leaned back against the countertop. "She'll have some when she gets back. We have a hard time meeting our calorie needs."

A smile pulling at one corner of his mouth, Peter looked all the way up at Bas. He shrugged and pulled out more slices of bread.

With a sigh of satisfaction, Bas set down the glass and went to work on the sandwiches. "So, you having any luck?"

"Not much," Peter said. "The catchphrase of the day seems to be, 'let me get back to you.'"

"Same here," Bas said. "This guy's Interpol fact sheet looks like Shade's—lots of open spaces. Even the photo they've got is some ancient black and white thing. You can't see half his face, or make out the other half."

"What's Curtis got going?"

"He's been steadily eating sugar, so he must be hacking somebody."

Shade appeared in the kitchen wearing a sports bra and micro shorts. She was pouring a glass of green goo before Peter noticed.

After a swallow, she said, "I called a guy I know and he told me some stuff, but it's just more hearsay." She made a sour face. "Ugh. That's awful, Bas. Next time throw some vanilla in there or at least some sugar."

In a snide voice, Bas asked, "You know a guy?"

She shot him a withering look. "He's ex-SIS and his son is currently SIS."

"Let's go upstairs." Peter grabbed the plates of sandwiches.

Shade downed the rest of the goo, and pulled a liter bottle of water out of the fridge. She cracked it open and chugged as they walked.

On the stairs, she snagged a sandwich off Bas' plate, instigating a jostling match between his wide shoulders and her hip check until she just slipped under him and sprinted up the rest of the staircase. Chewing a sandwich, Bas pointed at her flashing legs and nudged Peter.

"Yep, ripped," Peter agreed. "Another fine example of her OCD at work."

Bas rolled his eyes.

When they walked into the vault, Curtis yiped, "Oh!" around a mouthful of half-chewed Oreos and then started coughing.

Bas checked out the Oreo package. It was now down to three remaining cookies, and the milk glass was empty.

Shade handed Curtis the bottle of water. He took a long pull before handing it back. "Like I would drink out of that *now*?" she said, wrinkling her nose.

Curtis shrugged and took another swig, swishing debris around his mouth. "This just in," he said finally, handing Peter a sheet of paper.

Bas and Shade peered over Peter's shoulders at one line of printed text that read:

The information you seek will be provided to you by a contact in Fethiye, Turkey.

Peter growled and handed it to Shade. "Do I remember correctly, Curtis? Nemrovsky's last known address was in Fethiye?"

Curtis rummaged through a stack of papers and pulled out the creased fact sheet that Reid Amhers had given to Bas. "Yes," he confirmed. "Just outside Fethiye. They have a latitude and longitude listed.

"Where'd you get this?" Bas asked, taking the sheet from Shade.

"Uh…well, I sort of hacked SIS."

Shade gave Curtis an awed smile.

He ducked his head. "Yeah, well, it's not all good. I couldn't find anything, so I stayed in too long. They caught me. The screen just went blank and then that came up. It was like they were ready for me."

Peter shrugged. "We've been lighting them up all morning. Shade and I both called contacts there, and I had Al working on it from his end."

"This is not good coordination," Bas said.

"The problem is that we've been cooped up in this house too long and we're all going stir crazy," Shade said.

"Oh come on, you got to kill some people just the other day," Bas said, poking her.

"But your incendiary urges have been smoldering for days now, and the miasma is hanging in the air in the whole house." She leaned into him and shoved.

Bas gave her wicked look and was opening his mouth to fire back when Peter cut him off. He asked Curtis, "Why do you always look so amused when they bicker?"

"Duh? Because they're hilarious."

"You understand they're not really joking, right?"

"I try not to think about that part."

"Back to the subject…" Bas said. "Let's go around the room and share. Shade, ladies first."

She opened her mouth to say something acid and thought better of it. "I was told that Friend is not, and never was, SIS."

"Which source did this come from?" Peter asked.

She pulled out a chair and folded herself onto it. "That's the thing, it came from the son. His father put me in touch with him, so he was speaking to me on the QT, but maybe he just didn't have a high enough access. The father told me that he's heard the name in circles, but that I had the wrong acronym. He said Friend is, or was, CRW—the Counter Revolutionary Warfare wing of the SAS."

Curtis asked, "What's that?"

Peter answered, "Just what it sounds like. They're a fairly recent branch of the Special Air Service that have expertise in anti-terrorism, hostage rescue, siege-breaking, and sniper training."

Curtis looked impressed until he met Bas' bored gaze.

"That's more than I got," Peter admitted. "So far, all I've come across are the same rumors that Al and I heard before. He's RAF, he's SAS, or he was on their Special Projects Team, he cracked up and quit, he's a blackguard, he always works alone, he's the devil. But I still have one call out, and I'm burning a big favor if this woman comes through, so I almost don't want her to have anything."

Curtis jumped when the encrypted phone rang.

"Too much sugar," Bas speculated.

Peter picked up the handset and then said, "Ann let me put you on speaker."

"Hullo ducks." Her voice flowed out in a posh London accent.

Shade raised her eyebrows.

"Ann, thanks for getting back to me."

"So lovely to hear from you Peter, it's been yonks. You're calling in your favor, are you?"

"Unless you're feeling generous,"

She laughed merrily. "I'll think on it, shall I? Only, to be fair, I'm not sure I can supply what you're looking for. Because, you see, I've only the other side of the picture. However, I can tell you he's actually called Sebastien Mathason. I knew him at university, you see."

"You never actually worked with him? Was he ever at SIS?"

In a breezy chatterbox tone, she said, "No, never. At least, not officially. He came up through the RAF—family tradition and all that—and their special teams. The buzz was that he was someone's pet. Some muckety-muck gobbled him right out of the military, and into some elite special-services group. You know, one of those organizations like you have there, Peter. Figments?"

Peter made a noise of acknowledgement.

She continued her lighthearted patter. "Everything else I can tell you about him is personal and rather outdated. When we were in school in London together, he was a good-looking bloke, dark hair, stunning hazel eyes, nice build, decent shag, good dancer—lovely chap. Then I ran into him socially--oh--a few years gone, and didn't realize he was a big spy these days. He was mortified. Couldn't get away quick enough. He was putting on a Cockney accent for the chaps he was with, but he's really from North Essex-- Colchester. So, afterwards, naturally, I looked into him. And what you'll have heard is all I know--he went dark, he's a dodgy assassin-for-hire, and so forth. Hard to believe, really, because he was such a nice boy, and I've always considered myself a good judge of character, but there you are. Any road, I'm spanking late for a manicure, so, must run. Do give us a bell when next you're round here, will you love?"

Peter picked up the phone and edged away from the others to say a few private words before disconnecting the call.

"How do you know her?" Shade asked with a knowing smile.

Peter cleared his throat. "Never mind."

"She can really talk," Bas said, dazed.

"She really listens too," Peter said. "That woman ought to be declared a national asset. She hears everything sooner or later. She puts on a ditzy routine, but she's a damn good analyst, and I don't believe for one minute that she told us everything she knows. She's wanted to get out from under that favor she owes me for years."

"That was all from her personal knowledge," Shade said. "There was nothing in there that broached the professional realm except that bit about the 'muckety-muck.'" She frowned. "He's never been rumored to have a handler—isn't that what you said?"

"That's what everyone seems to agree," Peter confirmed.

"But she was suggesting he does," Bas said.

"Either way, she was the last card I had to play. Unless Al comes up with something, I don't think we're going to get anything else on this guy."

"We have a real name now. Routine information will be accessible. I'll look into that," Shade offered.

"On to Fethiye?" Bas asked.

"Looks that way," Peter said in a sour tone.

Curtis had been working while they talked. "I pulled up satellite imagery for the location already, using the latitude and longitude from the sheet. And, wow, Fethiye is gorgeous. Cerulean blue water, white sand beaches, mountains in the background. Lots of outdoor stuff to do. There's a marina and nightlife…can I go?"

Standing behind him, Shade dropped both of her hands onto his shoulders. And squeezed.

"Yeah, okay, I got it." He flinched out from under her hands. "So, uh," he continued, "it's a town around 70,000 population. Healthy tourist industry, so mixing in discreetly wouldn't be too difficult. It's very popular with the British. Bas, you think you can fake an English accent?"

"I'd rather not," he said.

"Outlying areas are small farmsteads, mostly livestock. Then you hit the foothills of the Taurus Mountain Range. You've got some heavy forest area initially, interspersed with open areas--just a few shrubs dotting a rocky landscape. There's only one road, and it looks like a dirt or gravel track. At the very least it's not in great shape and probably doesn't see much incidental travel, so any vehicle moving on it will be noticed. Geologically, it's all limestone out there, and unfortunately, the northern approach backs right up to a decent-sized mountain."

The three of them stood behind Curtis looking at the images he was pulling up on the monitors. When he zoomed in on the actual location, Shade tapped the screen and said, "Short of rappelling down, there's no access there, and the rear of the main structure looks like it's built right into the rock—there are actually archways or big-ass windows cut right in the rock face."

"No 'up' for you." Bas wore a smug grin.

"Guess we'll have to go with the B-S-U approach," Shade said.

Curtis decreased the zoom to an area view. "To the west of the house there are three outbuildings. Along the south, there's what appears to be a water tower, a fueling station—or some kind of storage tank--and a long low structure that's probably a garage. There's a helipad on the eastern side of the grounds. And off the grounds to the southwest there's another structure."

"Probably the hangar." Bas peered over Shade's shoulder.

"If that's a hangar, it's a big hangar. I'd be interested to know what he's keeping in there," Peter said.

"And the whole property has a wall around it. Can't tell from an aerial view what that's made of," Curtis finished.

"Probably something that involves animal dung, considering the primitive look of that area." Shade was wearing a look of distaste.

Bas quipped, "What? There's no pool anywhere? Hot tub? How about a golf course, or at least a putting green?

Peter shot him a stink-eye.

"This from the man who spends all his time cavorting in third-world countries," Shade said.

"That's where I *make* the money, I don't spend it there," he said with a wink.

Shade said, "Uh huh. Because there's no red-light district in the jungle. But whatever, talk to my bank account."

"Wait," Curtis said, sounding pitiful. "I don't have any snacks. Can we pause this until I get popcorn?"

Peter put a hand over his eyes.

Bas fired back. "Yeah, Posh Spice, I know. Since you're so plush, how 'bout you spring for a nice resort vacation once this is over? I'd like an on-call masseuse, maybe a manicure…" He examined his nails speculatively.

"Sure, baby," she purred. "And then I'll take you shopping. For shoes. For hours."

Bas asked, "I mean, how do you stand all this roughing it? Can't you just hear your pores screaming for a facial?"

"I'm versatile. But you'd be bored stiff trying to get through eighteen holes on a golf course—it'd look like something out of Caddyshack by the time you got done."

Bas leered. "I dunno, they tell me I'm pretty good at sinking a long one."

Shade's mouth popped open, and she swatted him on the shoulder.

"Time!" Peter bellowed. He made a time-out signal with his hands.

Bas had ducked, laughing, so Shade snuck in one more. "Just be careful in the cat box, wouldn't want you to end up with a bent shaft."

Curtis winced.

"Enough!" Peter bellowed. "Can we get back to business now?" He gave Bas a shove with his foot and smacked Shade on her bottom.

"Yes, dad," they said in unison.

Peter glared. "I think I'll sit this one out. I can stay here and handle the research and coordination while you two scout around and wait for contact."

"Works for me," Shade said.

"Sounds like a plan," Bas agreed.

Peter folded his arms across his chest. He gave each of them a stern look. "Can I trust the two of you to limit yourselves to recon until we have a better handle on this?"

Shade wrinkled her nose. "Did you just say that to me?"

Bas droned, "Yes, dad, we'll be good."

Shade aimed a sidelong expectant look at Bas.

Bas sighed. "And I'll need a fake passport, and probably Shade's help with a disguise since someone might tip off Nemrovsky, and I'm so recognizable."

Chapter 11

The closest Bas and Shade could get to Fethiye by air was the Dalaman airport in Turkey. From there, they took a bus overland to Fethiye. While Shade pretended to nap, Bas ingratiated himself with a group of tourists who'd come in for hiking and rock-climbing. He spent most of the ride picking their brains about the local terrain.

Shade disappeared into the sidewalk traffic after they arrived in Fethiye. They'd agreed she would remain invisible until they knew what they were dealing with. Bas carried both sets of bags to the check-in desk at the hotel.

During a daily, web conference session with Peter, Bas complained, "I feel like a sitting duck, and Shade won't let me go recon that compound. We've been here three days and I haven't even picked up any interest from the locals, much less this supposed contact, but Shade is convinced we're being watched." He was sitting at a table in the hotel room with his feet propped up, toying with a half-drunk cup of coffee.

"On what evidence?" Peter asked, looking doubtful.

Shade wasn't in the room, but Bas checked over his shoulder to be sure. "She's heard sounds outside the door at night, and once she thought she heard something at the window."

"But there was never anything there?"

"No." He hesitated, weighing whether he should continue. "She said she's smelled something."

"Smelled?" Peter repeated. "Bas, is she cracking up?"

"She said she came back to the room the first day, and the smell was thick inside. Then after each of these noises, she's noticed the same scent. She swore last night that someone was in the hallway, so we went out looking. Nothing. She claimed she heard the stairwell door, and then, I kid you not, she tracked the smell straight to the roof. She said she saw movement going over the roof in the dark. I was a heartbeat behind her, but I didn't see anything, and there was nothing below us on the street when we looked over the roof edge."

Peter ran his hand down his face. It stalled over his mouth for a moment. "I've been worried about her since

Colombia, Bas--all these weird little OCD things she's got going on."

"All I know, dad, is when the dog barks in the middle of the night, it hears something."

"You didn't see her in Colombia, you didn't see what I saw."

"Yeah, and maybe someday one of you will tell me what that was," Bas griped.

"You're right. It's time. If something happens to me, both you and Curtis need to know. You're the only one she'll listen to anyway."

"Bullshit. She hears me, but then she does whatever she's decided. You should've figured that out in Colombia. You've always gotten the relationship backwards."

"All I know is that in the past year her behavior has gotten a lot stranger, and she's been distancing herself from both of us. She's always been a borderline personality. The possibility of a break is something we have to be on the lookout for."

Bas said nothing, deeming the conversation pointless. Peter didn't begin to understand her.

"When you get back, I promise we'll talk, Bas."

"I'll keep an eye on her and keep you posted. She's hunting whoever it is. If there is someone, I have zero doubt she'll catch him eventually. She's got that fierce look, mad as hell, so I almost feel sorry for the guy."

"Where is she now?"

"Out strolling around."

"Is that wise?"

"She goes out every night around this same time. She's got a perfect disguise. You'd never believe it was her. I almost don't."

"Same time tomorrow unless you have a development," Peter instructed.

"Yep." Bas broke the transmission and shut the laptop. Shade was behind him. He hadn't heard her come in. He saw a pained look in her eyes before she turned away.

She sat down on the floor with her case of wigs and special effects and began peeling off her disguise. "It's leather, and coffee, and chocolate, and something like raspberry," she said. "It's an absolutely delicious smell. It's faint though--like it's sticking to something he's wearing, but he hasn't refreshed it."

"Raspberry?" Bas asked. "What guy would be wearing something chocolate and raspberry?"

She tucked everything neatly into the case and then snapped the lid shut. She went into the bathroom and he heard water running. She came out scrubbing the glue and makeup off of her face with a washcloth. "A smart man, who wants to smell delicious to women."

Bas scowled. "You think it's Friend."

"It has to be. I refuse to believe there's an operative out there good enough to elude me and that we've never heard of him or her."

Bas raised an eyebrow. "Ego much?"

"Oh screw you both." She started taking off her costume.

"You're telling me you want a threesome? That'd be awkward."

Shade ignored him while she changed and hung her clothes in the closet. She poured herself a cup of coffee and then sat down on the foot of the bed in a full Lotus position. She stared idly into the cup. "We've both noticed that Peter has a tendency to add two and two and stop at three," she finally said. "He doesn't always see the whole picture."

Bas listened warily.

"He's drawn a number of conclusions about me that I think he's basing on how he would've reacted or on accepted dogma. It smacks of a lack of imagination, I think. But that's consistent for him. It seems like he follows along with me only so far and stops listening before I've finished giving him information. He's got blind spots where both of us are concerned, and you know it."

Bas lowered his eyes and nodded. Then he teased, "So, you're not cracking up?"

"We all know I'm OCD, but he's mistaking it for PTSD."

"Post Traumatic Stress Disorder? I don't follow," Bas said.

"You listen to his version of Colombia first. I'm curious to see what conclusions you'll draw. And whether your memory comes back. I know the doctors said it was blood loss and head trauma, but you were awake part of the time. I think it's convenient you don't remember because it allows you to remain neutral. And I don't think Peter wants you to remember—or at least not if you're going to disagree with him. You're predictable, in his view. But in this case, I think on some level he's afraid you won't react predictably. But maybe that's me projecting. Where I'm concerned, he can't imagine what I'll do next, and he thinks that supports the theory I'm a sociopath. And then there's that asshole, Al, always spewing armchair psychology. Since I started out as damaged goods, they refuse to see me any other way."

"You're not any more damaged than the rest of us," Bas assured her. He re-opened the laptop and beckoned her over. "Now help me find chocolate raspberry stuff to drive women wild."

She rolled her eyes. "Yeah, that's not happening."

In an Oxford English accent he said, "Despite the hour, I'm glad you finally checked in. I w was beginning to think you'd done a bunk, as they say."

"They're watching me quite carefully. It's not safe for me to contact you from the compound."

"Nemrovsky suspects? How have you managed to tip him off?"

It was going to be another one of those conversations.

"I think Laurent may have unwittingly done so. It all started right around that time," he explained, rubbing the back of his neck to relieve the tension.

"Where are you now?"

"Sitting in a pub in Fethiye. I told them I needed to get laid."

"By all means don't let your onerous employment duties hamper your libido."

"Only I don't have the time, even if I were inclined."

"Have you been able to establish contact with Shade?"

"I'd an encounter with them earlier, and now they've just arrived in Fethiye."

"Excellent news. Do tell."

"They turned up at Rawlley's while I was there and crashed the party. And I do mean crashed."

"You've been to a party in upstate New York?"

"Nemrovsky had me meet with Rawlley to negotiate a deal."

"Ah. And so you were able to contact them while they were there?"

"Not actually, no."

"I'm disappointed. You were supposed to be the best, and we're just a bit short on time."

"To be honest, I wasn't at all sure it was her. I recognized Drake, but he was there with another man and a woman, and the second man threw me off. I've still no idea who he was. He didn't look or behave like a professional. So I waited, but then they were off."

"Did you at least get a good look at her?"

"Yes, but I don't know the description will do you any good, since I've no idea how much was real and how much smoke and mirrors."

"There must be a way to compile information, remove the variables, and come up with a common set of facial characteristics."

"Blond hair, blue eyes, tall, slim, but curvy and busty."

"That's half the world."

"Half the women at that party, any road. Which was obviously the effect she was after--the place was packed with models and minor celebrities."

"So, she looked like every other guest."

"She blended in perfectly, yes."

"And were they successful?"

"Based on the furor of the aftermath, I would say so. A bit sloppy, really. The firefight at the rear of the property was very audible and put a real damper on the guests' desire to linger. Rawlley had a number of bodies to dispose of and had to call in his computer expert. They definitely got into his safe room, if nothing else. Since the bloke was still there working when I buggered off, I've a feeling they managed a compromise."

"Ah," he said, sounding satisfied.

"Clearly, they're both still alive. It's jammy how those two always manage to land on their feet."

"This is why you must establish a connection with this woman. They're both there now, you said? What steps have you taken?"

"I needed to verify that it's actually them, naturally. So, I went round the hotel. I confirmed Drake's presence, but hadn't seen him with a female companion--he's not even friendly with barmaids and waitresses. And I thought it odd they'd be sharing a room."

"I see nothing odd about it if she's concealing her presence there."

"Right, but there's only one bed in that room. How many siblings do you know who'll share a bed?"

"And she's active at night, and he's active during the day? There's your answer."

He let it drop.

"If you were in the room, I don't suppose you thought to establish any monitoring there?"

"No point, really. Those two will detect anything I put in. Besides, they've been running a white noise generator at night when I've tried to listen outside the door."

"I assume neither of them would be stupid enough to leave a family photo lying about, so what did this delay to search the room accomplish?"

"Not much," he admitted. They'd security seals on the cases--the sort that'll tear when tampered with. If I'd opened them, they'd have known."

"This is all past tense--and now?"

"She's here. She twigged to the room entry somehow and has been stalking me around the periphery. Quite sly, she is."

"Then perhaps you could just stand still and let her catch you," he said in an annoyed tone. "Do I need to remind you what the stakes are here? What your orders are?"

The implied censure irritated him, but he kept quiet. "So that I'm clear, exactly how much am I to tell them?"

"Just enough to get them pointed towards accomplishing our primary goal. Then hang back and let them sort it out for themselves. This will give us a unique opportunity to observe their dynamics and how her mind strategizes which will assist us later on. Then only nudge them if you see them going off track, or about to make a mistake that would compromise the objective."

"Right." He had reservations but kept them to himself.

"Brief me once you've made contact." He rang off.

Chapter 12

Early on the fourth morning, Bas returned to the same cafe he'd frequented each day. He sat brooding in the sunshine and sea air at the same sidewalk table, reading a British newspaper he'd picked up at the hotel. He had the same buxom waitress, who gave him the same coy smile.

On his left was a crowded table of overweight American women in brightly-colored ill-fitting clothes. They were reviewing photos on their digital cameras and chatting loudly about the tour they were on. To his right was an elderly local man, clean but shabby, wearing a straw hat. He had a wispy beard, and deeply tanned and sun-lined skin. He was reading a newspaper and drinking coffee. Closer to the street were two thirty-something men poring over a map shared between them on the table. They were both physically fit, wore hiking boots, and had backpacks resting at their feet. The street traffic was light, and pedestrians were an even mix of locals and tourists.

The bells on the coffee shop door jingled, and Bas looked over in time to see it closing. When he dropped his gaze back to the newspaper, he found a slip of paper lying on top. The note read:

> *My compliments to Shade. When I see her, then you'll see me. -Friend.*

"Guy's got a death wish," Bas muttered.

Bas noticed that the little old man was gone, and he'd left his coffee and the newspaper behind. Gathering and folding his own newspaper, he walked around the corner of the shop into a narrow alleyway. At an intersection, he turned left into another alley and kept walking. He let the newspaper slide off the automatic in his hand and spun around. He and Jack Friend leveled guns at one another as the little old man's gun simultaneously lodged at the base of Friend's skull.

"We seem to have reached an impasse," Shade's voice announced through the old man's beard.

"Only it had to haf' been the wee old man," Friend said. His voice was low, raspy, and rolled out in a Cockney accent. "Well, as I've been hoping for a few words with you lot, why don't we agree to a temporary suspension of animosities?"

Shade cocked her head, listening to the accent fade in and out.

"You first," Bas growled, showing his teeth. He caught Shade's curious glance and jerked his chin in her direction, telling her to take the lead.

Shade's eyes flicked back to Friend, scrutinizing his movements as he lowered his arm and clicked the safety on the gun. With exaggerated care, he reached behind himself and tucked it into the waist of his jeans. He held up his hands. Shade took a step back, lowering her own weapon before Bas did the same.

Friend turned around. He was handsome in a wicked way. A black baseball cap was pulled low on his forehead above aviator sunglasses. He was wearing dark jeans, and a baggy, black t-shirt. When he lowered the sunglasses in what she took for a deliberately provocative move, Shade saw that Peter's friend had been right about his eyes. In the bright sunlight, they were more the golden side of hazel than green. His long dark eyelashes matched the color of his clipped hair, and he had a pouty little boy mouth. Aside from those girlishly-pretty features, the rest of his face was ruggedly masculine. A strong jaw and chin were shadowed by several days' growth of stubble, and his nose looked like it might have been broken at some point. Almost a head shorter than Bas, he was built like a bulldog with wide shoulders and narrow hips, and he seemed to have an attitude to match.

Transfixed by Shade, his exulted grin and gleaming eyes erased the bulldog analogy from her mind and replaced it with the thought that he looked like a wolf.

And she'd met him before.

He remarked, "Brilliant disguise, but I remembered you being bigger."

"Maybe I am." She tried to sound indifferent.

Bas had tensed, so she held his eyes until he settled.

"How the bloody hell did you keep tracking me?" Friend was still smiling, but he'd frozen in place.

"Chocolate and raspberry." She was picking up an undercurrent she couldn't identify and trying to parse whether they'd walked into a trap. Her first instinct was to shoot the man and leave, and he seemed to be sensing her animosity.

Bas' eyes were darting around the alley, giving the impression he'd picked up on her concern.

Friend laid on the Cockney accent again. "Garn. Thas' hard lines ta' me. She smelled me shaving cream that I hafn't used in bloody days." He scratched his whiskers to illustrate his point.

"You use chocolate-raspberry scented shaving cream?" Bas' tone expressed volumes of disgust.

"In truth, it's vanilla raspberry—the birds love it--but I likes a bit o' chocolate of an evening." He winked at Shade.

He was trying hard to diffuse the tension, so she went along with it. "And coffee and leather." She breathed deeply in spite of herself.

Bas gave her a look that said, *Seriously?*

Shade shrugged and took a step back.

Jack edged sideways and glanced between them, still on guard. "There are things I need to tell you both. If I may suggest a quiet spot for a bit of conversation, there's a back door to a pub just round the bend."

"*You're* the contact?" Shade asked.

With a sly grin, he said, "Skeptical? I never hear any complaints."

"There's a first time for everything," Shade said.

He raised an eyebrow and strode past Bas without a backward glance.

Bas followed Friend while Shade peeled off towards the front of the pub.

The little old man was already sitting in a rear corner of the dimly lit pub when Friend and Bas walked in. Friend didn't look surprised to see Shade there ahead of them.

The pub was small, but clean, with windows only at the front of the building. For the early hour, there were a surprising number of patrons. There was only one waitress and a bartender, but sizzling and clattering noises from a doorway next to the bar indicated the presence of kitchen staff, and the air was thick with the aromas of coffee and the local, spicy, Sujuk sausage.

Once coffees had been delivered, Friend leaned in too close and murmured to Shade, "I have to admit, I'm curious to see if I live through this encounter. The rumors of you being Kali, the goddess of death, or some such, abound."

"Mr. Friend, just cut to the chase. What is it you wanted to say?"

"You can call me Jack," he said.

"If you 'need' to tell us things, why have I been chasing you across rooftops for the past four days?"

"Personal ego. Also, a number of people would pay a lot of money for a description of your face."

She met Bas' eyes, who didn't look like he believed it either. "You're good at escaping, but you're not very adept at going undetected. Mr. Friend."

"And you seem to lack follow-through, Lady Shade." His eyes glittered.

Bas made a rude noise and duplicated the move Friend had used on Shade. "Look, restraining her follow-through has taken years off Peter Laurent's life, so if you're gearing up for a dick-swinging contest here, let me authoritatively tell you that hers is bigger."

"She didn't catch me." Friend shrugged.

"She had a gun to the back of your head. That's about as caught as it gets. The only reason you're not a dead Limey prick is because you might be useful."

The two men locked eyes. Friend put on a disarming smile and leaned back. "Well then, I'll haf to make meself useful." In a more serious tone he said, "First, a question--how is Laurent? It's my fault he ended up in that cock-up, and I am truly sorry about it."

Bas and Shade shared a guarded look.

"He's fine. How is it your fault?" Bas asked.

"Because I'm the one who tried to contact the two of you—you and your sister."

"She's not my sister. You did?"

Shade blinked.

Friend was studying Shade. "I can see even through the bang up cosmetic job that things are clicking into place. I'm impressed."

"And I'm impressed with your word games. So, you're the Puppetmaster," she replied.

He smiled. "I'll own it."

"There had to be a third party involved. There was nothing to be gained by either side targeting the other. Someone else had to be manipulating the whole thing."

"I didn't start out with that intention. But circumstances beyond my control and all that rubbish."

"You nearly got Peter killed," Shade said with a dark glare. "If we hadn't been in time—"

Friend interrupted, "Truly, it wasn't supposed to come off that way. I'd not heard back from either of you, see? I'd no idea he'd show up. And in rotten luck, I was off on an errand when he did. Nemrovsky's muppets exceeded their orders and picked him up…well, you know the rest of it."

Shade made some rapid mental calculations and then looked at Bas for his take.

Bas said, "Then we're done here."

Friend recoiled.

"Yes," Shade agreed. "If what you're saying is true and no one ordered it, then we already took out Peter's abductors. There's no continuing threat to any of us."

Friend's jaw hardened and he frowned. Talking quickly, he said, "But don't you see? It's too late. They've gotten you over here somehow. If you try to leave, they'll assume you're either in complicity with Nemrovsky, or that you've already relieved him of what they want. Either way, they'll come for you."

Shade scowled.

"Convince us," Bas said.

Friend paused and swept his eyes around the room.

"There is no one paying any attention to us, and there is no electronic monitoring in place," Shade said.

Bas said, "Story time." He stretched out and laced his hands behind his head, deliberately baiting Friend by flaunting his massive frame.

Friend straightened his shoulders and sat up. In a snarky tone, he said, "Once upon a time, a very highly placed member of the British intelligence community left a very disturbing suicide note before he blew his own brains out."

"I remember reading something about a suicide," Shade said, ignoring the boys' antics.

"To make a tedious story short, he admitted to having been blackmailed for a number of years. He also disclosed that he wasn't the only one in our government, nor the highest placed, and he went on to claim that there were others, within several other governments, who were in the same sticky situation. All compromised by the same individual, who had enough documentation of various dirty deeds to ruin the careers of a number of key people, as it were."

"Vassily Nemrovsky." Bas was folding a paper placemat into an airplane.

"Right-o," Friend said, still dishing out cheek. "So, a few unaffiliated gombos were dispatched in an attempt to confirm, or obtain, this very incriminating data. They bungled the job and got themselves dead as a reward, and Nemrovsky went on high alert making any further attempts very tricky. Their sole accomplishment was dying without implicating their employers. Enter…meself."

"He hired you to do what?" Shade asked.

"Counter them, of course. Provide him with inviolable security. I have a bit of a rep for that. You may have heard? And by-the-by, I confirmed that he does indeed have the goods. Naturally, I felt it was important to keep him off-balance after that since I didn't want anyone else getting their mitts on it."

Shade hissed, "You're the one who sent out all the solicitations. You got how many men killed?"

"Now-now, Alice, not so fast down the rabbit hole. The ones I sent in are all alive and well. Somewhere. They were catspaws intended to bring the pot to a boil. Their instructions were to go in, make a lot of noise, whittle down the defense if possible, and then play dead."

"There were confirmed deaths," Bas countered, still streamlining his airplane.

"Yes, but those were sent in by various wool-headed government types. I'm only guilty in that they all bought into my hype."

Shade guessed, "You inadvertently provided them with a cover story—an excuse. The ones being blackmailed would've wanted him taken down before any investigation disclosed their identities. And Nemrovsky would have started making threats, trying to identify who was responsible for the initial attempts, and word got around that operatives had been killed. So, they invented a fiction that it must be some conspiracy against intelligence agents. Once officially-dispatched assets were killed, it just hotted things up even more."

"Precisely. Threw a spanner in the works, that did. If he followed through on his threats to release the information without knowing which little piggy was in revolt, he was cutting off his cashflow from the other little piggies."

Shade said. "You set the whole thing up to get him to hire you to stop fictional attacks that you engineered."

"And it worked beautifully, except for one tiny, unforeseen glitch." Friend eyed the completed paper airplane and picked up a book of matches from the ashtray on the table.

"A massive body count of innocent operatives?" Bas launched the airplane at Friend.

"Codswollop." Friend batted the plane to the table and set it on fire. "That's not on my head, mate. That's survival of the fittest. Besides, some of the dead were assisted to that state by their own higher-ups to maintain the fiction. Or they were trying to capitalize on the situation--on the off-chance that someone might actually get Nemrovsky and let them off the hot seat."

Shade tweaked the burning plane into the ashtray and poured coffee on it. "We encountered a hit squad that may have been operating under those very parameters," she said, thinking of the hit on Reid Amhers.

"So, why are we here? You're in place, why isn't the problem solved?" Bas asked.

"He didn't know what to do with the information if he got it," Shade guessed.

"Right. I turn it over to…who? And all I accomplish is potentially lopping off the head of the Hydra—you're familiar with that myth, now aren't you?--only to have—how many more?--spring up in its place. Who's trustworthy enough to cauterize the monster and the people it implicates?"

"What kind of damage are we talking about?" Bas asked.

"Let's just say that the trails go under the doors of all the major players, and that widespread release would topple not only a number of high-ranking political figures, but potentially take down several governments as well. I've heard about your passion for all things incendiary, but even you would shy away from this level of demolition. It'd be anarchy, and I'm too fond of my creature comforts to allow that to happen."

"So it's a stalemate--if Nemrovsky follows through on his threats, he won't get any more money. If Nemrovsky is eliminated, the information might be released anyway--there're bound to be copies tucked away as insurance against that possibility. The only solution that neutralizes both parties is to get whatever he's got, and release it to people in a position to quietly mitigate or eliminate the subjects," Shade said.

"Having reached the same conclusion, I said to meself, what's a bloke to do? I'm just an uncouth scousegit from a wee island. I needs me a suave gent of wisdom with connections. Someone who can bring in a little finesse."

Shade coughed. "As long as you're dishing out blarney, go for an Irish accent. They're so much sexier."

He flashed a wolfish smile.

"You've seen what Nemrovsky has? You know where at least one copy is?" Bas asked.

"Not as such, no."

Bas made a noise of disgust, and Shade's expression mirrored it.

In a defensive tone, Friend explained, "I'm only a hired gun. I'm rarely left alone on the grounds, and I've never been alone with Nemrovsky. After the first attempt he started bringing in muscle—and keeps bringing it in. And he gives paranoid a whole new meaning--he actually has a food-taster. But lo, far more powerful men than I have wanted him dead for long, long years and yet there he still is. He's a cagey old bastard who cut his teeth on Cold War intrigue. No, I've an inside source who's confirmed absolutely what he's got, and I've pieced together the likely location."

"Likely?" Bas asked.

"Unless he's got it tattooed someplace private, it's the only possibility. However, if I'm wrong and he's stored it in a Swiss vault, well, we're all buggered."

"I can already tell I'm not going to like this," Shade said.

"He's wearing it round his neck," Friend said in a low voice. "He's got a sort of fancy gold gew-gaw set with gemstones. It looks like a piece of jewelry, but it's a flash-drive."

"Your 'inside source,'" Shade said. "It's the daughter. You have a reputation as a ladies' man and a 'decent shag' with the—what was your word?—birds. You're a Raven. How do you know she can be trusted?"

Bas snorted.

For an instant, Friend seemed annoyed. Then he blanked the expression. "I'm sorry? I'm a what?"

Sneering, Bas said, "A male agent who seduces people for intelligence purposes."

Friend clenched his jaw. "Pillow talk," he admitted. "Why would she lie? She told me the necklace is a flash-drive. I guessed the information is on a portable medium because she said he never goes anywhere without his insurance policy. And he *never* takes this thing off. Moreover, he's relocated twice now and clothes and his laptop are the only things he packs—and even those are handled by staff. Let's say the information was on his laptop, would he let it out of his sight? I've no doubt the originals are stored someplace secure, or maybe he's burned everything, but once the people implicated are dealt with, it doesn't matter how many copies he has—they're just so much rubbish."

"And you pulled us in because you want Peter to facilitate the dissemination," Shade said.

Friend's expression was inscrutable.

"There'd also have to be consequences," Bas pointed out. "If the information is turned over to the right people, they'd need to know there'll be a repercussion if they don't take action."

"That's easily sorted," Friend said, wearing a nasty smile. "And here's the last bit--you're on a deadline. Nemrovsky plans to relocate to the estate of an associate of his at the end of the month. In Cuba. The reason I missed Laurent coming in was because I'd been sent there to check things out. It would take a small army to penetrate that place, even if you could get into Cuba in the first place."

"I've done it," Bas said.

"A small team, I'd wager?" Friend said. "Once Nemrovsky combines his forces with those already present there, you'd have the makings for Bay of Pigs all over again."

Back at the hotel, Shade wished the web conference encryption had a profanity filter. Once she and Bas had relayed the details of their meeting to Peter, he launched into a stream of very loud colorful expletives. These were punctuated occasionally by statements like, "You have got to be kidding!" And "Why me?"

Lying in front of the laptop, belly-down on the bed beside Shade, Bas intoned, "Ask not what your country can do for you…"

"Oh, shut up. Let me think." Peter began pacing in and out of the camera's range.

"I hated him." Bas turned to Shade and jostled her with an elbow.

She patted him on the cheek. "Yes, dear, I know."

"You looked like you were going to lick him there at the beginning."

"I don't know what it is, but that scent of his is amazing. Oh, let's remember to tell Peter I wasn't having scent hallucinations, and that, gee whiz, not only am I not cracking up but *I…was…right.*"

Bas pulled one of his scowl-and-pout faces. "I hate him. I hate that we have to work with him. He's so--"

"Cocky, arrogant, overbearing, superior, irreverent, cynical, hotheaded?" Shade rolled over onto her back and yawned.

In a happy tone, Bas said, "Yes, all those."

"Just like you."

Bas faked a hurt look. "I'm way better looking."

"Yes, you are." Then she said, "Do we even want to do this? I mean, I'm just not interested in all this political crap."

"Personally, anarchy brings more work my way—"

"Children," Peter interrupted. He was back on the camera. "Do I understand correctly that he has no schematics of the grounds or the house? Just how're we supposed to get in if Nemrovsky's security is as tight as he's saying?"

"You have me," Shade said with an upside-down, Cheshire cat grin.

Bas gave her a sidelong look and then said, "He told us he's lodged in the guard barracks. Whenever he's been in the main house, he's been escorted. He gave us a basic layout from memory--doorways, hallways, the route to Nemrovsky's suite-- but he didn't know anything about the rest of the house."

"Can Curtis whip up an electromagnetic pulse bomb and we just fry the whole compound?" Shade asked.

"Who *are* you?" Peter quipped.

Bas gave her suggestion a thumbs-up.

"There's still all the manpower, guns, and weapons undetermined to factor in," Peter said.

"I'll call my team," Bas offered.

"Don't even start." Peter pointed at Shade before she could object. "There is no way this is a one-person operation. I don't think even a ten-man-team can handle it. And no, I don't think electromagnetic pulse bombs are something Curtis can manage."

Shade grumbled.

"I've got a guy--" Bas said.

"There's one more problem," Shade said, interrupting him. "I've met Friend before. I danced with him at Rawlley's shindig. He knows it was me. It might be too late, but I may need to eliminate him when this is done."

Peter let out a tired sigh.

Bas looked at her. "So, *that's* what was going on in the alley."

Peter said, "There's got to be some way to find out more about this guy. I don't like relying on an unknown. I'll beat the bushes. Shade, restrain yourself until we know more."

Bas frowned. "None of his actions make sense. He wants to get in touch with us specifically, but he said nothing to Shade when he was inches from her face at a party. He tests our perimeter for three days here without making contact, then tells us there's a big rush to get Nemrovsky before he makes himself an almost impossible target. He's in place but hasn't accomplished a damned thing. And we're supposed to believe he's turned on his employer. It stinks."

Peter said, "For all his nasty reputation, that is one thing he's known for--staying bought."

"Unless he was sent in," Shade suggested.

Peter mused, "Or maybe it isn't that he can't do the job, but that he won't because Nemrovsky really is the employer and he doesn't want to break his code of ethics. Maybe he wants us to get him out of the mess he's in? That's flimsy though. Maybe Al has come up with something on him."

Chapter 13

Bas told the hotel staff he'd be doing some hiking in the mountains to explain his absence, and then he'd made the transitions to get back to Virginia. Bas' team was already on standby, so the first thing he did when he arrived at the house was start making calls. Following his instructions, Curtis made preliminary arrangements for materials for the entire team and then worked with Bas to figure out the logistics of getting everything, and everyone, to Fethiye.

Shade was doing reconnaissance of the compound and outlying area, which was her strong suit and would keep her off the local radar. Bas seemed uncharacteristically short-tempered, and Curtis wondered whether he was upset about leaving her there alone or missing out on snooping around the compound.

Peter was still working on the Jack Friend anomaly, but Bas kept prowling around Peter's periphery until he took on a harassed air. Bas finally cornered him after dinner, and Curtis found out they were finally going to talk about Colombia. To his surprise, Peter told Curtis to sit in as well.

They waited for him in the attic, and when Peter walked in, Curtis saw that he'd poured himself a large glass of whiskey. He held it clenched in both hands after he sat down.

"When we got to the location, everything was wrong," Peter said. "The intel, the layout, and Shade kept saying there was even too much light. The guys in the unit kept acting like she was chickening-out or cracking up. She refused to go in-- said that she had a strong feeling about it. But the guys weren't willing to back out, and there was a lot of money at stake. So, Shade stayed behind, on a Ma Deuce—Curtis, that's an M2A1 point-five-oh caliber machine gun--intending to cover our fallback. Well, she was right—they were waiting for us. So, the fallback happened a lot sooner than any of us expected. After the fact, I found out our informant had sold us out for even more money. Still, our losses wouldn't have been as heavy if the unit had stuck to the plan. To make a long story short, more than half them went the wrong way and scattered. There was no way Shade could cover them, so she concentrated on the group that Bas and I were in—we'd stuck to the plan. A few from the other group nearly made it back to her position and started a firefight in her line-of-sight. That whited-out her night vision scope and forced her to cease fire. That's when Bas got hit in the chest. Four other guys in my group also went down because Shade was fouled by her own team members."

To Curtis, Bas said, "This is where my memory stops."

Curtis was picking up a bad vibe between the two of them and sitting on the edge of his seat. When Bas spoke, his eyes darted in his direction. Seeing Bas' grim expression, he looked away.

"They picked off the rest of the team like fish in a barrel. One of the guys, Benson, and I managed to drag Bas out. I figured he had a lung filling with blood and didn't think he'd make it. We got him to the trees, where Shade joined us, and we triaged him best we could. He'd lost consciousness at that point, and it was all Benson and I could do to carry him out of there. Shade was covering our trail, slowing down pursuit."

Peter took a big swig of his drink. "Out of twenty-five men, only the four of us made it out."

Curtis gave him a somber nod. He'd gotten the bare facts from Peter immediately afterwards, but no details. Talking about it must be painful, but Curtis couldn't understand why Peter seemed so uneasy.

"We came out on a knoll overlooking an open, grassy area. There was hardly any cover to the next section of trees, and the chopper was on the other side, so we stalled. They took out Benson at that point. There was no way Shade and I could carry Bas that distance, so she told me to go ahead, she'd stay behind and keep them off me. I told her it was a death sentence—there wasn't enough ammo left for her to hold out. She started screaming at me--she was really losing it. She actually pointed her gun at me and drove me down the knoll. She looked at me with those damned spooky eyes and said 'You will come back.'"

Curtis flicked a glance at Bas and knew he'd just heard the same thing. He'd blanched and stiffened. Curtis edged his chair back.

"She pulled it off," Peter continued. "She laid down fire that kept them off of me all the way across that field. I was well ahead of them at that point, but I couldn't run flat out all the way, and I got turned around in the damned jungle, so it took me some time to get back to the chopper. I hadn't heard any shots for a while, and I figured her ammo had run out just getting me clear. I figured they were both dead. I figured I'd fly over, but if I didn't see them..."

Curtis could hear a tremor in Peter's voice and the ice cubes rattling in his glass. He wasn't meeting anyone's eyes. Bas looked outraged.

"That flight... The sky was just starting to lighten, so the blood stood out black. The field was strewn with bodies-- dead men all around that knoll. And there she sat at the top, holding Bas in her lap, covered in gore from head to foot. I found out afterwards that she'd left their only handgun with Bas—a full clip. She'd done--all that--unbelievable horror--with just those blades of hers. She'd hunted them down one-by-one. You could see the perimeter she'd held, just by the blood. They hadn't even gotten close to Bas. I've never seen anything like it, I never want to again."

Curtis snuck another look at Bas who was staring at nothing, eyes darting back-and-forth.

"So, I landed the chopper. When I got to her, she stood up so slowly--sort of crouched like an animal. The look in her eyes--madness. The same look she had the day I found her. She had the gun in her hand, and I thought I was a dead man. Then she just said, 'You came back.' She didn't speak again. Not during the flight, not at the hospital. They stitched her up, and she sat by Bas' bed until she knew he was stable. Then she took off. I didn't see or hear from her again for months."

Bas said, "Shade was right." He rubbed his eyes before picking up the story. "She forbade me to die. She swore she wouldn't leave me. I wanted to, just so she could get out of there, but I couldn't make myself fire the gun. I heard it when she ran out of ammo—that click on an empty chamber. I heard her scream, and I figured they were on us, but after that I only heard other people's screams. I guess I lost consciousness for a while."

Bas took a deep breath and shook his head. Curtis wondered if he was trying to jostle the memories loose or stop them from coming.

"The next thing I remember is her giving me the automatic in case they got past her." Turning towards Curtis, but looking Peter in the eye, he growled, "The reason she didn't pick up any of their weapons was because she didn't want them to find her by the noise or the muzzle flash."

Curtis had a feeling it was about to get ugly and wondered if he should leave, but Bas was between him and the door.

"She kept coming back, and she'd talk to me--always saying the same things--" He cleared his throat. "Ah, hell. And each time, there'd be more blood until all I could see were her eyes." Showing clenched teeth, he said, "Those 'spooky eyes,' *dad.*"

Peter flinched and averted his eyes. His glass of whiskey was tipping to one side in his grasp.

"I was in and out, but she'd be there suddenly, in focus, telling me to hold on, checking the bandages, giving me water. The last time--I came to and she was holding onto me, making a noise--" he shuddered. "An awful sound. So, I knew it was over. She was crying, she'd taken the gun from me, and I knew she was gonna end us both. She'd given up. Peter wasn't coming back. Then we heard the chopper."

Bas straightened up, clenching his fists on his thighs.

Peter looked like he was bracing himself.

"I don't remember the flight, or the hospital. I didn't know she was there. When I finally came out of it, she was gone. I hadn't really seen her or talked to her until you went missing. I thought I had let her down. That she blamed me for the whole thing going wrong. That she couldn't stand to be around me."

"She cracked up, Bas. Al thought it might be a disassociative fugue. It didn't have anything to do with you. She went off on her own. She wasn't even sharing her activities with Curtis and me at that point. I wasn't even sure if she was working or just hiding out. I think the guilt just drove her right over the edge, and she lost it. Everything that happened probably brought back the old childhood trauma. It had nothing to do with us."

Bas canted his head at Peter looking exasperated. "You misunderstand her. It all makes sense now. She wouldn't have felt guilty at all--she was protecting us. She was probably terrified at the thought of losing either of us--because we'd been killed or because we were repulsed by what she did to save us. But your reaction is what drove her away. That's why she's been avoiding me--she's been afraid of how I'd treat her once I remembered—she couldn't bear the disapproval. I've been busting my ass these last few weeks trying to prove I wouldn't let her down again, and what she really needed was a damned hug."

Bas was keeping his voice even, but Curtis knew he was losing control. He'd suspected for a while that most of Bas' mannerisms were an act, he'd even heard him speak differently to Shade when he thought no one else was around, but he was slipping so much now that it sounded more like Shade was speaking.

"She stopped working with us because those men wouldn't listen to her, and they all died as a result. The entire situation, everything that happened that night, was because her teammates—you and I included, Peter-- ignored her advice and her orders because she was female. They broke the wrong way because they didn't trust her to man that gun—we both heard them making cracks about her not being strong enough. And on top of that, they got in her line of sight and endangered you and me."

He was getting louder and hotter. Curtis checked in Peter's direction and saw admission edged with guilt. It only seemed to make Bas angrier.

"She went off alone because she was heartbroken. And she won't work with other people anymore because they cause collateral damage that she can avoid. She's said that how many times?" His eyes targeted Curtis and then locked back onto Peter. "Hell, I would've left too, just based on the ingratitude. And I can't believe that I let you suck me into your delusion for a solid year! I really want to know--you've categorically avoided telling me the specifics until now, was it because you were so disturbed about what she did *to save both our lives*, or was it guilt? Because I heard what you glossed over. *You wanted to leave me and she refused.* She would've known I hadn't been shot in the lung, and she would've told you so. But because you thought she was cracking up, you wouldn't have believed her. You said it yourself--she started screaming at you and acting crazy. You know, just because you don't like her delivery, doesn't mean the message is invalid. You need to get that straight. And why did she threaten you? Was it because you were trying to make her leave too? Then you have the nerve to say what you said about her the other night? And she has to work with you, day after day, knowing you think that about her."

Peter closed his eyes, ashamed.

Bas stood up, towering over Peter in a fury, and crossed his arms over his chest like he was trying to restrain himself. "And I'll tell you one more thing. Did you ever ask her why she killed that Sheik when she was whatever-age-you've-decided-she-was? It's because that man ordered her mother and father killed, and I happen to think that's a pretty damn good reason."

Peter's eyes flew open. "How do you even know about that?"

Bas gave him a contemptuous look. "She told me. We've spent practically every day of our lives together since we were eight. *Except this past year.* She remembers a lot more than you think, but we know you want to pretend she doesn't because it scares you. Do you remember our nightmares?"

Peter nodded miserably.

"When you were away working, we'd crawl into each other's beds at night, to stop the other one's nightmares. Mine ended eventually. But I think she's got a whole new batch." Launching a final barb, he said, "And I wonder how well you'd be sleeping if she hadn't *shamed* you into coming back for us?"

As he stalked out of the room, he snarled over his shoulder, "Stop kicking the dog, Peter. We both owe her an apology and a thank you." He slammed the door, rattling the entire wall.

After a minute of shocked silence, Peter drained his glass and said in a shaky voice, "When he blows, he really blows."

Curtis kept as still as possible, sneaking nervous glances in Peter's direction. He couldn't think of anything to say to him that might make him feel less dejected, and he wasn't sure he wanted to. Peter was sitting with his head down, holding the empty glass. After a few minutes, he got up and walked out of the room.

Chapter 14

The wall around the estate was high, but constructed of mortar and rough limestone rocks. A scaffold of wooden beams and decking leaned against the inside of the wall, and two guards walked a perimeter patrol along the top of it. It only took Shade a few minutes to pick out hand and toeholds that would make it an easy climb.

She waited until a guard had passed and scaled up behind him. After pulling herself over onto the decking, she swung down through the timbers and dropped to the ground. In the shadow of the scaffolding, she plotted her course to the two buildings she suspected were being used as barracks. Choosing her cover, she set off at a crouching run.

The two buildings were constructed of the same materials as the wall. One of the two buildings was smaller, and all the windows were dark. She decided it must be the armory or some other storage building. Through the lit windows of the larger structure, she saw a living area on the first floor and off-duty men lounging around a television. She checked the positions of the two guards on the wall and began scaling the exterior of the building towards a dark open window on the second story.

The occupant was asleep in his bed, one muscled arm thrown over his face, bare chest rising slowly and evenly. She pulled herself through the window and crept across the plank floor. The sleeper shifted when she was halfway to the door. She froze. He'd moved his arm, and she realized she'd had the good fortune to climb through Jack Friend's window.

As she placed her right hand over his mouth, his left hand clamped down on her wrist and pulled her across him, flipping her onto her back on the mattress beside him. As he rolled to pin her, she kneed him in the stomach, uppercut him with the heel of her left hand, twisted her right wrist free, and brought her booted foot up to shove him bodily off the bed. There was a muffled thump as he landed on the thick, wooden floorboards.

He froze, and they both listened for sounds of a response. When he looked back at the mattress, she was gone. Crouching lightly on the balls of his feet, he peered around the dark room.

From her hiding spot, she saw he was wearing black boxer briefs, and nothing else. In the light from the window, every chiseled muscle stood out in sharp contrast. He was built like a swimmer, all lean muscle except the heavy shoulders and chest.

Her foot hooked out from under the bed, catching both of his ankles and toppling him once more. He caught himself and bounced out of range.

She surfaced on the other side of the bed, grinning, and stood for his inspection.

In the dim light, Jack Friend studied Shade, taking in the black leather jacket that seemed oddly thick through the forearms, a pair of form-fitting, black trousers with faint, black stitching that seemed to run in a chaotic pattern down the length. Rubber-soled, black boots were buffed matte to avoid any reflective shine. The boot soles added about two inches to her height. Even her hands were covered by thin, black gloves. She was wearing a short black wig that feathered closely over her cheekbones and forehead. It fit like a hood, and little of her face could be seen through it. Her eyes were dark this time, and he found that irritated him. Her lips weren't as full as he remembered from Rawlley's party either, and her eyes were less tilted. Her nose was perfectly nondescript and he wondered if she'd had it altered to look that way. Her upper body definition was concealed by the jacket. Her form didn't even look feminine until his eyes dropped to the curving hips and shapely legs.

He tilted his head to the side, eyes mischievous, mouth spreading into a slow, predatory grin.

Shade put her shoulders back and her chin up. Smirking back at him, she whispered, "Bring it."

They edged around to the foot of the bed and engaged in a series of thrusts and parries. Their kicks and swings met nothing but air as they bobbed and weaved, ducking out of one another's range. He blocked an intended groin-shot with a hard muscled thigh, and made a grab at her, but she simply wasn't there. She landed an open-handed thrust to his jaw, wrenching his head sideways, and he backed away. After shaking his shoulders out and jumping in place like a boxer, he sank into a crouch.

She smirked again and feinted in. Friend blocked her thrust and caught her in a headlock as she twisted away. She cocked her elbow and slammed it into the side of his head, breaking his hold and leaving his ear ringing. He backed away again, shaking his head to clear it. She darted in, landing shots to his abdomen too fast for him to block. She backed him to the door, and then eased off.

"Had enough?" she whispered.

"Never," he whispered back. "But I assume you came here for something other than a sparring match?"

"Call truce and we'll talk."

"Fine. Truce. But I could've had you." He straightened up and stepped towards her.

The spring-loaded ten-inch blades hissed as they shot out of her sleeves. "Not bloody likely, mate," she said, mimicking his accent, and then retracted them.

He raised his eyebrows, astonished, and said, "Show off."

She relaxed her stance, and he cocked an ear--the one that wasn't ringing--at the door to listen for footsteps. He moved to within a few inches of her and jutted his chin at her. "I cannot believe you tried to kick me in the goolies," he hissed in mock indignation.

Keeping her voice hushed she said, "Why? It's every male opponent's biggest vulnerability. I'd be foolish to scruple against using a highly effective tactic simply because of some male code of honor. I'm not male."

"Well, there's some question about that, isn't there," he said, stepping closer.

"Excuse me?" she said in a low tone.

In a voice just above a whisper, he said, "You've not heard that one, then? When they're not naming you Goddess of Death, Kali incarnate, or Medusa herself, they go on about how you're not a bird at all, you're some bloke in drag."

She had to clap her hands over her mouth to stifle the wild laughter threatening to burst out. "For realsies?" she asked, delighted. "You boys are so pathetic. Can't face being bested by a chick. That is just the--what is it you say? The dog's bollocks."

He brightened when he heard her descriptive. He leaned in next to her ear, and she could feel the stubble on his jaw and his breath against her neck. He murmured, "I'd have to agree, really. The girl parts I saw the other night were, indeed, the dog's bollocks. Ace, in fact." As she tried to step away, he grabbed her waist. "Then again, maybe you've just got a really nice set of implants and still have the knob."

One hand slid up the front of her leather jacket, likely feeling nothing but ballistic plates and zippered pockets, but she jerked backwards anyway and cuffed him on the side of the head. His other hand plunged between her legs and yanked her forward before she realized what was happening. He was grinning like a bastard, so she knocked his arm aside and her knee shot up again. He backed away fast, but she knew from his grunt that she hadn't entirely missed.

"She-devil," he gasped.

"Lech," she said. "Well?"

"Right. I'd have to say everything seems to be in order down there."

"Glad we got that settled. You pull any more stunts like that you'll be knob-less too."

"Oi! Cut a bloke some slack. You show up in my room in the middle of the night, me in my y-fronts, and then you whinge when I get the wrong idea?"

She pointed to her face in the dark. "This is me rolling my eyes."

He flashed the toothy grin at her.

"And speaking of underwear," she said. "Go put something on."

He straightened up and ran a hand from his chest to his six-pack abs, saying, "Ah, come on, there's not many can compare. Admit it."

"You forget I grew up with Basilius Drake. There is no comparison."

His expression went flat, and he walked over to a wardrobe and yanked out a shirt and some pants.

She heard footsteps in the hallway, and her eyes flicked to the open window. Without hearing him move, his arms wrapped around her, pulling her towards the wardrobe and away from the door. He kept his body between her and the door until the footsteps passed.

"Shh!" they said to each other.

Shade sat down on the edge of the bed while he pulled on the shirt and pants.

"So, what is it brought you out this evening, my little Kali? Couldn't sleep for pining for me, was it?"

Shade wrinkled her nose. "I have a few unanswered questions."

Friend rubbed the back of his neck. "Bugger, and me without coffee."

Opening an innocent-looking side-table, he pulled out a bottle of Scotch. He wiggled the bottle at her, and pulled out two glasses.

"No, thanks. I've still got to climb that wall and get back to Fethiye tonight."

He gave her a lopsided grin. "You're welcome to stay the night, but I'm not sure you'd be able to walk out of here in the morning—double entendre intended."

"Does this actually work on other women?"

He chuckled low.

She saw his eyes linger on the bedside lamp. When he flicked a calculating glance over his shoulder, she had a dagger poised to throw.

"How do you keep those bloody things on so well?" He fluttered his fingers at her black wig as if he'd never thought about turning on the lamp.

"Staples," she answered.

After he poured the drink, he deliberately sat down too close to her. She flinched. As she tucked the dagger back into her jacket, he ran a hand down her thigh. She jerked her leg away.

He said, "Let me see those fancy trousers." From his satisfied tone, it was clear he'd accomplished his objective and determined the stitching only looked decorative, it was actually pockets.

She slid further down the bed and positioned herself facing him.

Friend sighed and said, "My Q&A sessions with Natalya Nemrovsky were so much more enjoyable. For both of us."

"Let's start at the beginning. After attempting to contact Bas and me, and learning that Peter had come in instead, and gotten away, why didn't you try to contact any of us again?"

"I'll refer you to my earlier statements about being watched. And something about Laurent is what seemed to set Nemrovsky off, so he was the last person I was going to reach out to and run the risk of getting caught at it. You two killed off a chunk of his forces, so the same applied to you. Any road, after the temper of that strike, I knew you'd get here eventually."

She knew he was hiding something. And his excuse seemed weak. He'd attempted to contact both Bas and her originally through an online classifieds website. Why not use it again?

"If those were Nemrovsky's men on that island, why wasn't he there?" she asked.

"The island was offered to him as a secure location when he panicked and left Madrid--where we were before. When we arrived at the island, well, you saw it for yourself—security nightmare. He didn't even stay the night."

"Why did he leave men behind?"

"It was a trap. He wanted to see who showed up. And who did? A team of assassins."

"Who let it to him?"

"You haven't tracked down the ownership yet?" Friend laughed.

"A holding company affiliated with a certain lawyer sold it to a numbered Swiss account. When we tried to identify the account holder, we were pointed at Nemrovsky."

"Isn't that interesting," Friend said. "Yes, Liam Rawlley's partners offered it up."

"Even though they no longer own it?"

"I can't tell you anything about that."

She noted his use of the word "can't." She noticed him noticing her notice. She was willing to bet that the account somehow linked Rawlley and his partners to Congressman Harrison.

"Why not come here in the first place?"

"He's had quite a few improvements put in place while we scurried round. Yet despite them, how easily did you get in?"

"He can keep at it but I'll still get in." Then she said, "On to New York."

"I know exactly what you'll ask. I was at that event on an errand and happened to see your brother with a second man I didn't recognize."

"You already know he's not my brother," she said in an annoyed tone.

Friend paused, studying her. "Any road, I wasn't sure you were actually you. Then you vanished like Cinderella, and all hell broke loose. Simple as that."

Recalling Curtis' screw-up, she clenched her jaw. "What is Nemrovsky paying Rawlley for?"

"What do you think? Guns. Services."

"A Turkish hit team?"

Friend looked startled. "Not that I've heard, no. Who's he supposed to have ordered hit?"

"A list of low-ranking, and in some cases inactive, U.S. Government intelligence agents."

Friend's eyes stared off into the dark room. "Interesting."

"Just out of curiosity, what the hell was Rawlley's nuclear response to our presence all about?"

Friend chuckled. "You clearly missed the weapons."

"Don't tell me he keeps the arms he's selling at his *house*."

He winked.

"A personal question," Shade said.

Leering, he said, "At last! And yes, it's well over eight inches."

She made a skeptical noise. "Are you sticking with altruism as your excuse for turning on your employer?"

"Yes, and no."

She watched him make a slight movement of discomfort and then hide the telling behavior. "That's it? That's your answer?"

"Yes." He gave her a direct look, toasted her with his glass of Scotch, and knocked it back.

Frustrated, she moved on. "What's your role going to be in all this?"

"Ah. For Nemrovsky's benefit, I'll be pretending to impede you even though my interests are best served by ensuring your success. Afterwards, I imagine there'll be an assignment to obtain the data before you get clean away. If that fails, I'll concentrate on a couple of congruent projects that've been simmering on the back burner all this while."

She itched to write down his exact words. He was saying something between the lines by drawing out some words and inserting pauses before others. She tried to phrase her reply as carefully. "Then we'll be moving in the same circles and I'm sure we'll meet again." She knew her words scored because he was devoid of any expression.

"What's in the building next door?" she asked.

"Munitions." He shrugged.

"That's it, 'munitions?' Can you be a bit more specific?"

"I can't actually. I told you, I'm watched."

She jumped to her feet and panned her eyes around the room.

"No, I scan for bugs whenever I return to it. I only meant I'm escorted everywhere. So, what excuse do I have to be poking round? If I'm seen or caught, I could lose my position here. At minimum. And I have to remain in place as a last resort."

"What's the last resort?"

"I kill him, get the flash-drive, and run. But it's not bloody likely I'd make it out of here alive. That's why you've been brought in."

"Then I'll just take a tour as long as I'm here anyway," Shade said, in a pique.

"Right, let me arrange a distraction."

"What will that entail, exactly?"

"I'm a bit peckish--all this exercise, no doubt. I think I'll have a late-night snack and perhaps there'll be a grease fire. Will that do?"

"You cook?"

"I putter round the kitchen from time to time, yes."

She made an interested noise. "No," she said. "That'll draw too much attention to this side of the compound."

His eyes narrowed slightly, just a flicker, but she was aware she was being tested or assessed, and it amused her."Instead, how about a nice fall down the stairs on your way to that snack?" she suggested. "I want the boys downstairs focused on the interior of the building and away from the windows."

"Leave it to you to come up with something that causes me bodily harm." He set his glass on the bedside table and stood up. "And the guards outside?"

"Won't see me." She reached down her neckline, pulled out a watch face, and checked the time.

"You need a new wristband," he observed.

"I never wear a watch. Shiny face, luminous parts, ticking noise--that's a great way to be compromised by an opponent. Also, anything on my wrist would impede the blade mechanisms."

"The jacket is a very tricky bit of work. Must be difficult to replace. How many of them do you go through in a year?" He feigned an innocent smile.

"Well, that depends on how many times I get shot, Jack." She glanced out the window and then looked at the watch again. "Sloppy. They're running late."

Watching her tuck the watch away, he said, "Show me what else you've got in there."

"Didn't Kali kill the demon lord Raktabija?"

He tried to look crushed. From the door, he said, "Now?"

"Yes, please. I'll wait until I'm sure they're all captivated by your performance."

He eased the door open, whispering, "Oi! Have fun searching the room while I'm gone," and shut the door behind him.

She did search the room. She found a very high-end bug detector with a built-in white noise generator, two automatics and spare clips, an old-school lock-pick kit, a throwing knife, and a few other sneak-thief tools. Friend traveled light. She had more apparatus stored in her jacket.

His wallet contained a little less than 500 pounds, a UK drivers' license that identified him as Philip Davies, and a credit card in the same name. His passport listed the same identity. Since these were well-crafted fakes, she disregarded them. There was a slip of paper in his wallet with a long string of numbers printed in neat male handwriting. She took a photo of it with a small, low-light, digital camera she'd brought along to document the compound. Behind the credit card, tucked low in a slot, was a business card. The paper was cream linen and a heavy, expensive stock. Embossed in gold on the card was a phone number. She photographed that as well.

She found a leather bomber jacket hanging in the wardrobe above his stash of chocolate bars—he liked Hershey's. Since rumor indicated he'd been RAF, she supposed the jacket was authentic. It accounted for the scent of leather she'd noticed on him. The only other personal items in the room were his clothes and a shaving kit. She sniffed the raspberry shaving cream, laughing at herself. She pulled out a Post-it note, jotted a message, and stuck it on the container.

She heard a clattering noise on the staircase followed by raised voices and booted feet running on the floor below. It sounded like he'd made it good, at least.

Shade went out the window.

She let herself back into the hotel room a little after dawn. Pulling the laptop out of one of the suitcases, she set up a web conference session with Curtis, Peter, and Bas. She'd dragged them all out of bed, and Peter still looked half-asleep. He was sitting in the chair directly in front of the camera, Bas sat to one side, leaning away, and Curtis had his back to both of them at a different workstation. She was curious about the body language.

"Curtis, the first two photos I'm sending are things I'd like you to research. I found those in Friend's wallet and just want to know what they are and where they go."

Curtis said, "Got it."

"The others are detail shots of the various outbuildings and the compound as a whole. Bas, I have measurements for you as well."

"I'll work up a diagram," Bas said.

"Wait'll you see what he has in that munitions building, Bas. You'll have wet dreams. He's got enough armament in there to subdue Fethiye and move on to the next couple of towns. So, as you can see, that building will have to be taken out or things could get very messy. Also, there's a double-door archway into the mountain down-slope at the foot of the main house. It's big. Like, you could drive a semi through it. I couldn't get near it, and I'd overstayed my time as it was, so I have no idea what's in there yet."

"Okay, Shade, the photos are coming through now," Curtis called over his shoulder.

"Another thing that's very worrying--when I was leaving, along came three troop transport trucks. I had to pull off the road into the trees. Why does he have all these arms and troops coming in? Does that sound like a man who's leaving in a few weeks?"

"We know he has dealings with Rawlley. Maybe he's acting as a middleman for this guy in Cuba," Peter said.

"Maybe. But what about the trucks?"

"Are you sure they were full?"

"I didn't stop them to count heads, but the rear one was-- I got a good look through the back after it passed. And what else would he use them for?"

"To transport all those goods back out?"

"I don't think so. They've got nothing but canvas between them and the world--not the best way to covertly transport Stinger missile launchers."

Bas said, "I don't like it either. Keep an eye on that compound. Check back with the Limey prick, Shade."

Rolling his eyes, Peter said to Shade, "What is it with you and the nicknames?"

Shade stared at him. "It's an effective way to trivialize a strong emotional reaction, increasing my comfort level and concealing that emotional reaction from others, Peter. But Bas came up with that one all on his own."

Peter dropped his eyes.

Bas planted a fist on the worktable and leaned over Peter. "Did you rent a car to drive out there or...?"

"I borrowed it."

Bas winked. "You're freakin' rolling in money and you steal a car. And you call me an adrenaline junkie."

"I put it back. That's not stealing, it's borrowing. Besides, if I rent a car, they see the same one coming and going or parked nearby. If I borrow a different one--"

She heard Curtis say, "Woah!" as he began opening the image files.

Bas' walked over to Curtis' monitor. He whistled and then let out a few happy moans. "Can we steal some of this before we blow it all? Please?"

"How much does a Stinger missile weigh? About forty-five pounds?" Shade asked. I'm not humping that out of there."

Peter craned his neck towards the monitor and said, "Holy shit." He got up and walked away from the camera.

"There's more," Shade said. "Keep going, that building is two levels full up to the rafters."

Curtis said, "Wow, paranoid much?"

"The fact that he might not be paranoid is a lot more worrying," Peter said from somewhere off-screen.

Shade knew he was pacing.

"Hey, these aerial shots of the compound are nice," Bas said. "How'd you get these?"

"Up a tree," Shade said.

"Sweet. These are perfect," Bas said. "I'll get them printed out for the team."

Peter sat back down in front of the camera, blocking her view. His piercing blue eyes bored into hers. "Zyllah, is this a setup?"

She was curious about the shift in his manner. She guessed he'd heard some things from Bas that had shaken him up because he only used her other name when he was feeling emotional. She let him stew for a minute while they both thought whatever they thought about the other person.

"Not by Friend," she answered finally. "But I think Nemrovsky is up to something. Friend admitted he's being kept out of the loop. Which reminds me--I need to you think back to Crete. Run me through it again."

Peter looked puzzled, but he complied. "I flew in, checked into my hotel, and went to the rendezvous point--a greasy little bar right at the waterfront. No one showed. Bunch of sailors came in, started having drinks, asked me a few normal questions."

"Like what?" Shade asked.

"My name, where I was from, was I on vacation, how I ended up at that bar..."

"And you said—tell me the exact words--this is important."

Peter frowned, confused, and took a moment to recollect. "I told them I was from America, on a business trip, and that I was meeting--oh shit."

"What?" Shade prompted knowingly.

"I said I was looking for a friend."

"And then they assisted you outside, clubbed you over the head, and threw you in a boat."

"Pretty much."

"You got it now? They thought you were there looking for Mr. Friend. So, either you were there to kill him, their pet assassin, or you were there to meet up with him, in which case he's double-crossing the boss."

"You need to warn him, Zyl."

"I'm pretty sure he already knows. He said immediately afterwards, Nemrovsky started having him watched. You accidentally blew his cover without even knowing he was involved. What're the odds?"

"It's a stupid name," Bas said.

Shade debated telling them her suspicion that Friend had another agenda, but then she remembered the conversation she'd overheard about her mental state, and decided to wait until she had more evidence than a feeling.

"Moving along," she said. "Nemrovsky has five choppers in the hangar located off-site. Two are Mil Mi-24's and the rest are Huey troop transports that have been stripped of armaments. The Hinds are older birds. One of them is in worse shape than the other and might not even be flight-worthy. The other one looks maintained, is fully loaded, and seems to be the Israeli conversion--what was it called?"

Bas asked, "The Tamam Mi-twenty-four HMOSP?"

"Okay," Shade said neutrally.

"Man, can we steal that too?" Bas asked.

"We need to make sure those are out of play. I don't want that thing on our asses when we're leaving," Peter said.

"Agreed," said both Shade and Bas.

"There were only two guards at the hangar—not terribly alert, I might add. And two more guards on a patrol of the wall that surrounds the compound. That was at night. I need to check back in the daylight."

She yawned and rubbed at the dark circles under her eyes. Regaining her train of thought, she said, "There's a fuel depot at the southeast end of the compound--too distant to do any damage to the primary structure—and also a water tower. The gate could be rammed but that tactic would only be useful as a diversion. Once past the gate, you've got the depot and then nothing but open space until you hit the manor. Any vehicle penetration would be a sitting duck for their retaliatory response—like those Stingers. So, the only possible covert approach is the eastern side of the compound, through the woods, and we'd still have to get over the wall."

"And he's abandoning this site in favor of something more secure?" Peter said.

"It's far from impenetrable. A child could scale that wall. And I moved around fairly easily within the compound too. The problem is getting an attack force over it--twelve muscle-bound guys who look like ex-military bad-asses are going to be noticed. If we were prepared to launch a full-scale assault, we could reduce the entire compound to rubble in a matter of minutes without any risk to our personnel. But we can't do that because we have to recover the data he's got. And our team leader refuses to let me handle this on my own."

"We've already discussed that," Peter said.

"Oh, and there's no cell signal up there, Bas. So you'll need to add satphones to your shopping list if you want to be able to communicate with your men."

Bas grunted an acknowledgement.

"And I have no effing idea what's in the main house. That thing is lit up like a Christmas tree, there are cameras on a tight perimeter, and based on what Friend has indicated, guards and tighter security inside."

"Any luck finding architectural plans, Curtis?" Bas asked.

"I haven't had a chance."

"What are you people doing over there? Slacking?" Shade complained.

Peter sighed. "Researching your friend Friend and trying to line up support. I don't want to drop the Friend-thing entirely, but it'll go on hold now."

"Well, what've you found?" she asked.

"Using his real name, I got a little more intel than we had before, but mostly a whole lot of nothing. He comes from an upper middle-class family—used to be the snobby noble variety but it looks like the money is pretty much gone. Father was RAF, mother is a housewife. Nice ordinary childhood. He got good grades in school, went off to university where his grades dropped—probably boredom--and he quit and joined RAF. From there, he moved up fast through Special Teams and into CRW, and then he just drops out of sight."

"Probably when that 'muckety-muck' snapped him up," Shade said.

"Or he just went over to the dark side, so to speak," Peter said.

"When are you going back to the compound?" Bas asked.

"I'll do the same run tomorrow afternoon and check the areas I didn't get to tonight."

"Watch your back," Bas said. "He's got the skill-set to be a major pain in the ass."

"You have *no* idea," Shade agreed.

At about three in the afternoon, a knock at the door woke Shade. Since it was officially Bas' room, she kept quiet but closed her hand on her gun. The do-not-disturb sign was on the door, so it couldn't be housekeeping.

In a low voice, Jack Friend said, "Are you starkers in there, Shade? Or should I call you Zyllah?"

Sliding out of bed, she ducked into the bathroom. She jammed the little black wig on her head and combed it quickly around her face. With the curtains closed, the room was pitch-black. Leaving the bathroom door ajar would provide just enough light to keep him from banging into the furniture.

Gun in hand, she cracked the room door. "You bugged me?"

"Seems fair right about now." He held up the post-it note on which she'd written:

Sebastien, you need a shave.

She saw he had actually shaved. And he was wearing the bomber jacket and carrying a coffee. The full-spectrum scent wafted through the doorway, stronger than ever. "Are you insane to keep coming here? What if someone sees you?"

"Do you actually think you're the only person who knows how to sneak round? And if you're so concerned, why not let me in before someone does?"

She stepped behind the door and swung it open, shutting it as soon as he was inside. "If you turn on a light, I will shoot you."

"Clearly not a morning person."

"How were you even able to monitor a transmission up there?" she asked.

"I refuse to say."

While she searched her jacket for the bug, he lounged at the foot of the bed, perfectly at ease. She found it and threw it at him. Pulling out her own bug detector, she gave everything she'd worn the night before a quick once over and checked the room for good measure.

"I love the outfit, by the way." He was staring appreciatively at her legs while she wandered around the room in a pair of stretchy girl-boxers and a tank top that was filled to capacity.

"Yours is nice too. The bomber jacket is awesome, but you should go with a tighter t-shirt. Also, the inseam of those jeans really isn't displaying the wares as well as a shorter cut could."

"Only I need the extra space, you see."

"I'm *so* not up for this this early," she complained.

"Sucks being knocked up unexpectedly by dodgy buggers, eh? At least I let you get in a good eight hours. I'm operating on far less."

She translated out loud. "Woken up by untrustworthy assholes."

He smiled. "Close enough. You follow along well. Why is that?"

"You know, if you would've just stayed there, I was coming back tonight." She yawned. "Shit, this is the first real sleep I've had in days, and I have to be up all night again tonight."

"I knew it. Can't keep away from me, can you?"

"And by the way, I hate to deprive you of what seems to be a very self-satisfying little stunt, Mr. Mathason, but Zyllah is not my name."

"How is that, exactly?"

"Zyllah Laurent is an identity Peter established for me."

"You don't know your real name?"

"I didn't say that."

"You're not denying it either."

She started fiddling with the coffeemaker.

When she remained silent, he asked, "Do you know what the name Zyllah means?"

"Yes, and apparently you do as well."

"It's interesting that Zyllah is Hebrew for 'shadow' or 'shade.' Also interesting is that apparently people with this name are dynamic and versatile and like change, adventure, and excitement, and value their personal independence. They're natural leaders. They fight being restricted by rules and conventions and tend to be changeable, restless, and rebellious."

"I'm impressed. You know how to use Google. Are you going to read my horoscope next?"

He let out a long, low chuckle. "Yet you say it's not your name."

"Why are you here, Sebastien?"

"One day, I'd like to know how you sussed that. Only it's Bastien if you must keep using it. But I much prefer Jack."

"Great, I've got two testosterone-crazed adrenaline junkies in my life and one is named Bas, and the other Bastien."

"I suspect the irony goes deeper than even that." He sighed.

She gave him a puzzled look.

"I like them much better blue," he said about her eyes.

She rolled them and said, "I'll wear the green ones next just so you can be sure."

He squinted in the dim light, trying to determine if she was wearing contact lenses.

She turned around to pour the coffee.

"This view is fine as well," he said in happy voice.

She snorted, she couldn't help it.

He got up and walked towards the cup of coffee she'd poured for him. She set it down and stepped away with her own cup, keeping her face hidden.

"You're a bit barmy with that whole thing," he said.

"No, but I am quite serious about it. Honestly, I'm not sure I should let you live with as much information as you already have."

"Noted," he said. "Although, I've never fancied blindfolds, so it'll seriously impair my performance during nooners. Showering in the dark might be quite exciting, however."

"I notice you've dropped the Cockney slant."

"Now you know I'm an Essex boy, there's not much point, is there? It's not really fair, that. You could do me a world of harm with the information you've got."

"You know perfectly well I'm not going to tell anyone, unless you cross me."

"I'm to trust a cold-blooded killer but you won't."

"I'd like to remind you that I did let you in. But no, not while I don't know who you're working for."

"Fair enough," he said.

She noticed that he didn't insist it was Vassily Nemrovsky. Point scored.

Grinning, he said, "You can frisk me if you think I've come here with ulterior motives."

She held up the gun still in her other hand. "I already know you have *ulterior* motives—double entendre intended."

Dumping the fresh coffee into the cup he'd brought, he sat down at the foot of the bed. He switched to a serious tone of voice. "Three truckloads of troops came in last night."

"I know. They passed me on the way out."

"No, three *more* truckloads. And I heard more than one chopper go out as well."

"Is Nemrovsky still there?"

"Yes, he was out and about shouting at the workers this morning. Lots of wiring going on. Blokes climbing all over the wall. I wanted to warn you so you don't think you're going to stroll in as easily as you did last night."

She made a rude noise.

"Right, let me finish. The big man called me up to the house today. He got quite shirty with his head of security, so he brought me in to discuss the compound security. I played sullen and stroppy because I've been cooped up so long, not trusted, yada-yada, but since it's what I'm there for, I had to go along."

"Lovely. Give me a run-down."

"For starters, there will now be a checkpoint on the road a few miles out. He specifically asked about the woods so I had to recommend roving patrols. He thought that was a top plan, so he implemented it for the compound grounds as well and doubled the guard on the wall and in the house. But I still know nothing about the overall guard presence in the house, except the goons who never leave his side. Also, I expect you'll find that whatever I've told you, he'll have doubled--he's got all this manpower now."

"I'm still yawning."

"I'm still not done," he said. "Also new today, he's switched locations inside the house. I was taken to a main level sitting room for the meeting. We've always met in his office, previously. So, I asked my escort about it afterwards. Bloke's a little dim, but impressed by me. He told me Nemrovsky's moved farther back into the interior of the house. Inside the bloody mountain, sounds like. The new area has a vault door with a combination keypad on the entry to his suite and a guard station inside the entryway. He said the bodyguards are kipping there as well—that's sleeping to you, Yank. They don't open the door unless they like what they see outside."

"How many bodyguards does he have?"

"Just the two," he said. "I'll have more gen for you once I see what those workers were about."

"Where do your minders think you are now?"

"Told them I was on the pull." At her blank look he added, "Out looking for totty. To roger a bird. Rumpy-pumpy, a wank, a shag, a bang. Not entirely lying, was I?"

"After your tumble down the stairs last night, they bought that you were capable of fucking some woman all afternoon?"

"I am capable. Let me prove it." He patted the bed beside him.

"My standards are a little higher than 'capable,'" she said.

"Excel is my middle name."

"I don't call eight inches excelling."

"I said *well over* eight inches--"

"So, he's steadily bringing in more troops. And he's still maintaining the Cuba story?"

"Hasn't changed the plan."

"Shit, we're going to have to up our timetable. He's not leaving, he's digging in."

"Yeah, it's going all sixes and sevens. Yet I'm still alive. So he's not sure about me."

"I'd say you're in a lot of danger. You heard what Peter said last night about 'looking for a friend'?"

"Yes, bloody rotten luck."

After she chucked Friend out of her room, Shade showered, geared up, and made the trip back towards the compound. The enhanced security wasn't much of an inconvenience; it just made the trip take longer. She had to pull off the road into the trees further out in order to avoid the checkpoint; there were two vehicles stationed on the road as guessed by Jack Friend earlier. The rovers in the forest were easy for her to avoid. The wall was now lit by floodlights at regular intervals, but the doubled guards still didn't spot her going over the wall.

She'd finished her reconnaissance for the evening when she heard footsteps. This particular roving patrol was being fairly cautious and swinging a light into nooks and crannies. She ducked around the troop barracks, and seeing Friend's window open, she made a fast climb. The rover was just turning the corner when an arm reached out the window and hauled her inside.

She let him manhandle her to one side of the window and press her into the shadows against the wall. The rover paused but continued past.

He was wearing jeans but was bare-chested and she could feel a fast heartbeat through the slabs of muscle. He leaned into her and lowered his head to her neck. When his breath slid inside her collar, she shoved him backwards.

"Near miss," he said.

"Not even close," she disagreed.

"Everyone gets caught sooner or later."

"Not me. Are we talking about the same thing?"

A slow smile spread across his face.

"I need you to do something," she said.

"I'm yours to command," he said, throwing his arms wide. "Perhaps over there?" He gestured towards the bed.

"You said Nemrovsky sends an escort to get you."

Grumbling, he walked over to the bed and sat down. "Right."

"The guard just shows up here. Is it always the same guard?"

"No. I'd guess he calls the guard station in the house and they send whoever is handy." He patted the mattress beside him and gave her an encouraging look.

"With all the extra people coming in, a new guard wouldn't be a cause for concern," she mused. "Then I need you to steal a uniform. Whatever gear they normally wear."

"You're going to disguise yourself as a guard to get into the house? And speaking of disguises, where did you hide those breasts in your little old man disguise?"

"I've already been in the house and under it. We're running out of time."

He looked intrigued and a little impressed. "We had a visitor today at dinner--the son. Apparently, he came in by helicopter and then went back out the same way. I was called up there for the wining and dining hour. I wondered if he came in to take the information we want back out with him."

"It's still here. Or at least that necklace is still around the old man's neck."

"Is that so? I'm beginning to think you might be as good as they say."

"I'm better. Learn it. Know it. Live it." She grinned at her own words.

"*Fast Times at Ridgemont High*," he said, identifying her quote.

"Now *that* is impressive. But moving along—the son was probably disinformation. He wanted you to think exactly what you've thought."

"Maybe. Who's this uniform for, then?"

"One of Bas' guys. He'll be on the large side. After I run all this by Peter and Bas, I'll tell you more."

As she climbed out the window, he started to follow her. "Wait, why don't I come with you?"

"Not on your life. You're a totally unknown quantity Mr. Friend."

"Ah. Just hours ago it was Bastien. I'll hardly get known if you keep brushing me to the side."

She considered it and just said, "Exactly," and dropped out of sight.

Back at the hotel, once again sprawled belly-down across the bed with her feet up in the air, Shade logged in to another web conference. She went over Friend's visit, the alterations to the compound and outlying areas, and uploaded the latest set of photographs.

"Even if he continues to up the ante, the forest will still be the best way in. The only variable there is the time it'll take to hump a team of men with heavy gear through. Bas, you know your guys, I'll leave that up to you."

"You saw their dossiers. Ex-Seals, ex-Rangers--they can handle a fast march under load."

"Nemrovsky's building up daily, so we've got to move fast. I'm going to run myself ragged checking every day for new developments. Which reminds me—are any of your guys in the area now?"

"I got one guy who's in Athens screwing around."

"Which one?

"Wiley."

"Damn, he's one of the ex-Seals, right? He *looks* like military. I was hoping for, maybe, that guy Dutch."

"Dutch is in the States. He's the one who asked why we don't just wait and hit Nemrovsky while he's on the move."

"Because I don't think he's moving. The crap he gave out to Friend about the end of the month is more likely to be when he'll have all the fortifications complete. He wanted someone—us, as it turns out—to choose that very solution in order to buy himself time to get everything in place. Then when the end of the month rolls around, he's sitting there in a fortress and we're only set up to take him out en route to Cuba—where he isn't going."

"How soon do you need someone?"

"Yesterday. I want someone in Dalaman who can stay invisible and monitor the traffic there. The troop deliveries in the middle of the night vanish into that damned cavern under the house. I'd kind of like to keep an eye on what size force he's bringing in. By my calculations he's got around a hundred and fifty men there already."

Peter said, "They're under the house?"

"It opens into a big cavern riddled with passages. Probably some remnant of a Lycian ruin. They're all over this countryside. He's bunking the extra men there, and he's got ATVs and a tank down there too."

"What?" Peter said.

"That's the bad news," she said. "The good news is that one section was being used for storage before he converted this place into his private military base, and ductwork has been extended into the area. It goes right into the kitchens."

"I'm supposed to fit through air ducts?" Bas asked.

"You won't have to," she said. "But I did. It's like I keep saying, people always forget about 'up.' And we need to get this done before he remembers."

"Damn!" said Curtis. "Is this a picture of his bedroom? How the--?"

"Yes. Note the vault door, Bas. I'm going to need that blown. Who's your man?"

"That'd be Whitey."

"I'll need his shirt and pants size, please."

Bas guffawed. "Hell if I know. I'll find out."

"The other good news is that a few well-placed explosives should just about sheer that house right off the mountainside. Not to mention blocking up that cavern."

"Run us through your idea, Zyllah," Peter said.

"In a minute. Bas, I'm leaving the logistics up to you. I'd like you to develop two scenarios with your team dynamics in mind. One plan for everything-goes-perfectly and another for FUBAR. Because I expect that with all these variables, things will get fucked-up-beyond-all-recognition before we're through."

"Prepare to be dazzled, babe," Bas said.

"Just please be sure you brief them thoroughly. Make sure I'm not tripping over anyone this time around. Make sure they understand if they get in my way I will kill them and walk over their corpses."

"You have my word," he said.

"Dad, you've got to get us more support. I'm very worried about getting back out. I suspect from things Friend has said that there will be an attempt to intercept us. Don't argue with me, please."

She was surprised to hear him say, "We're already lining that up. Your boy Clemmons is pissed off in the most major way about that attempt on his life. He's quietly raised a ruckus that you wouldn't believe. The end result is that we're going to have some unofficial support on standby. We'll also have a satellite linkup for those satphones you wanted."

"Wow, and he seemed like kind of a pussy," Shade said.

"When will you realize you just have that effect on the sane?" Bas teased.

She flipped him a bird.

Peter said, "I'm also calling in a few dead men."

"I'm sure they'll appreciate the closure. You're always so thoughtful, dad."

He chuckled. "Smith, the Aussie, is an extreme mountain-climbing fanatic in his spare time. He said looking at the photos of your little hill that he'd most likely be bored stiff, but he was willing to help out. He and another guy—don't laugh, it's just a coincidence—Wesson, already started out from the other side, and should be in position in time."

"All right, that all sounds good. Here we go with the plan…"

Chapter 15

Once more at the local pub, mobbed by boisterous tourists swilling beer, Friend found a table in a dark corner to make his call. He ordered a pint of a local brew and a shot. He was supposed to be entertaining his bird and found himself nettled that the bird he'd planned to visit wasn't at home.

"What do you have for me?" he asked.

"She's gone," Friend said.

"What do you mean, 'gone?'"

"I mean she was here yesterday evening but tonight the room was empty—bags, everything. Either the operation is underway, or they've pulled out. You pick."

"Tell me about yesterday."

"First, she's completely surveilled the compound. Granted the security there is weak, but she's even managed to get a look at the jewelry round the old man's neck. She's got some sort of plan brewing, but all I know is based on what I can infer from her questions."

"Drake still hasn't returned."

"No sign of him, no."

"Does it seem that she's following instructions?"

"I can't say. It doesn't, no. Only it seems more like the other way round. She's not striking me as the sort to follow at all," Friend said.

"What do you mean?"

"She's got a very strong personality. I'm not sure 'back down' is in her vocabulary."

"What about her appearance?"

Friend gritted his teeth.

"The first night--short black hair, dark brown eyes, black ensemble from head to toe. The second night—same black hair, blue eyes, knicker-shorts and a tank top."

"I know you've been trained to be more perceptive than this."

"It's useless, as I keep telling you. Is that her hair? I've no idea. Her eyebrows and lashes are a nondescript brown color. She could be blond, she could be brunette. She could even be a redhead. Her skin is a mid-range color, but there's a wide variety of temporary tanning products. She has no freckles, tattoos, or identifying marks—or they've been removed. Her eyes change color on her whim. Her nose is perfectly nondescript as well—it's not wide, it's not thin, it's not long, hooked, or turned up. She has small, well-shaped ears. They're not pierced."

"Interesting," he interjected.

"Pierced ears would complicate a male disguise," Friend guessed.

"Her lips are full on one occasion, less so the next. I'd guess Restylane or some other temporary enhancer. Her chin isn't pointy, it's not square, it's not cleft. She has a firm jaw, but it's not particularly pronounced. Her face seems to be a perfect oval—like half the population of the bloody world--and she can make it look thinner or heavier, with cheekbones more or less pronounced, with a variety of tricks. Same goes for the shape and tilt of her eyes. They're wide-set and lovely, whatever color they are. Her teeth are straight, white, and also unremarkable."

"She was wearing only a tank top and knickers, you said," he said.

"I don't know how to estimate weight on a woman in her physical condition. I'd guess around eight stone, but muscle weighs more. She's got large breasts that she hides well, and a high tight ass. Gorgeous legs too, if you're interested. She has hands like a piano player. She likes French manicure—she's got it on her toes as well. And Bob's your uncle. Having said all that, she could still walk up to me on the street and I wouldn't recognize her."

"What have you been able to learn about their strategy?" he asked, sounding like the question had been more of an afterthought.

"Not much. Only it's going to be more than the three of them. They're planning on using me somehow. And the troops Nemrovsky is adding don't appear to concern her. My guess is they're going to hurry up execution before the whole thing goes pear-shaped."

"Excellent. Soon we'll be able to move on to the next phase."

"I hate this assignment. I've never felt so useless and in the dark. I could easily get the damned flash-drive, kill

Nemrovsky and be away, and so could she. Yet we're going through this ridiculous exercise."

"There's no assurance you'd get out alive, nor her. Has she said she thinks she can do it? Why do you suppose she doesn't try?"

"My guess is for the same reason—she's been ordered not to do so."

"So, she does take instruction."

Friend refrained from commenting.

"Contact me when you have more details. I particularly want to know how they plan to exit Fethiye."

Friend ended the call and thought about all the things he hadn't mentioned. In the end, he found he didn't care, and shrugged his unease away.

Shade had changed her mind about stationing Wiley at Dalaman, opting to perform surveillance of Nemrovsky's compound herself from the woods nearby. Peter had disagreed, but Bas had supported Shade, knowing that she was both right and well able to conceal herself in the terrain. The only drawback was that she'd been out-of-touch for days. They planned to rendezvous with her prior to the start of the maneuver to receive the latest intelligence, but as of their departure they had only her original information.

Once they'd all loaded into the chopper heading for the drop point, Bas began giving the team an intensive briefing. Peter was listening in from his seat in the cockpit next to his buddy, Mack Havers, who was piloting them from Rhodes, Greece. Shade had provided coordinates for a clearing she'd found on the east side of the compound, within the forest. They all felt the location was far enough out to be circumspect, and Bas' had assured Shade his team would have no problem with the rigors of the long hike to the compound. Havers' instructions were to circle back out, refuel at Dalaman, and then take a more direct route to the extraction point.

"And here's the most important part," Bas said. "There're two things you need to remember at all times. First: never, *ever* get between Shade and Peter, or Shade and myself.

You do not want her going through you to get to either of us--and she will. Second: I know you're all bad-asses, but trust me when I tell you that she is badder. If she tells you to do something, do it. Do not hesitate. Do not ask her questions. Do not share your thoughts with her. Peter and I are the only ones who may disagree with her. If you do not follow her instructions, you will probably die. You will definitely never work for me again. Twenty-two men were killed—our entire unit--the last time she worked with a group because they wouldn't listen to her. The only reason Peter and I made it out alive is because of her."

Shade was waiting for them in the shadows of the trees. She looked well-rested and immaculate. She was wearing her black outfit and had camouflage paint on her face in a kaleidoscopic pattern. The paint job blurred her features effectively, and in the darkness she would be nearly invisible. Her eyes were dark, and under the beret, her hair was braided and tucked beneath her collar.

"Whatcha' been up to, sweetheart? You smell better than these guys do," Peter said after they'd unloaded the chopper.

"I found an abandoned farmstead. Sheep or goats by the smell of it. But there was water and a fireplace so it was like a little mini-vacation."

"Were you able to take out the helicopters? I really don't want an aerial pursuit."

She gave him a level look. "Yes, I disabled them. They shouldn't have any idea until they actually try to start them up."

She tossed a rolled bundle to Bas. "You decide who's fetching Friend, but they need to fit into that uniform." She approached him and rapped experimentally on his flak jacket, then turned to Peter and did the same. She smiled when she heard the sound of the body armor underneath.

"You're becoming a bit of a mother hen, Shade," Peter said.

"Here's what you asked for," Bas said, handing over a backpack.

"Were you able to get everything?"

"Yes, ma'am. Including the sat phones. We'll each have an earpiece, and Curtis is listening in too."

She rummaged in the bag, extracting some things and stowing them in her jacket or pants, then zipped it up and hefted it onto her shoulders.

"Gentleman, the woods are heavily patrolled," she said in a clear voice. "I will be scouting ahead. If you can take out the rovers silently, do so. Otherwise keep your heads down. We do not want our presence known until we're all in position. If everyone sticks to the plan, I'm afraid you're all in for a boring time."

Most of the men were looking at their shoes, the trees ahead, anywhere but directly at Shade. A few were giving her sidelong glances out of the corner of an eye, but they'd look away quickly if she caught them at it. They'd heard her reputation.

Shade had read all their dossiers and took advantage of the time to match the live versions with what she remembered from their files. She picked out Rabbit easily. At five-foot-six, he was by far the smallest man on Bas' team. He had a compact build, was lightning fast, and could fit into even the tightest spaces. Caucasian with brown hair and blue eyes, his unusually large ears had earned him his nickname, and he used them to detect an adversary long before anyone else heard anything. He was the team's usual point man. He was standing beside his partner, Whitey, the explosives expert. Whitey had gotten his nickname from his prematurely white hair, pale skin, and light blue eyes. Since Whitey was half-deaf from one too many detonations at close range, Rabbit filled in as his ears.

Snake and Wiley, the two ex-Seals, were both tall, muscular, black men, close to Bas' height. As she looked them over, Wiley met her eyes once, briefly. Wiley had come to Bas with his partner already in place. Both of them were physically intimidating, and had intense don't-fuck-with-me demeanors. They were smart and proficient but prone to independent thinking. Bas suspected they wouldn't be with him much longer as they'd both been making noises about starting their own business, and they were well-qualified to do it: Snake, the other half of the pair, had degrees in business and in economics. In

Shade's opinion, their style of operation was more mayhem than finesse, however.

Beyond them were the two Carloses, Guera and Lavarre, also known as C1 and C2. The dark-haired and dark-eyed Latin men were both easy-going, had a bent for communications equipment and gadgetry, but had become closely-bonded friends who mostly kept to themselves.

She was pleased to see Chavez again. His performance had been faultless the last time out. His partner, Andre, had a comparable conduct record but with a twist: these two were very popular with the ladies, but according to Bas, Andre was as big a douchebag as Chavez was a sweetheart. An almost pretty, light-skinned, black man, Andre was always trying to jive someone and a little vain about his appearance and grooming. Bas had said he was also prone to whining.

She wasn't thrilled to see Red. As his name implied, Red was a redhead and had the stereotypical temper to match. A quiet man until he blew, he had a tendency for moodiness and also berserker behavior in combat. Shade hadn't wanted him included on the mission, but he had medic training and was partnered with Dutch, who she did consider an asset. A mix of Asian, African-American, and Native American, Dutch wore his hair in a long ponytail and had an unflappable personality. He rarely spoke or smiled, but was adept at guerilla-style tactics and an excellent tracker. The standing joke was that he singlehandedly fulfilled Bas' Equal Opportunity Employer quota. Acting as the rearguard along with Bas, he would prevent any ambushes from behind.

Bas called over his shoulder, "Rabbit! You will be tailing her point. And I do mean *tail*."

Rabbit came forward when Bas called his name, but by the time he looked around for Shade, she'd already faded into the trees. He made an admiring noise and disappeared after her.

They'd been walking for about thirty minutes when Bas heard a sound like a body impacting on the ground. He and Dutch peeled off and backtracked. Shade was crouched over a patrol, cleaning off a dagger.

"Looks like you missed one," she whispered.

"You're supposed to be on point," Bas said.

"Rabbit thinks I'm still up there. I'm much faster than you all, so I'm orbiting." She chucked a handheld radio to Bas and said, "This will come in handy. I'll get a few more and then we'll be able to listen in once things get going."

When he and Dutch looked up, she'd gone. Dutch grunted once, and the corner of his mouth twitched.

After another fifteen minutes, Bas paused to let Dutch catch up and asked, "You see her?"

Dutch said, "Nope. But she got another one."

"They've probably been chapping her ass for days and she couldn't do anything about it until now." He shrugged. "She's working off her mood."

About an hour in, they stopped for a rest. The men were all carrying gear that almost doubled their body-weight, and it was a warm night. Water bottles came out of packs.

When Bas checked in with Peter, he was asked, "You seen her?"

Bas said, "Just the once."

Peter pointed to two bodies off to the side of their route. "At this rate, there won't be any left when we get there."

C1 said, "That girl is voodoo."

C2 said, "Glad she's on our side," and crossed himself.

They continued on this way, occasionally seeing bodies but never encountering any patrols themselves, until they reached the edge of the woods. Bas called a halt and checked the time.

Rabbit materialized, looking spooked, and sat down under a conifer breathing a little hard. "I never once saw her," he said. "She's like a freakin' ghost."

Peter approached Bas and asked, "Where is she?"

"Why would I know?" Bas asked.

"I thought you two had that Spidey-sense thing going."

"It's more like sonar. She pings me, not the other way around. If she doesn't let me know where she is, I don't." He had a feeling then and looked up at the tree beside him. She dropped out of the branches, landing lightly in front of him. "Up."

She nodded.

Rabbit made an 'O' face.

"We're ahead of schedule," Peter said. "We can be late to extraction, but we don't want to be early."

"Break here then. It's clear," Shade said.

They spread out, picked cover, and hunkered down. Wiley and Snake volunteered for watch. Some checked their gear, others took out power bars and water, each to their own inclinations. Shade sat down beside Bas and tucked her face into his neck for a nap.

Chavez eventually wandered over and sat across from Bas under another tree. "I know you told us your parents were dead, but how'd you get hooked up with Laurent?"

Bas jutted his chin at Shade. "Actually, my father abandoned my mother and me." He gave Peter a thoughtful look and then shrugged. "He may still be out there. My mother died of cancer when I was eight, and I was sent to live with my aunt. Her husband was a mean asshole. He hit her. He hit the four, mean, little assholes he'd fathered. I was just another mouth to feed. The rule of the house was the biggest bully was his favorite, and I was the youngest and smallest. My mother had never hit me or even raised her voice to me, so it was like I'd landed on another planet."

Peter said, "Hard to believe he was ever small or helpless, huh Chavez?"

Chavez grinned.

Bas said, "Yeah, well, anyway. The three middle cousins and two of their friends caught me on some back street in Stockholm one afternoon and were knocking me around when Shade came along. She just…attacked. No warning, nothing. Before I knew what'd happened, all five of them were on the ground, bleeding and crying. I'd never seen anything like it--- anyone so angry. She was like this tiny dervish of rage. You could almost see it coming off her like heat."

They all looked at Shade, leaning still and silent against Bas. She seemed more like a shadow Bas was casting.

"She stood there and taunted them afterwards, saying they'd just been beat by one little girl. She said if they were so tough, why didn't they get up or defend themselves from one little girl? Nobody got up. When I asked her why she'd helped me, she said, 'problems should be solved by those who see them.' When I asked her where she'd learned to do that, she told me about Peter. I begged her to let me come with her, and she did. It took us a while to convince him, but here I am."

Peter said, "She wasn't really good about the word 'no' even then."

Shade stretched and yawned. "I didn't just happen along. I'd been following you. You looked sad and lost."

Bas looked at her, surprised, and she kissed his nose.

"How old were you?" Chavez asked Shade.

Peter answered for her. "We don't know. She didn't know how old she was when I found her. We think she's about the same age as Bas."

Shade had gotten to her feet and was dusting herself off.

"Should be about time to move out, sweetheart," Peter said. "Anything else we need to know?"

"The troops have been steadily coming in. He's increased the manpower on patrols, as you've seen, and the number of troops deployed around the compound at any given time. I'd estimate that he's at least doubled the total number I reported to you last."

The men gathered around to listen.

"None of the other improvements will impact us, since I don't intend for us to be maneuvering in there. He keeps increasing the fortifications though. I think we've moved just in time. I want to stress that it's critical we blow that ammunitions building. The fuel depot and other structures are secondary targets just to cause confusion. We do not want those weapons coming into play in this operation--we have too small a force here. Any questions?"

Chavez spoke up. "Bas said originally that you thought this guy had been targeting specialists and govvie intel types but now you think it's the other way around? They were all after him for this information he's got."

"That's right," Peter said.

C2 interjected, "Bas said someone even tried to pull in Shade and him."

"What if the first story was right? How do we know this isn't just some kind of set up to net all of us at once?" Andre asked.

Rabbit said to Andre, "I'm sorry--who are you, again?"

"Yeah, Andre, it's not like you're on anybody's most-wanted list," C2 added dryly.

"Except maybe that brunette in Panama, but I think she only wanted to un-man him," Chavez joked.

"I saw you smile," Bas said sotto voce to Shade.

Shade elbowed him and said to the others, "If everything goes smoothly, most of you won't ever go inside those walls." Turning to Andre she said, "But if you're worried, Andre, just stay behind me."

Hoots and jeers broke out. Andre scowled but kept his mouth shut.

Chapter 16

Bas signaled eight men to split off and take up concealed positions around the wall. Peter was in charge of the exterior group and the snipers, Smith and Wesson, who were already in place on the mountain above the compound.

Shade had discovered a natural fissure in the mountain that led through a series of caves into the area under the house. Once the first group was moving into position, Bas, Dutch, Whitey, and Chavez followed Shade into the caves.

Shade's group had a tense moment when the passageway narrowed between two stone protuberances. Shade and Chavez slipped through easily, but Bas got stuck between the two rocks. Shade found herself thinking that the entire mission might have to be scrapped until he lost enough weight to wiggle free…stuck between a rock and a hard place…and her mind kept spinning out witticisms until she ended up on her knees on the stone floor convulsed in silent laughter. Bas was so irritated with her that he tore himself loose. Scooping her up with one arm, he carried her like luggage down the passageway, still shaking with the effort of suppressing her howls. She'd almost gotten herself under control when she looked back at Chavez. He was a reddish color, lips pressed into a hard white line as he tried not to laugh, and the sight set her off again.

When the passage opened out into the main cavern, Shade and Bas took out the two guards sitting by the entryway with Bo shuriken. Bas hit first, but Shade's aim was more precise. They traded looks before Bas waved in the rest of the team. Whitey donned the uniform Shade had provided and then slipped out to retrieve Jack Friend. The uniform included a cap, but his coloring was still too pale and Shade hoped it wouldn't be noticed. When he was safely away, she joined the others who were already at work planting explosives. Bas meticulously wired the entryway to the improvised troop housing area himself. They wanted all those men contained until their team was clear of the hot zone.

Shade led them through the passageway that tied into the house. Once they were inside the storage room, Shade opened an unsecured door leading into the kitchens.

Bas whispered, "Seriously?"

In a quiet voice Shade said, "Nemrovsky probably doesn't even know this is here. What lord of the manor visits the kitchens? And his chief of security either forgot about it, or has lost his ability to be objective about the vulnerabilities. Jack would've pointed it out, but he was never allowed in here."

"Oh, it's 'Jack,' is it?"

"Smartass," she said. "Run along and B-S-U."

"Thank you," he said in a sober tone that had nothing to do with what she'd just said.

In the same tone she said, "You're welcome, California." She put a hand on the body armor covering his chest, directly over the scar from the near-fatal bullet, and then moved on.

They found the kitchens dark and empty. Bas' signaled his team to proceed out into the hallway to a centralized location Shade had described. Shade climbed into a service access hatch to make her way along pipes and ductwork to her intended destination.

When Whitey came over the com indicating he and Friend were in position, and Shade confirmed her readiness, Bas' team set off a small explosion that started a firefight in the middle of the house. Their intention was to draw all the house guards in their direction. Chavez hit the button detonating a blast in the entry to the cavern barracks, preventing those troops from entering the fray. When the barracks on the compound grounds emptied, responding to the ruckus, Smith and his partner began picking them off from on high. They fired in a few grenades just to add to the chaos. The exterior teams then began firing on the walls. Peter had them work in a sequence starting from one side of the compound and then drawing off responders to another side by the action of that team. At Shade's signal, Whitey and Friend detonated the explosive on the vault door to Nemrovsky's suite. When the bodyguard came out firing, they were taken out by a second blast.

Shade had a gun to the back of Vassily Nemrovsky's head before he even knew his guards were down. The white-haired Russian was overweight, red-faced, and caught completely off-guard. Before the door blew, Shade had observed him sitting at his desk in pajamas and a silk robe, enjoying a nightcap while he surfed the internet. He'd jumped to his feet, but indecision had held him static. She reached for the necklace, gave it a yank, and broke the chain.

"Let's confirm this contains what I came for," she said.

"Ah, a woman," he said. "You would be this Shade I have heard so much about."

"Sit," she said. "Keep your hands on the desk. If you do as I say, quickly and quietly, you may live to enjoy the money you've swindled all these years. For my part, I don't care. I'd as soon kill you as look at you."

She dangled the necklace over his shoulder and said, "Plug it in."

Once he'd attached it to the laptop, she reached over his shoulder and typed an address into the web browser. Curtis was waiting to remote in. He took control of Nemrovsky's laptop and began rummaging through the contents of the flash-drive.

Nemrovsky watched, bemused. "The things you can do with computers these days."

"Do hurry along," Shade said, keeping her gun trained on Nemrovsky and hoping Curtis was monitoring the com.

Curtis voice broke in. "Yes, it's here. At least it looks like it. Damn, Shade, I don't know exactly what I'm supposed to find, but it's not garbage and there's a lot of it."

"How did you know?" Nemrovsky asked, unable to hear Curtis.

Shade snorted at the irony. "A little bird told a friend." She snatched up the necklace and zipped it into her jacket.

From the open doorway, they heard shots fired and returned. Shade knew that would be Friend stationed down the hallway. Whitey crashed into the room, firing repeatedly in the opposite direction. Capitalizing on the distraction, Nemrovsky launched his chair backwards, hoping to catch Shade off-guard, but she slid away. He kicked the rolling chair in her direction, and she was forced to sidestep again. Whitey turned and fired a shot into the room, aiming towards Nemrovsky, and she ducked. The house shook and rumbled, becoming unstable from all the explosives. Whitey staggered off-balance, Shade grabbed at the desk, and Nemrovsky teetered into a bookcase, which swung, and he was gone behind it. Shade couldn't tell whether he'd been hit or not.

"Dammit," Whitey exclaimed.

Shade shrugged. "I got what I came for."

Friend kept grinning as the three of them outflanked the opposing force and fought their way back to Bas' position. Shade thought he was acting like a kid who'd finally been let out. It was too bad the house-guard weren't much of a match for them. She could still hear gun and artillery fire coming from outside the compound, so presumably everything was progressing smoothly. Bas' group fell back and met them at the kitchen and they went out the same way they'd come in.

As they passed into the storeroom, Friend asked, "Is Nemrovsky still alive?"

"As far as I know," Shade said. "I couldn't tell if Whitey got him."

"Then I may need to vanish at some point," Friend said.

"You can't possibly stay here. The guards will tell him you participated."

"I nicked a page out of your book. No one who's seen me is alive to tell about it." He was still grinning from ear to ear.

"Copycat," she said, and moved out.

As they all retreated down the passageway, Bas set off another charge he'd planted in the kitchen to prevent pursuit. The floor shook under their feet again. Chavez spared a nervous glance for the ceiling.

"We need to get out of here," Shade yelled.

Chavez, Whitey, Dutch, and Friend were clear of the passageway and heading for the doors of the cavern. Shade was exiting the passageway with Bas bringing up the rear. He would detonate the charges intended to immobilize the tank and ATVs once they were clear.

Shade heard yells from behind them revealing that some of the guards had made it through the kitchen prior to the last blast. As she turned around, Bas took a bullet in the back and went down. He caught himself, pivoted around on one knee, and opened fire. Shade back-tracked and took up a firing position to one side of the passageway. A portion of the overhang sheered away and came down on top of Bas with crushing force. The impact blew dust in all directions.

Firing blindly, Shade rushed to Bas. He was unconscious and had a heavy stone slab pinning one leg. Rubble covered him but it appeared that most of it had broken apart as it fell. She began shifting the stone, but before she could completely free him, fire started from down the passage again. She threw herself to the ground and dug into her pockets for a couple of explosive limpets. Triggering her left blade, she grabbed the gun in her right and charged back down the passageway seeing red.

They tried to jump her as she turned a corner created by fallen stones and met the slash of her left arm. She fired randomly with the right, and then speared the next man who leaped out at her. She hacked or shot four more before there was stillness. Slapping a limpet onto the wall, she strode back down the passage to Bas.

It took her one last heave to get the stone off him, and then she had a real problem. No amount of slapping or shaking would wake him, and he was almost double her bodyweight.

Chavez, Dutch, and Whitey were pinned down behind a truck. They'd been forced to take cover when they drew fire leaving the cavern. They'd lost track of Friend shortly after they'd gotten clear. Their egress orders were to proceed to the northwest part of the wall which had been blown out when the ammo dump was detonated, a charge planted earlier by Whitey, but none of them had seen Shade or Bas exit the cavern yet. The ammo dump and fuel depot were still engulfed in flames, and other portions of the wall were also down. It appeared to have crumbled like cheese under the onslaught from the guns and the RPGs fired from Smith's position.

Ducking under a flurry of fire, Peter skidded in next to them. "Why are you still here? Where are Shade and Bas?"

"Sir, we thought they were right behind us. And we've been unable to go back for them. Every time we stick our heads out, we're taking fire," Chavez said.

Peter got on the com to Smith, and soon after they had coverage on their location.

They all swiveled their heads towards the cavern entryway as another detonation rocked the grounds. There was a massive flash of orange light, and a cloud of dust and smoke roiled outwards from the doors. Behind the haze dispersing into the courtyard, they saw Shade dragging Bas. She had her back to the compound, shielding him with her body. The muscles in her legs stood out in sharp relief from the monumental strain of dragging his weight, and the cords in her neck were outlined by the harsh, orange light. She was baring clenched teeth as she heaved him along, and her eyes flashed crazily even through the distance. The dust churning in the air created an illusion of smoke pouring off of her.

Chavez and Dutch were already running towards her, but Peter, dazed, had to fumble his gun up to join Whitey covering them.

Chavez threw his assault rifle to Shade when they reached her. She caught it and initiated suppressive fire out into the dark. Dutch and Chavez hefted Bas between them and began backtracking to the truck. As they retreated, and the compound defenders began retaliatory fire in earnest, Shade made a throwing motion twice, and explosions sent dirt and rock flying into the air, providing a covering cloud. From above them, Smith followed suit, firing in grenades that thickened the cloud's opaqueness.

"Just keep trucking!" Shade bellowed at them as they neared Peter.

Whitey preceded them to the torn wall, and Peter lagged behind to cover them.

Once they were clear of the compound, Peter ordered the men positioned on the far side to fall back. The remaining positions would continue the assault, falling back in turn. Shade retrieved her backpack from Peter's original location. She'd passed it off to him before going into the compound. After digging in the backpack, she began laying down mines to slow pursuit. Bas had instructed each position to do the same as they abandoned their location. They knew their intended withdrawal route would take them through mostly open country where they could be easily tracked, but they only had to buy enough time to make it to the rendezvous point where Havers would be waiting with the helicopter.

When the team reached the rendezvous point, Havers wasn't there. Worried glances went around the group, and men checked their timepieces.

Peter's attempts to raise Havers on the com went unanswered. "Curtis, you still listening in? We need air extraction yesterday."

Faint and crackling, Curtis answered, "I'll see what I can do."

Sitting slumped on the ground, Shade said, "The detonator for the tank was buried when the ceiling collapsed on Bas. So that thing is still a contender. I think I got most of the ATVs with that last blast, though."

"Is that what happened to him?" Peter asked.

"Nothing but a mountain can defeat Basilius Drake. Is he coming around yet?" she asked Red, who was checking him over.

"He's twitching," Red said. "Looks concussed though, and his ankle might be broken. I'm not sure about this wrist either."

Chavez said, "Havers needs to hurry up. That is one heavy son of a bitch and I'd rather not have to hump him across country. Pardon my French, ma'am."

"Leave him be and see to the others while we have a minute," Peter told Red.

Red started with the two Carloses, who both had flesh wounds. He bandaged a graze on C1's thigh that didn't seem to be bothering him much, and moved on to a deep furrow along C2's forearm from a shard of flying rock. C2 said it wasn't serious, but it was bleeding a lot and affected his grip. Their position had been furthest from coverage by Smith and they said they'd taken some heavy return fire. He bandaged Rabbit's right shoulder for a through-and-through in the meat of his deltoid muscle. Aside from a few other scrapes and bruises, Red pronounced they were all in pretty good shape.

They heard a blast coming from the direction of the compound, and all heads turned towards it.

Andre said, "Now, whaddya' wanna bet they're freeing up those troops, gents?"

"Any other bad news, Shade?" Peter asked.

She thought for a moment. "Well, Nemrovsky is probably still alive, but no, nothing I can think of. It went according to plan until the ceiling came down."

"Why is it always me?" Bas grumbled, finally starting to come around.

"You're a big target," Shade said. "It's hard to miss you."

Rabbit said, "I have movement."

A landmine along their back trail exploded.

"We can't sit here, we're too exposed," Peter said. "Shade, get us to some cover."

"There's some sparse forest south of here. But I mean *sparse*. Big rocks, a few trees, and not much else.

"It's better than being sitting ducks," Wiley said.

"This is a good spot for a chopper pickup," Snake added. "But it sucks for a firefight."

"Get him up," Peter said, indicating Bas.

"Somebody forgot to FUBAR the helicopter," Shade said to goad Bas. She stood up and stretched out her cramping legs.

Sitting up, Bas gave her a shocked look and said, "That's so not fair! How the hell was I supposed to FUBAR the helicopter?" He pointed at her. "You talk to Peter. Havers was supposed to be able to handle himself."

She turned away so he wouldn't see her smile.

He said to Red, "Get me up! Splint the ankle, it'll hold. Honestly, my fucking hip hurts worst of all."

"You only use one hip for fucking?" Andre wisecracked. "'Cause I put both of 'em into it." He made a grinding motion to demonstrate.

Another landmine went up from the east.

"That's two approaches," Rabbit said. "They're surrounding us."

"Move south," Shade said. "That's our best cover."

When they reached the area, the cover was thin but sprawled out on both sides of the southbound dirt road. They all fanned out and tried to choose defensible positions.

Shade, Wiley, Snake, and Dutch remained mobile while the others dug in, taking out patrols as they were able. Rabbit scouted the periphery. It quickly became apparent they were being overrun.

When they heard the sounds of trucks moving towards their position from further south, Shade cursed. To no one in particular, she said, "I knew I should've stationed someone in Dalaman. He's got more troops inbound. What do you bet that's what happened to Havers?"

Snake's voice announced, "We are totally cut off to the south."

Rabbit came on and said, "It's open on the northwest side--they looped east and joined up with the other group and are coming at us from over there."

Wiley, in Shade's line of sight, turned towards the northwest.

"Belay that!" Shade shouted. "That's a dead end. It's a sheer cliff with no way out. They're herding us in that direction because they know it. If they're smart they'll send troops down the ravine below it to cut us off. Can we trickle through on the northeast side and get back to those woods?"

Wiley eyeballed her, nostrils flaring as his logic and his orders conflicted. He ground his teeth and turned back, obeying Shade.

Dutch's placid voice said, "They've got the tank en route from the northeast with more troops."

Peter said, "Shit!"

Shade hung her head. "Northwest it is. If we can make it, there's a ruin right at the cliff's edge. It's the only defensible spot. There're the remains of a wall and some piles of stone, but then it's a sheer drop."

Bas' voice said, "Chavez, Andre, you're going to guard our rear. Dutch and Rabbit, pull back fast. C1 and C2, you're going to haul ass with me to that cliff and fortify. Everyone else, move as you're able."

When Bas and the Carloses reached the location, they found it scattered with boulders and loose rock piles. Except for one horseshoe-shaped section of wall, the ruin was just that: tumbled blocks of stone. The terrain was uneven, with gullies running through it, and there was almost no vegetation. With Shade's preference for highly-mobile, guerilla-style combat in mind, Bas understood why she didn't consider it a viable location. It could be held for a time, but only by entrenching. And against a much larger force, with ammunition running low, it was a death trap.

C1 was cussing under his breath.

"Here to me!" Shade yelled from behind the wall. She shrugged out of her pack and began rummaging in it.

C1 and C2 deposited Bas behind the wall and began freeing up ammunition from their packs.

Bas' ankle had swollen to twice its normal size and he was barely able to put weight on it.

"Lucky for you, I FUBARed this cliff," Shade said. She pulled out what looked like a coil of rope from her pack, and after strapping on a harness, she tossed the rope to Bas. "Tie that to something," she said. "I'll be right back." Then she dove off the cliff.

C1 leaped to help Bas secure the line to a boulder.

C2 ran to the edge with a horrified expression and watched as Shade fell, arms spread, legs together, her hair unraveling and streaming out behind her as the line played out above her. He crossed himself and muttered under his breath, "Angels don't fall out of the sky."

Shade righted herself as she fell, and the bungee cord stretched almost to its limit and slowed her. As she neared the ground, her arm flashed up and a blade severed the line. She absorbed the drop with her knees and pushed off into a sprint.

The ravine was a dry streambed and littered with piles of rock and a few shrubs. She dodged and hurtled, but as she'd warned them, there was a unit of Nemrovsky's men moving in from the north end, and she had to run right past them. They started firing when they saw her. She took a bullet in one leg, tumbled, rolled, and was back up running, but with a limp. C2 flung himself almost over the edge of the cliff and laid down covering fire as Bas rolled and elbowed himself into position, and C1 joined them. The three of them forced the shooters to stay under cover until Shade had passed their location.

"Man, she's fast," C1 said.

Red arrived and slung his pack on the ground. "This location sucks!"

"Like she said." Bas crabbed back towards the wall.

Wiley ducked his head, shimmied out of his pack, and joined Snake piling up rock.

"Where the hell is she going?" Rabbit said, laying out clips of ammunition.

"To save our asses, would be my guess." Chavez slammed a fresh clip into his gun.

Peter hurried over to help Bas. It took all his strength to drag him back towards the wall. "Do you know what she's doing?"

Bas made a noise in his throat when his ankle bounced over a rock. He grated out his guess. "Helicopters."

"She'll never make it all the way back there!" Peter said.

"You better hope she does," Bas said through gritted teeth.

"Dig in!" Peter shouted.

Chapter 17

Their only advantage was that the incoming troops weren't bulletproof. From the safety of the rocks, they could pick off any attacker who got too close. But they were outnumbered and most of the incoming troops were well out of range, so their adversary could afford to outwait them. And then there was the little problem of the incoming tank, as Rabbit pointed out.

A few enterprising souls had attempted to crawl through the maze of rocks and had gotten past their perimeter. Dutch had suffered a deep arm slice from an attacker during one of the attempts. Wiley and Snake were reconnoitering their perimeter but individuals still got past them.

They received heavy fire if any of them showed an available body part, and projectile rock chips knocked off the boulders by ricocheting bullets were almost as hazardous as the bullets themselves. C1 wrenched his shoulder diving for cover from one hail of splinters.

Andre called, "Clip!"

Chavez said, "That's my last one. Make it count."

"Where the hell is she?" Peter asked no one in particular.

"That's it guys! Here comes the tank!" said Rabbit.

Bas said into the com, "Shade, baby, we're about outta' time up here."

Crackling with static and background noise, her com came alive. In a jittery voice, she said, "Fighting the updraft!"

Every head turned to Bas in confusion, and he said, "Down! Down! Down!"

As they dove for cover, the air filled with the thunder of pounding rotors. The blades seemed to come up over the cliff's edge in slow motion as Shade piloted the camouflage-painted, Hind, attack helicopter up the precipice. As soon as the Gatling guns cleared the edge, there was a supernova of light as she opened fire on the front ranks, edging the battle-scarred gunship forward over her team. She launched missiles with a percussive air noise before they whistled away. The cannons followed for the big bass boom that blotted out their hearing.

They could see her gritted teeth through the gunner's cockpit window as she fought the stick without a pilot, trying to keep the tail down and the chopper level, while maintaining the barrage. There was blood running down the right side of her face beneath a tracking helmet. The helmet panned the whining armaments wherever she turned her head. Voids appeared in the troop lines assembled beyond them. The guns screamed and pivoted. Whole sections of men vanished with sprays of blood as she relentlessly obliterated the opposing force.

The Hind swayed from side to side as she hovered, like a bird of prey bating protectively over its nest. Tornadoes of dust, generated by the buffeting winds from the rotors, swirled up into the churning air. Hot smoking shells were streaming down on their heads like rain from hell, and through the staccato percussion of the guns, they heard the air-splitting shriek as she released the anti-tank missiles.

The first missile exploded the tank into two airborne parts, and the second obliterated the base of the machine, sending shrapnel flying into the rear lines of the troops arrayed against them. A circular void appeared in the middle of the ranks. More men retreated from the devastation, scattering in every direction. Shade laid on the guns again and began edging the chopper vindictively forward as their attackers' lines folded.

"Shade! Do not pursue! Evac us now!" Peter bellowed over the guns. "Bas, don't let her do this again!"

Bas aimed a black look at Peter but yelled, "Shade! Time to kiss a sunset pig. Will you?"

"Bas, get up there and keep her in check! Chavez, C2, get Bas into that chopper, he's the only one who can restrain her!" Peter barked.

"Move! Move!" yelled several of the men.

An incoming soldier, screaming berserker-style, leaped over the rocks aiming at Chavez who'd stood up to climb onto the chopper. Shade swung the tail around, and Chavez ducked. Blood sprayed over half the team as the three-blade tail rotor sliced into the attacker. She spun back, evidencing wobbly control, and laid on her barrage again. C2 wasn't the only man crossing himself at that point.

Blasted by grit and the wind of the rotors, Chavez climbed onto the stub wing and got the pilot's canopy open behind Shade. Snake and C2 hoisted Bas up to the cockpit. Once

Bas had climbed in, Chavez edged back to the bay door. Bas angled the helicopter to allow for easier boarding, but this left the starboard side exposed. Chavez took up a machine gun position to provide coverage as the other men loaded in, but the opposing forces were still in disarray from Shade's onslaught.

After he took over the primary piloting controls, Bas said, "Shit! That wind is really something!"

"That damned precipice draws like a chimney," Shade said, her voice vibrating in the turbulence.

"What's all the smoke?" Peter climbed into the flight-technician's jumpseat behind Bas.

"Well, I had to do some quicky wiring, and this thing is an old lady. Guess she isn't up to being put through her paces today."

"Will she get us out of here?" Peter asked.

"Out of here, but how far after that, I don't know. You work on that from back there, why don't you?" Shade said.

Bas gritted his teeth, trying to hold the chopper steady as the men boarded and threw in gear. "She wasn't designed to carry this kind of load either, so factor that in."

Bas had put some distance between them and the compound, but they were still nowhere near the Rhodes airport where they'd originally planned to debark. The smoke in the cockpit had been gradually increasing, the men and their gear were cramped in a cargo compartment only designed to accommodate eight, and the chopper was beginning to wallow and shudder. Bas was losing responsiveness.

"It's either put down or crash," Bas said.

"Looks like a clearing over that way," Shade said.

"Do it," Peter agreed.

"We're only a few miles from Dalaman," Bas suggested.

Peter thought about it. "Yeah, but we don't know why Havers didn't make the rendezvous—that airport might not be an option for us."

Bas put down in the center of the clearing, the Hind shaking and stuttering. They were surrounded by heavy forest. Red had started treating injuries during the flight, but they took the time after landing to finish providing medical attention, and to situate the wounded men as comfortably as possible in the cramped interior.

Whitey's injury was the most serious. He had a leg wound that was bleeding sluggishly and the bullet was still in his leg. Red suspected the bone might be broken. Shade had a through-and-through in her thigh that she'd bandaged, but she was walking on it. Both Carloses were injured, and Dutch needed stitches for the knife wound. Bas had to be helped out of the cockpit by Snake and Wiley.

Standing outside the chopper, Peter was trying to raise Curtis on the com. "We can't be out of satellite range yet." He looked up at a sky that was still dark. "What the hell is he doing?"

"I have a strong feeling we won't have to sit here for long," Shade warned.

They both looked at her.

"I might be wrong," she said.

Peter winced, and Bas shouted, "Able bodies out, establish a perimeter and keep your heads down. Rabbit, how's the shoulder? You think you can make it to Dalaman and find out what the hell happened to our original ride?"

"Will do." Rabbit checked his gear and hopped out of the helicopter.

The ambulatory men jumped out of the troop compartment with Shade right behind them.

Peter helped Bas into the compartment, and had just finished checking the other men's bandages, when Curtis finally came on the comm.

"You can expect unofficial air support shortly." They could barely hear him through the spatter of static.

"How soon is 'shortly'?" Peter asked.

"I'm honestly not sure. Apparently a Navy chopper was standing down but is now en route. They won't tell me anything, but they wanted to know whether you were out of the hot zone. They're not prepared to engage, only transport. I don't understand all this military stuff," he explained.

"Shade?" Peter asked.

"Acknowledged," she chimed in.

Snake's hushed voice said, "Unfortunately, we have movement."

"Confirming that movement," Wiley said in the same low tone.

"Me three," whispered Andre.

"What the hell?" Peter exclaimed. "How could anyone know we're here?"

They all heard a shot, and Chavez said, "They're trying to close the circle."

"Red?" Bas queried.

They heard the rattle of sustained machine gun fire.

Sounding disgusted, Shade's voice said, "Overkill. I have him."

Peter leaped out the compartment door and ran into the woods, hoping Red cooled off before Shade got to him. They had only what ammo remained in the clips and no clear idea how long they had to hold this position.

The darkness within the forest was nearly absolute. Peter could feel a presence ghosting among the trees, but he hadn't actually encountered anyone. Moving without a sound, Wiley approached him as Peter was doubling back towards the chopper.

"Who's back there with the wounded?" Wiley asked.

"No one will get near that chopper as long as Bas is in it. Shade will get them first, and in the unlikely event she doesn't, he will."

"Man has a busted ankle," Wiley challenged. "Woman's been shot in the leg."

"It won't matter."

When an unknown man leaped through the compartment door, multiple guns hesitated before pointing at him. Only Bas had actually fired when a dagger imbedded itself precisely at the base of the man's throat. The man went face first onto the deck and laid there in widening pool of blood.

Shade leaped into the compartment favoring one leg.

"You're slacking," Bas said.

She pointed at her bandaged thigh. "Hey, big hole. Remember?"

They both looked at the man.

"These are not Nemrovsky's troops," she said.

"I figured as much," Bas agreed.

"Need anything?" she asked brightly.

"Nope, we're good here." He glanced around at the other men, checking. When he looked back, Shade and the body were gone. The blood still remained.

Whitey said, "She scares me."

Bas said, "Glad to hear it. Guess my doubts about your sanity were unfounded."

Whitey gave him a dirty look.

Shade watched Peter making his way back through the woods towards the chopper. She had a little pile of bodies stacked and was squatting beside them.

"What's this?" he asked.

She made a vague noise. "I had the time, so I thought I'd tidy up."

He squinted at her.

"I'm checking them for intel," she said, aggrieved.

"Anything?"

"Not much in their pockets. But they're English."

Peter sighed. "Is anyone not out to get us?"

They both turned their heads towards the distant beat of helicopter rotors.

"That'll be our ride, gentleman," Bas said over the comm.

"Hallelujah," said Peter.

"One of them, anyway," Shade muttered.

The two of them walked towards the clearing, standing well back until the Huey touched down and powered down the rotors. Shade wasn't a bit surprised to see Jack Friend piloting it. She wasn't pleased, either. Beside her, Peter was on edge, having sensed her uneasiness. The other men were trickling into the clearing and glancing around uncertainly as they picked up the tension. Bas hobbled and hopped over to join Shade.

"Coming to our rescue?" Shade asked after Friend had climbed out of the chopper.

"Just call me White Knight."

She had to admit he wasn't dressed for any kind of engagement. He was wearing the bomber jacket over a white Henley shirt and faded blue jeans. From the way the shirt clung to him, he wasn't wearing a vest of any kind. And he was highly visible even in the dark.

"Why'd you leave?"

"My services were no longer required, so I stole this." He indicated the Huey with a flourish. "Only it took me a bit of time to undo your clever botch job."

"How's Nemrovsky?" she asked.

"Still alive when I left."

"He just let you go?"

"I convinced him that the best thing at this point was for you to succeed in releasing that information and removing his victims from power. I told him your need for revenge would topple all the people involved. Then I pointed out that he has enough money to live quite comfortably for the rest of his life, and now he has the opportunity to do it in relative peace. He's old. He didn't want to spend his twilight years locked in a stone prison of his own making."

"You do have a gift for fast-talking. How'd you know we needed a ride?"

"I didn't, actually. I saw the muzzle flares and came in for a closer look."

"In an unarmed helicopter," Shade pointed out.

Friend was spared answering by the sound of a second helicopter arriving.

The incoming pilot announced, "This is the US Navy Mustang 264. I will be extracting you fine gentlemen today. Please haul your asses on board. And I respectfully suggest you hustle since I am presently in violation of Turkish airspace."

"We'll be taking that one," Peter announced.

"You don't want to do that," Friend said.

"Sounds legit to me," Wiley countered.

Friend shot him a look and then said to Peter, "Ask where it originated from."

All around, skeptical looks were directed at Shade.

With a note of desperation, Friend said, "You're mere miles from Dalaman, so you've got cell coverage. Get your man on the phone and ask where your ride is supposed to be coming from."

"Who has a phone?" Shade asked, still studying Friend.

Peter rummaged in his flak jacket and produced a phone. As he dialed Curtis, he moved away from Friend.

Bas hailed Rabbit on the com and asked whether he had a phone on him.

When Rabbit's call came in, Peter switched over from the call with Curtis. "Uh huh."

"Well?" Friend stood with his arms crossed over his chest, wearing an expectant expression.

"Curtis said this chopper should be coming from Rhodes—that's our support from Clemmons. Rabbit says Dalaman is a mess. He saw Havers, alive, but looking like he'd been roughed up, and he was being held at gunpoint. The chopper is grounded, and there are signs there was some kind of firefight between god-only-knows-who. I told him to head south and we'll pick him up on our way out."

"That's how they've known where we were," Shade said. "Havers com-link."

Peter walked towards the landing Chinook and had a brief conversation with the pilots once they were down. "Thank you seamen," he said, unable to determine the pilots' rank because they were both wearing plain clothes. "I can't tell you how much we appreciate you sticking your necks out for us. We had transport arranged but our man never showed."

"I was told he had mechanical problems," said one of the pilots. "It's no problem, sir, since I'm currently piss-drunk and I stole this helicopter for a joyride. After official apologies from our Government to the Turkish authorities, I'm sure I'll be court marshaled to a nice, sandy beach somewhere."

"Thank god Dalaman is so close and you were able to get to us so fast. We have wounded we need to get to a hospital," Peter said.

"It's a short flight, sir, we'll have those wounded tended in no time."

Peter leveled his gun at the pilot's head. "Unfortunately, there's going to be a delay."

Bas muttered, "They're as American as I am."

Snake and Wiley, personally offended by the Navy impersonation, weren't gentle securing the two pilots.

"What do you think, sweetheart?" Peter asked, looking at Friend.

"I don't trust him completely. He's got some other agenda."

Friend looked away, but they all saw the wry smile before he hid it.

"Look at it this way," Friend argued. "I can assure you you'll remain in possession of what you stole, and survive to use it. Can you say the same about those pilots?" When no one said anything, Friend offered, "Point a bloody gun at my head, if you like. I'll take you wherever you need to go."

"Sure, because you need to know exactly where we go…why?" Shade asked.

"The hell with that, any of us can fly these choppers. Leave him here with the other two, and let's get out of here," Bas said.

"And then he's sneaking up on us again. I'd rather keep my eye on him," Peter said.

"I find it interesting that we were under attack until shortly before you arrived," Shade said. "But where are they now?"

"I can honestly tell you that I had nothing to do with that," Friend said.

"Let's go," Peter said. "We'll tie him up and take the Chinook. It's faster, it's armed, and they're expecting to see it at Dalaman. It'll buy us some time before they figure out we're not landing there."

"Leave the pilots?" Bas asked.

"Yes," Shade said. "If I'm right, their *mates* in the trees will come in for them when we're gone. Friend here might just be our ticket out of this."

"Finally, she catches on," Friend said.

He got three piercing looks.

Once they'd secured the pilots, loaded the chopper, and lifted off, silence reigned while everyone thought hard, or didn't think at all. Shade was counting herself in the former minority.

"What's next, then?" Friend asked into the void.

"I don't really see any reason why you need to talk," Bas said from the pilot's seat.

The Chinook cockpit was a side-by-side arrangement and Peter was in the secondary pilot's position talking to Curtis about their current transportation. Shade was sitting in the troop compartment, which was open to the cockpit, directly across from Friend. He'd let them truss him with zip ties without protest, and he was sitting comfortably on the bench seat wearing a smug expression. Shade was staring at him mercilessly. He was staring brazenly back. At Bas' statement, Friend smiled and lowered his eyes.

"I can duct tape his mouth shut," Chavez offered from beside Shade.

When he turned his attention to Chavez, Friend looked amused.

"We stick with the original plan," Shade said. "Our first order of business is to get those documents released to the right people. Until then, they're going to keep coming at us—a diverse lot of them apparently." She added, "Unless we get lucky and they keep fighting one another."

Friend raised his eyebrows and nodded.

"How do you keep it all straight?" Shade asked him. "The mish-mash of loyalties and agendas?"

"I've no idea what you're talking about," he answered. "My agenda has always been a straight line. Maybe we've just finally found something that the great Shade isn't good at—political intrigue."

Chavez leaned forward menacingly, and a few of the other men raised their heads in the dark compartment.

"Bah! I admit it," she said. "I hate politics and the pretentious assholes who think they run the world."

"No desire for power or fame?"

"I don't exist. So, no, fame wouldn't suit me at all. As for power, it's a fleeting thing that's easily removed—by one bullet."

"Sounds like you'd prefer anarchy and chaos, then. Why undertake this mission?"

"They threatened my family."

"Some view emotional attachments as a weakness to be exploited," he said.

Shade wanted to stick something sharp into him—he had used the careful phrasing and enunciation again. "Warning noted," she said. "But I believe I've made it clear it'll be the last thing they ever do."

"Brown again," he said, staring into her eyes and sounding heartbroken.

"Ugh."

Bas and Peter both stirred restlessly, and Peter looked back at her over his shoulder. Shade got up and went forward. The sun was just lighting the sky. She switched seats with Peter.

As Peter started to leave he said, "Shit. What's that up ahead?"

"Three Seahawks," Bas said. "They can't be from Dalaman, they're coming from the wrong direction."

Over the radio they heard, "Attention, this is US Navy X-ray Six Foxtrot, plus two. We have orders to render assistance as needed and provide escort to rendezvous point."

"We've heard that before," Peter said.

But the pilot was continuing, "Code word…" he paused, and in a questioning tone said, "Curry Mantra?"

Peter let out a whoop. "That's our boy Clemmons!"

'Better late than never," said Bas.

Shade said, "Like we need any help *now*."

Peter gave her a stern look which she met with an insouciant one of her own.

Closing her eyes, and nestling into the seat, Shade said, "Don't forget to pick up Rabbit and tell someone about Havers. Wake me when we get there."

Chapter 18

The three Navy helicopters escorted them to a private helipad on the Greek island of Rhodes. Clemmons was waiting there in person, along with a task force of Navy personnel and a few representatives from other agencies. Peter climbed out first and met with Clemmons while the team off-loaded the wounded. Clemmons had transportation parked on the tarmac to convey them all to a local hotel where he said a medic would attend the wounded. A rowdy bunch of ostensibly off-duty Marines would be providing an escort as well.

With her beret hiding her hair and pulled low over her face, covered in blood, grime, camouflage paint, and in the dawn light, Shade was able to unobtrusively exit the chopper with the rest of the team. Using Jack Friend as a shield, she climbed right into a waiting car. She'd cut the ties on Friend's ankles but left his hands bound, and she retained custody of him until Bas and Peter joined her in the vehicle.

They pulled in behind the hotel and entered through a service door so that hotel staff and guests didn't become alarmed by armed bloody men in combat gear strolling through the lobby. Shade disappeared into the night.

Friend didn't see her go, but immediately noted her absence. "What's she up to, then?"

"Don't you worry about it," Bas said. "She'll join us later."

Peter said, "For once I agree with her inclination."

Clemmons joined them in their suite. He and Bas immediately set to work on the contents of the flash-drive while Peter took a shower. Bas had his swollen ankle propped up, waiting on the medic. Friend had been shoved into a chair, hands still bound, and Bas was keeping an eye on him. Peter had refused Clemmons' offer to put Friend somewhere for safekeeping.

Considering the trouble the data had caused and the amount of effort it had taken to retrieve it, once Bas segmented the records by nation of origin, the time it took to zip the files and send them to pre-established email contacts was anticlimactic.

Bas told both Clemmons and Friend, "It's done. It's been sent to a short list of government contacts. Peter already told these people what's coming and what'll happen if they don't take immediate steps. It's also been sent to a few friends who'll take steps of their own if those people don't. Isn't the internet great?"

"I'm curious to see if the Senator's name appears on that list. Or General Ratcliffe," Clemmons said.

Bas looked up at him. "I can't speak for Peter, but Shade and I don't care. We set out to get Peter back and make sure none of us were threatened again. That's done. What happens after this doesn't interest us."

"You're not at all concerned about the damage to our infrastructure?" Clemmons asked.

Bas shrugged. "We're not Americans."

Clemmons took a step back. "There's still the possibility someone might take vengeful action against all of you."

With a hard look, Bas said, "Not if you people do what *you're* supposed to do."

"Laying low would still be a top plan until things are underway," Friend said. "Until all the players are sorted, and they know it's too late, they'll keep trying to get to you."

Peter emerged from the bathroom fully-dressed and toweling his hair dry. "Shade is taking care of those arrangements now, unless I'm mistaken." He looked at Bas for confirmation, and Bas nodded. Peter's eyes slid over to Friend. "I think you're going to be guesting with us for a little while longer."

As Peter showed Clemmons out, a dark-haired bellboy with a tiny mustache arrived at the door. He was pushing a cart loaded with luggage and limping. Once the bellboy was inside the room, Peter closed the door.

Shade said, "Okay, this is all the stuff you left on your way in plus the bags I had shipped here from Fethiye."

Friend's head whipped around at the sound of her voice, and he took in the disguise. "Brilliant!"

She tapped her bellboy hat in a salute. "Bas, the medic will be in to see you next. The rest of the guys are all taken care of and are dispersing by ones and twos." She opened her uniform jacket and pulled out a piece of paper. "Here's what you three need to do." She handed it to Peter. "Oh, and Friend, the bag you had in the Huey is here as well."

As she went out the room door she said, "Bas, you've got time to get cleaned up, but then you need to move out."

The medic told Bas' that he had a bad sprain but the ankle wasn't broken. After wrapping it in a brace and giving him a shot for the pain, he told Bas he could walk on it. Clemmons and his men were still in the hotel, presumably guarding them but actually guarding air. Bas had gotten word that the entire team had already checked out, and their small group was sneaking out right beneath their warders' noses.

A taxi was idling outside the hotel's delivery door when the three men walked outside. The sun was fully up and casting dark shadows in the alley. As Peter stooped to climb in, Bas focused on a red Maserati tucked behind a trash dumpster. A moment later, a brown, four-door sedan angled in front of their taxi and screeched to a halt. Bas shoved Friend into the backseat beside Peter and pulled out a gun. A stunning redhead stepped out of the Maserati wearing a tan pencil skirt, a white silk blouse, and leopard-print stilettos. Four armed men exploded out of the brown car. The redhead put bullets into the two men on her side of the car, and Bas took out the two on his side.

"Pathetic," Bas said.

From inside the taxi, Peter yelled, "Now, who the hell sent *them*?"

Shade, climbing back into the red car, called out, "Who cares?"

The shaken taxi-driver couldn't wait to be rid of them at the airstrip and drove off as soon as they had all climbed out of the car. Bas watched the car speed away and then followed Friend's gaze. The red Maserati had preceded the taxi as they made their way across town and was parked beside a small private jet waiting on the runway. Shade was just getting out.

Peter balked in the hatch staring at the extravagant interior of the jet. Shade breathed out a pleased sigh as she wandered down the aisle. Individual soft, gray, leather seats lined one side, swiveling to allow conversation with those seated beside or behind, and a long, narrow, leather bench seat ran along the windows on the other side. All the paneling and trim were solid wood, shined to a high gloss. They discovered an on-board bathroom, and a fully equipped kitchenette with a mini-bar.

They deposited Friend on the bench seat where they could all keep an eye on him. Once they'd settled in and were underway, Friend asked Shade, "Don't you all usually split up to travel?"

"Don't play stupid. You know perfectly well why we're doing it this way," she said. She kicked off the stilettos, and leaned back into the cushions of her seat, flexing her toes.

Friend wore a sage smile.

Peter asked, "Does someone want to clue me in? Not that I mind, as long as this is coming out of your pocket, not mine."

"She's watching over you," Friend said. "It's touching, really."

"I have reason to believe they're going to make a try at either you or Bas," Shade said. "And the jet isn't coming out of anyone's pocket. It belongs to someone I know. The pilot will drop us and go home, forgetting all about this trip."

Bas said, "You believe we're at risk because *he* told you so?"

"No, because he implied it in a very sneaky roundabout way. And it makes sense in combination with a few other things that he also didn't come right out and say."

"Yet, do I hear a 'thank you?'" Friend said. "No, I'm bound and dragged round, and still complying very reasonably while my hands slowly develop gangrene."

"I'm lost," Peter said. "We did what we set out to do, we're laying low until word gets around…"

"There's something more going on," Shade said, and got up to cut Friend's bindings with a small knife from her bag.

"Ah, now I see what you've done," Friend said as Shade leaned over him. "You've actually got latex or something glued onto your face. That's brilliant, really. Perfect bloody makeup job. I can hardly see it."

"Airbrush," Shade said. "But you didn't even notice the green contacts and I wore them just for you."

Bas, watching the exchange, was smiling, but not in a nice way.

Peter said, "Can we go back to what you just said?"

"Sure," Shade said, "But maybe now isn't the best time." She patted Friend's unshaven cheek to make her point.

Peter grumbled and got up to make drinks at the mini-bar. "Who's joining me?" he asked.

"What are we gonna do with him?" Bas asked, holding up a finger to request a drink.

"Hit me," Shade said to Peter. And then to Bas: "He's not going to try to get away. At least, not yet. But I don't trust him for a minute, so when we land, I want you to knock him out."

Bas looked much happier.

Friend affected an expression of mock distress. "More bruises, she wishes upon me." And to Peter: "I'll take a Scotch if there's any."

"Could be much worse," Bas pointed out to Friend. Then to Shade: "Why *is* he still alive, anyway?"

"Later," she said.

Friend still managed to look superior as he sat rubbing his wrists. "I have a question. That was very coordinated at the taxi. How do you two manage to be so smooth?"

Bas glanced at Shade, but she was eyeing Friend with an inscrutable expression and swirling her drink, so he answered, "We've been drilling together since childhood. We know what the other will do."

"You've been together since you were children," Friend said in a leading tone.

"Yeah. And…?" Bas said, glancing at Shade again.

Peter had taken a seat after passing out the drinks and propped his head on one fist, listening.

Friend paused, sipping at his drink. "You're sort of like twins at this point. You even refer to yourselves as twins do—'we this' and 'we that.'"

"Peter was away a lot, working. We were shipped around and left with one person or another. We only had each other. But we're nothing like twins."

"It's just it's quite something—the synchronicity—when you're working together. Word is the pair of you would have the advantage over almost anyone you came up against, having been trained from childhood, you and your sister."

Automatically, Bas opened his mouth and said, "She's not—" but a slight movement from Shade stopped him, and he finished instead, "—part of a pair. The two of us together are just overkill for most jobs. That, and our style differences, is why we don't work together."

"Ah, I thought it was some lovers' spat." Friend wiggled his fingers.

"No, nothing at all like a lovers' spat," Shade said in a monotone.

Friend picked up on her warning and changed tack. Putting on his jovial smile, he summarized, "So, you've got your areas of specialization but as a by-product of your childhood circumstances you come together with precise synchronization. You clearly think of yourselves as a pair, yet you claim you're free agents. And Peter is the de facto handler of the group but doesn't always have a handle what the two of you have got going on."

Bas narrowed his eyes.

Shade heard the weird tone again that meant there were clues to be had. She had an idea what he was trying to say between the lines and fired a warning glance at Bas.

Friend caught the look and nodded to himself.

Peter leaned forward in his chair and in a stern tone said, "The dynamics aren't really as simple as that."

"Oh, I can see that. Indeed," Friend said, downing his drink. "There's always been quite a bit of propaganda circulating about your group, but you may discover increasing focus on your bona fides. And I'm aware there's an unacknowledged additional player, as well. I'm quite curious to see the impact on your team.""

Shade said, "You'll have to remain mystified."

Peter turned to Shade and said, "Okay, now I see what you were talking about."

When Friend went to the on-board bathroom, Bas said in a low voice, "He thinks he knows something."

Shade said, "He does know something. He knows several somethings. And he's also a very accomplished doublespeaker. "

Peter said, "He's all but screaming in our faces that someone is very interested in how we operate, when he already seems to know. What about 'bona fides'? That's the term for proof of identity. Someone's after Curtis?" Peter frowned, puzzled. "Why doesn't he just come out and say what he wants us to know?"

"He can't," Shade said, not bothering to disabuse Peter's notions with her own suspicions. "It's the whole code of honor crap. He's being employed by somebody. What I can't figure is whether they're the only somebody."

Bas said, "It definitely isn't Nemrovsky. There's no angle left for Friend there, and even if the guy wants revenge, he wouldn't hire Friend. "

"Nemrovsky was just one layer," Shade said. "I think he was sent in there—I suspected that early on and firmly believe it now. Out of all the potential specialists in the world, he targeted our team. You saw the setup in that place. Even allowing for a difficult egress, he could've done that job alone. And even if he couldn't, any combat-trained team would've sufficed. Why did he need us so specifically? And I don't believe for a minute that he's not as well-connected, if not more connected, than Peter is."

"He sure didn't have any trouble coming up with a network when he needed to fabricate hits on Nemrovsky," Bas agreed.

"So, why are we keeping him around and letting him observe exactly what whoever-it-is probably wants to know?" Peter asked.

"Well, dad, like you said, if we cut him loose he'll be sneaking around the periphery. He's still got a job to do and I'd like to know what it is. You heard him back there--his 'agenda has always been a straight line.' The more he asks, the more he gives away. We just need to be very careful what information we expose him to."

"He's targeting you," Bas said to Shade. "He's not interested in all of us, just you. And looking back, it always was just you."

"My gut says the same thing," Peter said. "Listening to him talk to you on the helicopter…"

"That's not it though. Or that's not all of it, at least. Let's just watch him for a day or two. He's very clever, but I think he's going to slip up shortly."

"Can you help him slip up?" Bas asked.

"If I have to," she said.

"Good," Bas said. "Can I knock him out now? 'Cause he's annoying the shit outta' me."

Peter said, "Damn, what was I thinking when I took you two in?"

Chapter 19

Smith, the Australian sniper who'd assisted them in Fethiye, had offered to let them lay low at his sheep ranch until things cooled off. Peter had recommended the idea, pointing out that the ranch was located a million miles from anywhere in the middle of the Australian bush. Smith wanted to be able to see enemies coming in, and he'd built a setup that would send them right back out again.

When he picked them up at the Sydney airport, Smith presented himself as an enthusiastic, happy-go-lucky man. His first name was Tristan, but he hated the name and insisted everyone call him Smith. Shade judged him to be in his late forties or early fifties, but too much time in the sun had prematurely burned deep lines into his brown skin making him appear older. His hair was sun-bleached to the color of straw, and looked like he'd hacked it all off with a machete. There was a liberal peppering of gray in his sideburns and the stubble on his jaw. Bushy gold eyebrows hooded squinting brown eyes, giving him a raptor-like look that was at odds with his personality. His big frame was sparsely-fleshed with ropey muscle, and he stood only a few inches shorter than Bas.

His home, located dead center of his land, was a wooden farmhouse with a wraparound porch and a metal roof. Smith bragged that he'd added the second story himself, and a crow's nest for a 360 degree view in every direction. He admitted he did a little target practice from up there.

Inside, Shade wandered around purring. The house was rustic and homey with exposed-beam ceilings and pine-paneled walls and floors, polished to a golden shine. At the rear of the house, massive picnic tables and wooden chairs were scattered around an enormous stone fire pit.

Bas had taken great delight in rendering Friend unconscious at the airport. Once they'd gotten far enough out, even if he had woken up he wouldn't have known where he was. As it happened, Friend stayed out until they'd actually arrived at the ranch. Smith carted him to the upper level of the sprawling, ranch house and dumped him on a bed.

"Do we need to watch him?" Peter asked Shade.

Smith answered, "What for? He tries to walk outta' here, he'll be dead of dehydration before he sees another soul. We'll hear him start a Jeep, and as you may have noticed, I've got a good long eye with a rifle. Now, who wants a cold one?" He strode off, presumably towards the beer.

"If anyone says the words 'shrimp' or 'barbie,' I will shoot them," Shade said. "The word 'crikey' is also off-limits. I suppose 'G'day, mate' is inevitable."

"You could use a nap, sweetheart," Peter suggested.

"That is a fantastic idea," She limped towards the staircase.

"Why on earth are you calling me at this number?" she asked.

"Ask me yes or no questions, quickly," Friend murmured.

"You're out of Nemrovsky's?"

"Yes."

"You're with Laurent's group?"

"Yes."

"I gather things aren't totally amiable?"

"No."

"Have you been able to report to Oxford?"

"He knew I'd try to stay with them."

"Sorry, ducks, that wasn't really a yes or no question as it turned out," she said. "Were they able to get the information and send it out?"

"Yes."

"Do you need assistance?"

"No, and you couldn't send it if I did."

"Why? Where are you?"

"No idea."

"Clever girl," she said.

His answer was an emphatic, "Yes."

"Keeping you on your toes, is she?"

He chuckled low.

"Ah, you're starting to fancy her. Careful, love. Hm, I might be a wee bit jealous. But any road, are we still on track?"

"Yes." He paused, listening, "Wait, it's too quiet. Damn her. Better go."

He turned off the phone and opened the bedroom door. Shade was standing just outside. "It's uncanny how you do that," he complained. "The floor creaked at least fifty times just walking from the bed to the door."

"Who were you talking to?" she asked, taking the phone away from him.

"An old friend," he said. "Just checking in."

Shade tried to pull up the last number dialed, but he'd already deleted it from the history. "Bastard."

She moved into him fast, knocked the air out of him with a hit to his solar plexus, and spun him up against the wall with a slam. She kicked his legs apart, slapped both of his palms on the wall, and had frisked him thoroughly before he'd even gotten his wind back.

"You missed a spot," he said, wheezing.

"I've seen you in underwear, so it's clear there's nothing else in there but the little bit you were born with."

"Oi, she cuts me to the bone," he said. "Double entendre intended."

Responding to the noise, Bas appeared in the doorway, glowering.

"It's okay, I have it in hand," Shade told him.

"Well, not really, not *it* anyway," Friend said, leering.

"I can put him out again," Bas offered.

"Too late." She tossed the phone to him. "We missed this."

"Who'd he call?"

"I don't know. And I only heard yes or no from him. Asshole."

"I'll tell Smith."

"No worries, mate," Friend quipped in a credible Australian accent. "I swear. No one's coming. I don't know where I am, anyway. The middle of the Outback, is it? I thought I saw a kangaroo."

Bas had removed the battery from the phone. "They could've been tracking you with this."

"No one is. I swear it."

Bas gave him an ominous look and left the doorway.

Shade slid her hand between Friend's legs, and he sucked in a quick breath. She said, "Just like I thought, nothing there."

"Give it a minute," he suggested.

He was laughing as she shoved him out of the room and down the hallway. When they reached the staircase, she said, "Go downstairs with the other boys. And stay there."

Shade went out to the front porch after her nap. She was leaning against the railing, serenely contemplating the panoramic view, when Friend came out the front door and joined her. She was still wearing the redhead disguise.

"How long can you keep that up?" he asked.

"Longer than you can keep it up, I'm sure. If your sole reason for allowing us to kidnap you was to wear me down and see my face, you're in for a disappointment."

"It wasn't, but it might be a fringe benefit."

"The only fringe benefits available to you walk on four legs and make a baa-ing noise. Go catch one."

"Honestly, the witty repartee is more than enough to keep me hanging round. It's not often I come across a bird who's stacked, saucy, and who'll kill a man as soon as look at him."

Peter wandered out onto the porch with a glass full of whiskey. "Hell, he's as bad as you and Bas. Maybe I should adopt him too."

Friend threw his arms wide, and with a big smile, said, "Dad."

"Don't encourage him," Shade said. "He follows a predictable pattern of working up his courage with smartass comments before he hits on you, and I don't think you want that."

Friend assumed a tragic look and said, "You wound me."

"No, I sure don't," Peter said to Shade. "But you could take him back upstairs and screw his brains out. I'm pretty sure he'll tell you anything we want to know at that point."

"Oh shut up." She stalked back into the house.

Friend said, "Please tell me at least *you* know what she looks like."

"Yep, she's scary-ugly," he said, staring out at the landscape with a mild smile on his face. "For your own peace of mind, you want her to keep wearing those masks. Not to mention your longevity."

Smith and his ranch hands put out a huge spread of food that afternoon in the area behind the house. By the end of the meal, everyone was in awe of how much food Bas and Shade had put away.

"You should've seen my grocery bills when these two were growing up," Peter said, drowsing beside the firepit.

Smith slapped a hand on his thigh and said, "Beaut! Pig roast tomorrow! Maybe two!"

Sated and relaxed, they took Smith's advice and sat enjoying the oranges and blues of the Australian sunset, and drank steadily through the evening. Smith kept pouring the liquor, and eventually only the five of them were left. The men kept the conversation revolving around shop talk and women.

Shade was curled in a chair with her head propped on a fist. She kept dozing off and startling herself awake. Bas leaned over and poked her. "Why don't you go to bed?"

She murmured something noncommittal and then said, "I don't think I have the energy to climb the stairs."

Bas set his drink on the ground. He grabbed both her hands, pulling her upright, and slung her over his shoulder. She was laughing and shrieking, "Your ankle!" and beating her fists on his broad back as he carried her into the house.

When he came back a short time later, he said, "She's out."

"Good. She needs to recharge," Peter said.

"That's me lying low tomorrow, then." Friend rubbed the knot on his head. "I don't think I can take her at full strength right now. She nearly kicked my ass last time."

Peter looked over with an interested expression.

"She started it," Friend said defensively.

"She usually does." Bas dropped back into his chair. He threw the sore ankle over the arm, and let out a huge sigh.

"Let me ask you something," Friend said to Bas. "You've been sparring with her since you were small, right?"

Bas raised his eyebrows and nodded, a knowing smile spreading across his face.

"Do you ever actually land a hit on her?"

"Not often, no," he admitted.

"Does she land them on you?"

"Not often, no."

Friend looked confused. "Then how do you decide who won?"

"Oh, I always win."

"Bloody hell, how?"

"I cheat."

Peter sat up, startled, and shot a scornful look at Bas.

Smith made a tutting sound and got up to pour another round of drinks.

Friend sat waiting for an explanation.

Bas guffawed. "You don't actually think I'm going to tell you how to beat her, do you?"

Peter asked Friend, "Was this an unarmed fight?"

Friend said, "Yeah, completely unarmed as I was in my knickers at the time."

Peter persisted. "But she was unarmed?"

"It was just a bit of fun--bare knuckle."

"And she beat you?"

"Not that I want this repeated outside this circle, mind you, but yeah, she would have done. But we called it."

"What's your training?" Peter asked.

Friend assumed an insulted look. "Old man, if you've a mind to go a few rounds, just say the word. Otherwise, trust me when I tell you there's not many could've done what she did. Girl's fast—offensively and defensively."

Peter's gaze was speculative as he eyed Bas and Friend.

Following Peter's train of thought, Smith said, "I've got a fenced area behind the barn that we use for shearing where the lads can have a go in the ring."

Friend groaned. "Bed it is."

Bas said, "Baaa-baaa. I think one of your sheep got loose, Smith."

"Right, then," Friend snapped, heaving himself to his feet.

The next morning, yawning sleepily, a redheaded Shade strolled into the dining room. She was still limping, but the dark circles were gone from her eyes. The rest of them were showing the effects of their late night.

Shade's eyes flicked over the cuts and contusions on Bas and Friend's faces at the breakfast table. "Inanimate objects or fists?"

The two men grinned at each other over their coffee and then winced.

She brightened and grabbed Peter's arm. "Who won?" she demanded.

Peter patted her hand and shook his head sadly.

Smith came in carrying a platter piled with bacon and another of toast. "Jack did. But it was close."

Shade narrowed her eyes at Bas. Shaking her finger at him, she said, "Ah hah!" She jumped up and danced around, pumping her fists in the air. She stopped suddenly and froze. "Wait! How much did they have to drink?"

Bas made a blowing noise of dismissal.

Friend tilted his head from side to side and then shrugged.

"For their body weights, I'd say about the same." Peter looked offended. "But Bas has a bad ankle."

"Poo," Shade said. "I have a bullet wound."

"Up to taking on the champion?" Smith asked Shade as he doused his eggs with hot sauce.

She opened her mouth to reply, but Friend said, "Ah, not today, mate. I'm hung over and sore."

Grinning, Bas elbowed him. "Wuss."

Shade slid onto the bench and started loading up her plate. "Pansy."

Friend just pressed his lips together.

On the second day, Shade wandered outside barefoot and clad in a short flower-print dress, compliments of a former guest. It was a little too tight in the bust, and too big in the waist, but she didn't seem to care. She had appropriated a wide-brimmed straw hat from Smith and had her hair tucked inside. Enormous dark sunglasses concealed most of her face. Still, Friend discerned she had done something to it.

She sat down on the ground to chat with Smith. He was cooking their breakfast on the open flames of a grill built onto the fire pit. She had her skirts tucked into her lap and was showing a lot of long bare leg while leaning back on her palms. Smith scrubbed a hand through his hair every few minutes and kept shifting his rangy weight uneasily. He was laughing and flashing a snaggle-toothed smile at her. They were discussing Howitzers and their mechanical difficulties. That part was a little disturbing, but it was the first time Friend had seen Shade looking so relaxed.

"She's quite chirpy today," Friend said from his seat across from Peter at a picnic table.

Peter was reading a newspaper he'd gotten off one of the ranch hands. He glanced over at Shade before replying. "She hasn't slept regularly for a long while now, and she was living in the woods for several days before the hit on Nemrovsky."

"Is that where she was?" Friend said.

"She really pulled more than her fair share of the load on this last op."

"And that'd be on my head," Friend admitted. "She comes across wound a bit tight though."

"You've only been around her when she's working," Peter said, turning the page.

Bas slid into an Adirondack chair like it was a throne and announced, "I'm so bored."

"Take a run through the brush," Peter suggested.

Bas eyed the bush country as though considering it.

Smith tuned in and shook one of his cowboy-booted feet in their direction. "Mind the snakes, if you do."

Shade looked at the ground around her and then got up and walked quickly into the house. A few minutes later, she reappeared with a good-sized knife in her hand. As she walked back over to Smith and sat down again, it vanished somewhere onto her person.

"Atta girl," Smith said.

Bas snorted, and Peter just went on reading his paper.

"Did you hide the kitchen knives when she was small?" Friend asked.

"Not if we wanted dinner," Peter said.

Shade purred, "Smith, I meant to say, you are such an excellent cook. I just love a man who's good in…the kitchen."

Smith chuckled and reddened.

Bas and Friend both snorted.

That evening, Friend was out on the front porch, drink in hand, leaning against one of the support posts and staring out at the open terrain.

"I've never seen so many stars," he said as she approached soundlessly.

"You're getting pretty good at catching me sneaking up on you. I'm not sure I like it."

"Sometimes the void of silence is the clue."

"You'll have to explain that to me sometime."

"You're taking your father's earlier advice now, are you?" He tossed back the rest of his drink.

"I listen to people's advice, but I make my own decisions," Shade said.

He set the empty glass on the porch railing, turned around, and put both hands on her waist, pulling her closer.

"Who were you talking to on the phone?" She braced her hands against his chest but then snatched them back.

"I told you, an old friend." He captured her hand and lifted it to his lips, kissing her palm before she pulled it away. His eyes danced, mischievously. "Take the contacts out."

"Answer my questions," she insisted.

"We could conduct a barter, but I don't think you'd like where it would lead," he said, running delicate fingers down the curve of her neck.

She turned and looked at the door behind her.

"They're all out back—Bas and Peter," he said.

She shrugged. "Bas could turn up and you'd never hear him coming."

"I find it hard to believe that man can move that quietly." His lips grazed her neck and traveled down to her collarbone.

"We had the same training."

"Peter has no idea, does he?" Friend said, kissing the divot at the base of her throat.

"About…?" she asked.

"About you and Bas."

She shifted her weight, and he felt the smooth glide of muscle under his hand.

"You think you know something but you don't," she replied.

"You're very quick to correct anyone who refers to you as brother and sister." His fingers undid the top button of her dress. "And you call Peter 'dad' to his face but by name to each other, or others."

"It's the simple truth. Peter prefers to think of us as a family unit, so we've always tried to give him that comfort. But we both remember the families we had before him."

"A very interesting dysfunctional family. But then I suppose most are."

"Why are you here?" she asked.

"You brought me here," he answered, as the second button was undone.

"Who are you working for?" She leaned closer.

His hand slid inside her dress and down to her bra. "Lace," he said, fingering the edge and sounding surprised. And then, whispered against her ear, he said: "You're immune. This is just a waste of time. You said it yourself, no one else can compare."

"That was an ex-lover's plane that brought us here," she said.

His head came up, and he narrowed his eyes. "Ah, now you're just lying to me." One finger slid under the lace.

She shivered and leaned into him. "I never lie."

His finger kept stroking, his mouth hovering inches from hers. "Yet another thing we have in common."

"But you're right," she whispered. "This is a waste of time. Because if you were serious about any of this, you'd have me pinned against that post right now instead of all this tender delicacy. You're not the scoundrel you pretend to be, Mr. Friend."

His hand dropped and he forced her back a step. When he tried to move away, she caught him around the waist, spun them both, and pulled his hips hard against hers as she backed into the post behind her. Holding him against her, she snatched one of his hands and brought it up to the heavy weight of her breast. She angled her hips against his and heard him let out a quick breath.

"You belong to someone else," he said, leaning into her.

"I say again, Bas doesn't own a plane."

His lips pressed lightly against hers and lingered for a moment. She put her hand on his chest and traced the curves of muscle down his abdomen. She tucked her fingers into the waistband of his jeans, tugging his hips tighter against hers. Her other hand slid down to his ass.

"Why are you here?" she asked.

"To guard you," he whispered, parting her thighs with his own and pressing in. He slid her hand down the front of his jeans. "See? I never lie."

"It does seem to be well over eight inches, just as you promised," she said. "Why do I need a guard?"

"You're being hunted. He wants something from you. He thinks he can control you through Peter or Bas." His open mouth trailed down her neck, and his hand slipped inside her dress again.

She slid her own hands under his shirt and up his smooth muscled back, feeling him tense and then relax. "What's his interest in me?"

He kissed the swell of her breast. "I think he knows who you are."

It took all her self-control not to recoil. Instead, she bit gently into his neck and he responded with an involuntary shudder of pleasure.

"Why do you think that?" she asked, continuing to make soft slow bites along his neck.

"He keeps asking questions about your appearance. He's obsessed with your history. It's like he's trying to prove something he believes about you."

"Who is he?" she asked in a low dangerous tone.

Friend exhaled and backed away from her despite her attempt to stop him. He caught her hands and kissed both of them. Then he leaned back in and pressed another feather light kiss on her lips. Dropping her hands, he said, "That's why I didn't want to tell you. You mustn't go after this man. You'd ruin everything we've worked for." He kneaded the back of his neck and then fled into the house, letting the screen door slam.

Shade buttoned her dress, grabbed Friend's empty glass, and went through the house to the backyard. Smith had the fire pit going and was standing too close to the blaze, tossing odd bits of kindling into the flames. Bas and Peter were reclined with their feet up and drinks in their hands.

Bas said, "Where's Friend?"

"Probably in a bathroom jacking off," Shade said, taking a seat between them.

Peter made a rueful face. "Shade you've got to go easier on us menfolk."

Smith called out, "The hell you say! What a woman!"

Shade beamed in Smith's direction, and he winked back at her.

"You suggested it," Shade reminded Peter.

"I was kidding," Peter said.

Bas said, "He's working a honey trap. She's countering his Raven with her Swallow."

"Come again?" Smith asked.

Peter said, "I did not teach you two these things." To Smith he said, "A honey trap is when an agent attempts to get information out of someone by seducing them. A Raven is the term for a male agent using those tactics, and a Swallow is the female version. And he does have a rep for that kind of behavior."

"What'd you find out?" Bas asked Shade

"Someone is hunting me for some purpose, he's going to try to get at me by using one of you, and Friend thinks the guy knows who I am. Friend says he's here to 'guard me' and keep that from happening."

Peter sat up, dismayed. "That's not possible. You know how we searched for information after I found you."

"Still," she said. "It's not inconceivable to suppose that somewhere in the world somebody knows something about that stolen child."

"You know that would most likely be a trick—a trap," Bas said.

"Of course." She gazed down into the empty glass in her hand.

"Let him cool off for a while and then try again," Bas suggested. "He's probably already changed his mind."

Peter scowled. "Sometimes, I'm afraid you two are heartless."

"Hey, it was your idea," Shade said. "And we're just secure in ourselves."

Looking Shade in the eye, Bas said, "She won't hurt him, but she will get answers out of him."

"Well, I might hurt him a little," she admitted.

Shade waited until the rest of the house was asleep and then went padding down the hallway in her bare feet and a t-shirt. In Friend's room, she found him leaning against the window frame. He was facing the doorway, his back to the starry sky this time. He was shirtless, but still in the jeans. He was so tense that he looked like he was carved out of marble in the starlight. His eyes glittered in the darkness.

"Round two?" He saluted her with a half-filled glass.

"Had time to regroup?" she countered.

"The score-keeping is a little muddy, but you're not as far ahead as you think," he said.

"I'm quite sure you're just as tricky as I am," she said. "But I am ahead."

He set the glass down when she reached him and made a grab at her. "What's this?" His hands slipped under her shirttail and encountered only soft, smooth, bare skin. They caressed up and outwards, grasping her hips.

"I couldn't sleep, so I wandered this way." Her fingers skimmed up his stomach to his chest.

"I have something guaranteed to wear you out," he offered, grinding her hips against his.

"There's that bravado again," she whispered in his ear, tracing her lips across his earlobe and down his neck. "But we both know you choke at the finish line."

"I prefer a clear field, not stealing from others." He'd thrown his head back and his eyes were closed.

"Oh, please," she scoffed. "I've heard your reputation. You've done your fair share of stealing."

"And you?" He opened his eyes and looked down at her.

"I've had my share of lovers, yes."

"All in the past year, I'd bet," he said. "Did *they* get to see your face?"

She smiled up at him, her eyes dancing wickedly.

"Blue," he observed.

"Who are you working for?" She pressed a hard kiss under his chin.

"I've already told you I won't tell you his name." His fingers explored the depression made by her spine and then pressed into the small of her back.

"That's not who you're working for. You gave up Nemrovsky because he wasn't your employer--I still can't figure why you stuck to the end like you did, though. And you've given this other man's agenda up as well, so he's not your employer either."

"I see someone did their homework about me." He sounded pleased. His lips wandered down her neck. "In Nemrovsky's case there was a potential that he'd let it be known that I double-crossed him. My reputation would have been damaged in the eyes of others, even though, as you've pointed out, he wasn't really who I was working for."

"And you seduced his daughter, Natalya, for information about him," she said as a reminder, holding his head against her neck.

"Natalya is a lovely person but I didn't particularly care for her." His hands roamed up her ribcage.

"And so, despite all your lascivious words and actions, you're holding me at bay because you think I don't particularly care for you."

He leaned back, his demeanor growing chilly.

"You don't even know me," she said.

"Oh, but I do. We're just alike, you and I."

"Not if you scratch beneath the surface," she said.

He tangled his hands in her hair, pulling her head back. "You're always so damned unaffected."

"Oh, I'm not unaffected. Want me to prove it?" She guided his hand to her hips before he pulled it out of her grasp.

"This is your hair," he said, massaging his fingers against her scalp. He made a move to pull her closer to the window, into the light, but before he realized what was happening, she'd spun him and knocked him onto the bed. "You know, it bruises a man's ego to be tossed about by a woman half his size," he said to the ceiling.

She climbed onto the bed and straddled him, letting her hair slide like curtains around her face. "Oh wah," she said. "Your ego is so over the top that anything I could do would only reduce it to the neighborhood of normal."

"Why do I continue to put up with such a cold piece of work?" he asked.

"Because all your simpering little birds bore you to tears. You like that I don't give a rat's ass what you think and give back exactly what you dish out."

In one smooth move, he locked his arms around her and flipped them both back down on the bed with himself on top. "That's better," he said, tugging her shirt up.

She'd unbuttoned his jeans and was working on the zipper.

"Bloody hell, you give no quarter, do you?" He bowed his head against her chest and made a low sound when her hand slipped into his pants. He wriggled out of his jeans, kicking them off onto the floor. His mouth closed on her neck while he yanked her shirt over her head and flung it aside. Her arms wrapped around his back. Pushing her flat on the bed, he wedged her thighs apart with his hip. His lips pressed down onto hers as their hips melded together. He broke out of the kiss as they began to move, his eyes closed, and his brows clenched. "My god, you're magnificent," he said. "Ask your damned questions. You've this much time."

"Who is this person hunting me?" she asked.

"I won't tell you his name," he muttered.

She arched her back and wrapped her legs around him, pulling his head down into a kiss. His arms slid beneath her, holding her so tightly she could barely breathe. "Tell me about him, then," she gasped.

He buried his face in her neck and murmured, "He's highly placed in the infrastructure. His actions have raised questions for years. We know he's dirty, but we can't prove it. Even when others have attempted to implicate him, he always manages to walk away unscathed."

"So they sent you in to catch him," she prompted.

"We hoped to get evidence on him with the Nemrovsky-action, but it was too risky to turn the information over to him. I went for the double-play. He's obsessed with you. It was easy to encourage the idea of bringing you in. Those were his men you encountered in the woods afterwards, and they were at the airport to counter Nemrovsky's support as well—they're who had your man, Havers."

"If you know all that, why haven't you been able to make anything stick?"

"He always has plausible deniability. Or someone else to take the fall. And he's leading a double-life. I know who he is, but I can't prove that he is who he is." He reached under her knee, hooking her leg up, and shifted his weight to give himself more leverage. "You'd better hurry," he said with a grin. "You're running out of time, fast."

"What does he want with me?"

"Something illicit. Something he thinks you're uniquely qualified to do."

"Why not just hire me?"

"No, the money trail," he grunted. "He can't have a money trail. He needs a way to make you do it without leaving a trace."

"He needs a woman," she murmured. "As you've pointed out, the only real difference between us is gender."

"And thank god for that difference." His voice was strained and veins stood out on his forehead and neck. "But it's you specifically. There's something about your history, something he's desperate to know. He's obsessed with your appearance. There's more there, but I don't know what."

"You said you think he knows who I am."

"I think he suspects, and is trying to confirm it." His breath was gusting out and sweat was making both of them slick. He adjusted his angle again, and she pulled him in tighter.

"Hurry," he warned. "You hold me like this, it'll be over in minutes,"

"Works for me," she breathed. "Who are you working for?"

He let out a choked laugh and kissed her stubborn mouth. "No one that means you any harm. I'm to keep you safe, remember?"

Her orgasm washed over him first, triggering his, and they both gasped and clutched at each other with steel arms and legs. When he relaxed against her, she kept her legs locked around the heavy weight of him and massaged the knotted muscles in his neck and shoulders.

He grunted with pleasure and muttered, "You are so bloody talented."

She cradled him against her while he kissed her neck. "What is it your employer wants me to do?"

He raised his head, grinning. "Ah, no more questions. Time's up."

She shoved at him, and he let out a deep chuckle.

"No one can say you're not a man of your word," she complained.

He rolled off of her, scrubbing his face and still trying to catch his breath. "I think you may have ruined me."

She pushed herself into a sitting position and stretched, easing tight muscles. "Not yet."

Sated and sleepy, his half-lidded eyes traced her curves.

"You've been sent here to enlist my help," she said. "You're only guarding me for as long as it takes to pull me in on whatever scheme your employer has in mind. Why not just tell me?"

"Nope, I've already given you far too much. Tell you what, you let me see your face, and I'll answer any question you put to me." With a complacent smile, he closed his eyes.

"Oh, sure," she said. "Do I have your word on that one?"

"Yeah, why not?" He opened one eye.

She reached over and clicked on the light.

"Bloody sodding hell!"

Chapter 20

Friend was sitting at a picnic table with a cup of coffee cooling in front of him, nursing a hangover and brooding, when Peter staggered out the back door the next morning. Further down the same table, Bas leaned over a plate piled with food, wearing a smug expression as he chewed.

"Where's Smith?" Peter asked Bas warily.

"Off somewhere inspecting the sheep," Bas said between forkloads. "He said he'd be back later this afternoon."

Humming, Shade sat down beside Peter with her own plate and began shoveling in food.

Peter did a double-take when he saw her wearing her own face and hair.

"Fresh air," she pointed out with a sigh.

"Is there any *honey* for this toast?" Bas asked, choking back a laugh. "It makes it so much easier to *swallow*."

Friend kept his eyes lowered, fixed on his cup of coffee.

"Oh, hell," Peter said, looking at him.

"I persuaded Mr. Friend to give me a few more details," Shade said around a mouthful of food.

Friend looked up at that point and shot her a foul look. She raised her eyebrows without pausing her chewing.

Bas' shoulders heaved in silent laughter.

"I did try to warn you, son," Peter said to Friend.

Friend met his eyes, his expression blazing mad, and then went back to staring at his coffee.

"You'll need to stay here a while longer," Shade said to Peter. "Any objections?"

"Not as long as you keep me informed."

"Good. They're going to make a try at one or both of you, and I'd like you safely out of reach so that I'm free to maneuver. Mr. Friend and I will be going to London to turn the tables on this person."

"Are you going to have support for this?" Peter asked Friend.

Friend shifted his gaze in Shade's direction.

"Answer him," she said.

To Peter, Friend said in a clipped tone, "Yes. We'll be doing exactly what they wanted—with a little twist that Shade's come up with."

Peter shrugged.

Shade studied Peter for a long moment, fork halfway to her mouth, and then shot a significant look at Bas. He acknowledged it with a slight shake of his head. Neither of them bought Peter's easy capitulation.

"We'll pack and head out tonight if we can get a commercial flight," Shade said. "Friend has a flat in London where we'll be staying. I'll leave the address for you."

Peter nodded. "I could use a little rest, to be honest. And it's very peaceful here. I might need to buy myself a spread like this for my retirement."

Shade wore a disguise as they traveled. Friend found that he was almost relieved her face was hidden again. Every time he looked at her, he was reminded of his own colossal misjudgment. If anyone found out what she'd done, his career was over. But as soon as he'd start brooding or trying to work out how to mitigate his compromised circumstances, she'd sidle up against him with a hip or the softness of a breast to jar him off-balance again.

They were playing a happy couple returning to London from a vacation Down Under, and he found himself repeatedly falling for her little displays of affection: a caress, a swift kiss, an arm around his waist, or her hand stroking his thigh. She was almost kittenish—the kind of kitten that would grow up to be a man-eater, mind you--and it was wearing him down.

When they got to Dubai, their connecting flight had been canceled. They opted to get a hotel and finish the trip the following morning.

While Shade was showering, he pulled out the cell phone she'd returned and dialed the same number as before.

"Odd hours," her sleepy voice said over the line.

"It's pretty much all sixes and sevens, now," he muttered.

"Tell me."

"She's coming in, just not quite the way we'd planned it," he said.

"Still, good news," she said, sounding pleased.

"I'm completely compromised," he said.

"I did warn you," she said. "Still, it may yet work out. And it just might be the best thing for you."

He sighed. "You don't understand, and I don't have time to explain. She's in the shower."

"Why on earth aren't you in there with her?" she asked with a naughty laugh.

"My manhood is feeling a wee bit bruised," he complained. "She outmaneuvered me and I walked right into her set-up like the biggest punter there ever was."

"You'd better buck up then, love. You'll not keep her on board that way," she said. "Does Oxford know yet?"

"No. I'll check in with him once we've arrived at my flat. I don't want to risk her ducking off and leaving me empty-handed."

"Give us a ring when you're there," she said and ended the call.

He put the phone away and collapsed on the bed with his arms over his face.

Shade said, "Did you check in?" Wearing a fluffy white robe, she climbed on top of him. Her hair was dripping water down her back, and her eerie eyes were half-lidded. She straddled him and rocked appealingly.

"Oh, no you don't," he said, sitting up and attempting to remove her by main force. "I'm not falling for this again."

She laughed and wrapped her legs around his waist, clinging like a burr. She shushed him and stroked his face, peppering him with tiny kisses until he subsided.

"I won't ask you any more questions," she said, kissing him ardently on the mouth while her hand slipped between his legs. "I promise. Because I'm too freakin' tired to think."

He growled at her and bit her lip.

Then the robe came off, and somehow his pants were undone, and she was pushing him down for another go. He just laid back and held onto her hips.

He slept through the entire flight to Heathrow. She'd kept him at it all night. She'd even woken him from a sound sleep and started him up again. She was insatiable. He hadn't even made it through a shower without an interruption, although the hot water pounding on his back while he kept her pinned face-first against the tile had been one of the better moments of the past twenty-four hours.

She kept up the kitten routine all the way through the airport, the minicab ride, and into his flat. She fairly purred wandering about the place with a bug detector, admiring this and that, and it occurred to him to say, "You don't even have a home, do you?"

"We never had a home growing up. We moved from place to place constantly with Peter. It was a pain, but the alternative was being left with someone else permanently, and we didn't want that."

He noticed that she hadn't actually answered the question. He followed her into the bedroom where he found her stripping off her clothes.

"I recall you said something about showering in the dark?" she asked.

And they were off again.

When he woke the next morning, she wasn't in the bed. He found her in the kitchen, humming and cooking breakfast, looking completely unlike the woman he'd been with the night before.

She'd gone to market and picked up things while he slept. There was even a stack of Hershey's bars sitting on the countertop. He knew he should be pleased by her thoughtfulness, but it just annoyed him more, really. He didn't know where she got the energy. After watching her consume an unbelievable quantity of food, he had a better idea.

"Is it time for you to make that call?" She eyed him over her coffee cup once they'd finished eating.

"I'd better do, yes," he said. "He doesn't always answer or get back to me right away."

It turned out to be one of those times. He left a message on the voicemail saying, "Shade is with me. Call with instructions at your convenience."

She watched him through the green contact lenses, and he found he almost did prefer them.

"He'll probably check your story," she said.

"Right, and you've been seen entering my flat and walking round the market. He'll know someone is here. Might take a bit of time though," he said.

She wandered around the table and leaned over his shoulder, running her hands down his chest. "What shall we do in the meantime?"

And they were off again.

He was coming back from the market--the woman could *eat*--two days later, when his phone rang. He got into the flat and waved her over before accepting the call.

"She's there with you," he said. "How did you manage this?"

Friend and Shade traded glances, noticing his first statement wasn't a question. He'd clearly used the time to have someone verify Shade's presence. Based on Shade's sly manner, Friend had a suspicion she'd probably caught some poor bugger at it.

"We're shagging. What can I tell you? I'm a charming bloke."

"Where is she now?"

"In the flat. I'm just returning from market." He wasn't really lying.

"You've seen her face."

"She's got those bloody disguises or she keeps the lights off. If I try anything crafty, she'll stick something sharp into me." He grimaced, hoping he was believable. He had the miserable thought that this was something he was going to have to learn to lie about for the rest of his life, however long his life might last with her around. Bloody-sodding-Peter had been right.

Shade smiled and nodded encouragingly.

"Look here, pick a spot, I'll bring her round. You talk to her yourself," Friend said.

"She'll never consent to the assignment without some form of incentive."

"Then what is it you need done? I'll take care of it myself."

"I appreciate your enthusiasm, but that would be impossible."

"I can tell you from what I've seen, she'll turn in your hand if you try to coerce her. Blowing up an island would be just a start. You'll be looking over your shoulder for the rest of your life if you go after Drake or Laurent."

"You seem to be representing her interests. Developed a fancy for her, have you?"

"Don't be ridiculous. In my line of work, I cannot afford to get attached. I'm just giving you the benefit of my professional advice," Friend said.

"I'm comforted to hear that. I'd hate to think myself at risk—our relationship would be brought to an abrupt and unpleasant end if I so much as suspected it. Especially after the fiasco of our last venture. Fortunately for you, I was told by my agents there that you were taken hostage while attempting to recover the information. So, I can't fault any aspect of your performance." In a tone of disbelief, he mused, "Who would have guessed Peter Laurent would opt to release it at no cost? However, I am pleased to discover that you seem to have landed, once more, on your feet. Frankly, I was concerned I might have to take steps."

Friend clenched his jaw.

Shade was staring at the phone with an almost frightening expression.

"You say you can bring her to me. She'd just come meekly along, then?"

"Why not? I tell her I have a discreet client who'd like to give her a piece of work. Tell her I've an established relationship with the client, would she meet with him?"

"And then she refuses the assignment. I believe we've come full circle." He sighed.

"To tell the truth, I think she fancies me. I might could persuade her," Friend added.

"I'll think about the alternatives and get back to you." He rang off.

Shade said, "He has an odious, little voice. Small man, if I'm not mistaken. Pinched, narrow nose. No resonance in his vocalizations at all. Over-educated, or he wants everyone to think so, at least. He's very self-confident in a foolishly arrogant way."

Friend studied her suspiciously. "Yes, small man, narrow nose, over-educated, arrogant. Calls himself Oxford in trade circles."

"He wants me to kill someone. Someone only a woman can get close to," she said.

"It's a good bet."

She walked over to the abandoned grocery bags and peered inside. "What did you bring me for dinner?"

"Shade, you cannot kill this man."

"Who says, Jack?" She carried the groceries off to the kitchen.

"We need him exposed and prosecuted," he said, following her.

"Why?"

"It's what I've been ordered to do."

"Those are your orders, not mine." She began unloading the bags and fussing about in the kitchen.

"If you kill him, and he does know something about your past, you'll never learn what it is."

"Then I'll have to make sure I find out everything he knows before I kill him," she said in a pragmatic tone. "As you may recall, I'm very good at getting men to talk. And I have a variety of methods to suit the circumstances."

He abandoned the topic and crossed his arms over his chest. "I saw Bas when I was walking home," he said.

"If you saw him, he wanted you to see him. Did he say anything?" She hopped up onto the counter and pulled Friend between her legs.

"No, just stepped out, let me see him, and stepped away." He discovered that his hands were sliding up her thighs.

"He's been here all along." She plucked at the collar of his shirt.

"I guessed as much."

"I imagine Peter's lurking somewhere around here too, the worrywart." She began smoothing the frown lines on his forehead.

"I thought you wanted them to stay somewhere safe?"

She sighed. "Yes, but in my experience, the closer they are to me, the safer they are."

She slid down off the counter against him, the friction setting his blood flowing again. She was unzipping his pants before his mouth closed on hers.

Afterwards, he helped her tidy up the kitchen and cook their supper. "We're getting progressively more violent," he grumbled. "I'm not sure the cabinets will be able to take much more of that."

"You're frustrated with me," she said. "But it'll all work out, you'll see."

"It's like my head's packed with wool lately." He sounded petulant even to himself.

"I understand," she said. "But if it makes you feel any better, you're posing quite a distraction for me too, and normally I don't allow that."

He knew she was up to something. She was deliberately keeping him distracted. Every time he started to have a clear thought, she'd do something to divert him. And the most unnerving thing was he found he really didn't care. He was like an addict who'd do anything for his next fix. Just looking at her was like the slow drip of an exquisite chemical cocktail.

Sautéing vegetables in a skillet, she said, "I have a few more questions."

"What, no pinning me on the bed and grilling me while I'm helpless in ecstasy?"

"Kind of like you did to Natalya Nemrovsky?" With a wicked smile, she added, "Besides, you won't be ready again for a few more minutes."

"You're bloody evil, you are."

"Yes. Where did this man come from?" she asked. "What's his history?"

He sighed, resigned. "If we're right, he started in MI6, back when it was MI6. He worked his way up foreign intelligence. There was a stink about him looking the other way on illegal foreign activities, white slavery, drugs, guns, that sort of thing. Allegations were made, followed by a cover-up, and he did a runner and disappeared for a while. Came back squeaky clean and moved immediately into intelligence work again. As I've told you, every time someone has gotten close to pinning anything on him, he's managed to dodge it. All the shady deals are done using the Oxford identity, and no one's seen him to prove it's the same man. All my communications with him are by phone. I'm not the first to attempt to expose him, but I'm the most deeply buried. He's had me do little things for him, but so far nothing significant enough to bring him down."

"White slavery, you said."

"Right. In the Middle East. Gun sales were there as well. During that era, everyone was mucking about in the Middle East."

"What's his ethnicity, the person you suspect?" Shade asked.

"He's English, but of Indian derivation—that's India proper to you, Yank."

"So, he's got darker skin?"

"Yes, black hair, dark eyes, brown skin, a little man, as I said."

"He dresses well—custom-made suits from Savile Row--that kind of clothing?"

"Yes, Zyllah. What do you know?"

"Lots of things, Bastien. Like…this has to cook for a few minutes, and you should be reloaded now, so…"

They went spiraling out to the living room and ended up tangled on the sofa.

When Shade was finally asleep for the night, Friend dragged himself out of the flat to ring his contact. If this kept up, Shade would be the death of him. He made it as far as the bottom step of the walkup and then just sat down. Good enough. The street was deserted, and he had a clear line-of-sight in every direction.

After the briefing, his contact said, "My god. This might work. He's so obsessed with her that he just might consent to meet in person."

Friend said, "Right, and her reputation is ironclad. He'll have no reason not to speak freely with her."

"We'll have a positive ID, and once he tells her what the job is, we'll have him."

"Not if she kills him first," Friend pointed out.

"You can't restrain her?"

"Not a bloody bit. She's like a force of nature. By the look on her face, she plans to kill him."

"He might talk her out of it if he does have the information she wants," she said.

"How could he know anything about who she is? You said she was stolen as a child."

"And then again, it's possible he's lying," she tempered.

"I'm not sure using her in this operation is a top plan. She's a bloody wild card." He sighed. "I'm reluctant to admit it, but I can't stop worrying she might not be entirely balanced."

"I think you've misjudged her, love. There's nothing the matter with her, she just doesn't have the same mores as the rest of us. She's a realist—she sees a problem, and she solves it in the quickest and most final way possible. And her solution isn't completely untenable. She doesn't work for us, after all, so there's no blame to us if he meets a sticky end."

"Then you're telling me to just let her go about it as she will."

"Let's see, shall we? Ring me when he commits."

When he crawled back into the bed, Shade said, "Well, what's the news?"

"Green light, go," he muttered, exhausted.

"Which contact were you speaking with?" she asked.

"The one you don't need to know about. Apparently, there's not much concern about discarding my original orders."

"And what were your original orders?"

"To seduce you and win you over to our side."

"Well, oops. That mostly worked out."

"I had a few challenges, didn't I? I thought the whole thing was scrapped when I saw you and Bas dancing at that party."

She made a sleepy, noncommittal noise.

He kept quiet, holding his breath. He let it go. "It wasn't supposed to work out this way. I was only ever intended to talk you into acting as a spy. Find out where he was, confirm his identity, and steal, or catch him at, something compromising that he can't wriggle out of."

"That would have taken a lot longer. Meanwhile, my family is at risk and you're stuck in an assignment that's making you miserable. My way is much faster. And it's final."

He pressed his lips together, hearing a déjà vu from his phone conversation.

She snuggled against him, fitting their curves and angles together, and twined her leg through his.

"I'm done in. I don't think I can possibly get it up." He kissed her hair and tightened his arms around her.

"Good, because you've finally worn me out." She yawned.

"Amen."

She let him sleep through the night, but his cell phone rang at an inconvenient moment early the following morning. Shade reached across his prone form beneath her to the nightstand and grabbed it. His hands roamed her body while she turned it on and handed it to him. She leaned down over him to listen in on the call, and her full breasts pressed against him. Her hair cascaded around both of their faces and he breathed in the intoxicating scent.

Trying not to sound winded, Friend said, "Yes?"

Oxford's voice said, "Ask her to stop by the lobby desk of Herridge Hotel. There will be an envelope there for her." He rang off.

Shade was a little breathless herself. "He's just trying to get me out in the open."

"Will you go?" Friend asked.

She sat up and tossed her hair over her shoulder. "Of course. But I'll need a ride."

"I've got your ride, right here."

Shade walked into the hotel wearing the little black wig, sunglasses, the leather jacket turned to its beige silk side, jeans, and a pair of boots. It was an older hotel, but immaculately maintained, and decorated with beautiful antiques in a rose and gold theme. A bustle of hotel staff whisked around the small lobby, wheeling luggage trolleys across waxed parquet floors that radiated a faint lemony smell. The guests she observed all appeared relaxed and content.

Bas was seated in a rose brocade armchair in a sunny open lounge area adjacent to the lobby. He was reading a newspaper and wearing a disguise that had turned him into a heavyset, older gentleman with a beard. Steam rose from a china teacup and saucer on the small table beside him. An actual elderly man and his wife were seated nearby, sharing a newspaper and a pot of tea, and two businessmen were talking on cell phones in different corners of the room. No one showed the slightest interest in Shade, and her eyes found nothing that held her attention. She and Bas shared a look, and he gave her an all-clear. She felt a little pang of separation. She wondered how Curtis was doing. He was probably happy to have his house to himself again.

She retrieved the envelope from the clerk at the front desk and went back outside. Friend was waiting in his car on the cobblestone turnabout.

Once she'd climbed in, he said "That's it?"

"That's it."

As they drove away, she opened the envelope and pulled out a photograph of a young girl. It appeared to be a professional school photo. The girl seemed to be around seven years of age, and had blond braids, wide blue eyes, and a sweet little button nose. Her mouth was a pink rosebud.

"Is that you?" Friend asked.

"No, I don't think so," she said in a thoughtful tone. She didn't notice Friend's dismayed expression when he realized she had no idea what she'd looked like as a child.

She flipped the photo over and found a post-it note that read:

If you would like more information, we should speak. Arrangements will come through the previous channel.

"She looks…familiar." Shade stared at the photograph.

Friend took another look. "She looks a bit like you but—no. Did you have a sister?"

Shade blinked. "I need to make a call. Give me your word you won't repeat what you hear. It's personal and totally irrelevant."

He sighed wearily. "Fine, you have it."

She dialed Peter's number and waited. Cocooning herself in her jacket, she lowered the car window and leaned into the fresh air.

"What's up sweetheart?"

"The other girls—the ones who were recovered—you said they were sent home to their families."

There was silence on the line as Peter puzzled out her words. "You mean the compound. Yes, they were all sent home. All the live ones, Zyllah. Quite a few people were killed in the explosion. Don't you remember?"

"I remember this girl," she mused aloud.

"What are you talking about? What brought this up?"

"He gave me a school photo of a young girl who resembles me. But she looks about seven."

"Too old to be you," Peter confirmed. "He must think it's you. Let him keep thinking it."

"Missy," Shade said in sad voice. "Her name was Missy." She put her hand over her mouth.

Friend glanced over, worried.

"Thanks, dad. I'll call you when I have more. Tell Bas."

After she'd turned off the phone, Friend asked, "You all right then?"

She leaned back against the headrest and closed her eyes. "Yes. He's given me a photo of a dead girl named Missy who was also kidnapped and held at the same location with me. He must know she wasn't returned to her parents and is assuming I'm her. He thinks he'll use information about this girl to bribe me into doing whatever this job is. We'll let him go on thinking that. It'll play perfectly." Then she said, "I wonder if her parents know what happened to her?"

"Do yours?" he asked.

"Mine are dead. They were killed when I was taken." She looked at the photo again and then put it back inside the envelope. Squaring it on her lap, she placed both hands on top of it.

"I'm sorry," he said. "I didn't know."

She nodded absentmindedly and made a show of rallying. "Your handler doesn't know everything, apparently."

"I don't have a handler," he said. "Not per se, anyway."

"Sure doesn't seem that way," she said.

"Oh, and what's Peter, then?"

"A pain in the ass, mostly." She smiled fondly. "But he doesn't give assignments, he just passes options along. I decide what I want to do. That doesn't seem to be the case with you."

"Maybe I'll jump ship and come work with you lot," he said.

She chose not to comment.

Shade practically pounced on Friend's phone and flung at it him when it rang the following morning. She'd been pacing the flat like a caged tiger all morning, making the place seem a lot smaller. He could almost see the wheels spinning in her head, but she wasn't sharing.

"Mr. Friend," Oxford greeted him. "How is the young lady today?"

"She's quite interested in hearing more about the photo and would like to meet," Friend said, as Shade and he had discussed.

"Copy down this address. We'll wait until dark for the comfort of all parties. Shall we say ten sharp?

"We'll be there." He disconnected the call and grabbed his car keys off the coffee table. "Right. We'll want to check out this location first."

She gave him an odd look but said only, "It's so nice not having to explain these things." As they were walking out the door, she said, "Don't forget you're supposed to call in now, secret agent man."

Chapter 22

Friend arrived at the construction site promptly at ten. Shade had left the flat hours earlier. As he'd showered and dressed, he'd felt repeated jolts from the sight of the empty shelf in the shower, the open space in the wardrobe, and then the empty drawer. She'd apparently loaded everything out without saying a word to him. It was clear that the idyll was at an end.

According to the signage they'd read earlier, the location Oxford had picked was a new office-park. Concrete jersey barriers and a chain-link fence surrounded the perimeter to protect pedestrian traffic and discourage trespassers. Piles of boards and metal beams were stacked neatly around the site. Areas of excavation stood out as inky blots on the ground. Mounds of dirt, rock, and broken concrete made a haphazard mountain range at the rear of the lot, inhabited by the looming shapes of cranes, dump trucks, and other construction equipment that had been abandoned where it'd stopped earlier in the day. As he walked in, the bare bones of the structure loomed over him like a metal skeleton against the night sky. Scaffolding spider-webbed the framework giving the workers access to the upper levels, and rough floors had been nailed over some areas. More noticeable in the darkness, he heard torn plastic sheeting making a rustling noise in the breeze.

The only light came from well-spaced streetlights and a few glowing windows in the office buildings that lined the street. He couldn't see a moon in the sky, and the starlight was eclipsed by the glow from London's city lights and the fog hanging in the air.

Since he was expected, Friend made no attempt to conceal his arrival. In an open area, he saw a table and three chairs had been set up. A white cloth covered the table, and a single candle burned in the center. Steeling himself for more theatrics, he sat down in one of the chairs and waited.

A few minutes later, a small man wearing a dove-gray business suit, dark tie, and a bowler hat stepped from behind the forest of girders on his left side and approached the table. He had a neatly-groomed, full, dark beard covering heavy jowls. His nose was long, narrow, and flattened downward at the tip. He had rather fleshy lips. Under the impeccable tailoring of his suit, he hid a portly midsection. Friend saw the flash of a gold watch beneath white cuffs that bore gold cufflinks. He was flanked by a gorilla wearing a dark suit.

Just outside the circle of light created by the candle-flame, the small man stopped and in Oxford's voice asked, "Will she not be joining us after all?"

Friend answered, "Just because you can't see her, doesn't mean she isn't here."

Oxford nodded and stood in place, rocking on his heels. His hands were in his trouser pockets.

Shade was standing a few feet away on Friend's right. He hadn't seen where she'd come from. Unmoving, she stood wearing her black outfit, the dark wig, and a pair of sunglasses. Friend wondered how she could see anything at all. She'd also done something deceptive to her features.

"Ah!" Oxford called out. "Here she is now."

Shade looked pointedly at the table, so Friend snuffed the candle.

The gorilla pulled out a chair for Oxford. He sat down primly and crossed his legs, folding his hands on his knee. Shade pulled out her own chair, and Friend noticed that she deliberately set it further back from the table than his own. She sat gracefully and appeared perfectly at ease, but she was sitting at the very edge of her seat, all her weight resting on the balls of her feet. Her hands were placed on the outsides of her thighs to allow clearance for the retracted blades. She was poised to spring, and Friend hoped Oxford didn't make any sudden movements; he needed this assignment concluded successfully.

"Good evening," Oxford said. "I appreciate the courtesy you've extended by agreeing to meet with me. I understand that you do not routinely conduct business in-person." In the dim light, he peered intently at Shade as he spoke. His avarice was almost tangible.

"You claim to have information that may interest me."

"Yes, and I am willing to trade this information in exchange for your professional services."

"I'm listening," Shade said.

"Mr. Friend, if you would be so kind as to step away from the table until we complete our transaction?" Oxford said.

Shade's only reaction was to turn her sunglasses towards Friend. Shrugging, he walked to a distance that was theoretically out of earshot, but wasn't.

Oxford leaned towards Shade over the table, his hands grasping at the edges, and said in a low tone, "I admit I am rather disappointed. I came here prepared to face you, but I see you have chosen to conceal your features from me."

Shade said, "It wasn't discussed and isn't a stipulation I'll ever comply with. I can certainly leave—"

"No, no," he interjected. "Well, on to business then." He leaned back, seemingly at ease, but his hands were clenched so tightly in his lap that the knuckles stood out white. "I have a particular target in mind who has presented me with considerable difficulty over the years--one woman. The undertaking will require a great deal of finesse on the part of the specialist. Their actions must be completely clandestine--there can be no trace of foul play. Since these qualities are your trademark..." He shrugged.

"It's a woman?" Shade asked. "Then I don't understand. Jack could more easily attach himself to a female target."

"The problem is one of location, I'm afraid. Due to this person's varied routine, it is necessary for her *accident* to occur in a location that is not accessible to men. And it absolutely must appear to be an accident."

"Statistically speaking, seventy percent of accidents occur within a ten mile radius of the home. Within the home, one third of all accidents occur in the bathroom, and women are injured there seventy-two percent more often than men. I wonder if you should rethink your plan."

Oxford smiled. "You do know your trade. However, it must not occur in or near the target's home."

"Is there a family? You're concerned about witnesses?"

"That is not the concern, no. But the condition is not negotiable."

"You said it was a location only accessible to women," Shade prompted.

"The target observes no predictable pattern in her day. Her work hours are irregular and her place of employment nearly impenetrable. The only regular habit that my subordinates have been able to confirm is a weekly spa appointment. Membership is exclusively female. I believe you can see the possibilities there."

"Of course," said Shade.

Oxford reached inside his jacket, and Shade tensed. He froze. "I have an envelope with the particulars, if you would allow me...?"

She nodded.

Oxford placed one manila envelope on the table and slid it towards her. In his other hand, he held a second envelope. "Inside, you will find a photograph of the subject, pertinent details, and the address of the location where I would like the accident to occur. "This envelope," he held up the one in his hand, "contains information relevant to you personally."

"And I don't get it until the job is completed?"

Oxford smiled.

"How do I know there's anything in there of use? And how did you come by the photograph I've already been given?"

"Some years ago, I was employed as a courier for a particular foreign dignitary. My diplomatic status made frequent trips to the Middle East unremarkable, and I was able to transfer--ah--various items with ease. Once a potential customer had specified his preferences, it was customary to provide photographs of the available options for the customer's review. The chosen merchandise would then be obtained and transport arranged. Thus, there was no lengthy storage burden upon the seller. I brokered numerous transactions for him and his associates, and the photograph came into my possession in that way, as did the background information that I am willing to trade to you. I believe you will find the subject research quite thorough."

"And of course there's more you're holding back to entice me to donate my services again."

Oxford pursed his lips and gestured vaguely. "It was so long ago. Sometimes things do turn up in storage, or misplaced somewhere. Who can say?"

Shade leaned over the table with her head cocked to one side. She showed her teeth as she said, "Customer preferences, merchandise, and storage burdens. They were children. Kidnapped children and young women sold for horrible purposes. She died, did you know?"

Oxford was fingering his gold watch, wearing a wary expression, but he was still transfixed by Shade.

"That little girl died—her name was Missy. She had arrived just two days prior. And do you remember Susan? She was a very kind teenager who looked after all of the littler children who were shipped in and back out again. She died in the middle of the night from what you did to her, and there was nothing I could do to help her. And you sit here in front of me and think that I'm going to make a deal with a creature like you?"

Friend heard the hiss of the blades and Shade exploded out of her chair, sending the table flying. She buried one blade in Oxford's thigh, skewering him to the chair, and pressed the edge of the second blade to his throat, choking off his scream.

His bodyguard only then registered her movement and began to draw his weapon. Friend was taking aim when he heard a soft wet noise, and the bodyguard sagged to the ground, clutching at the knife protruding from his throat. Friend caught a glimpse of Bas' pale hair as he faded behind a girder. Friend strode forward, snatched the envelopes off the ground, and shoved them inside his jacket. Standing behind Shade, he kept his gun at the ready, his eyes scanning the area.

Oxford was whimpering and begging, "Please, please!"

Shade pulled the blade out, and he shrieked and clutched his leg with both hands.

"I wasn't sure it was you at first," she purred in his face. "You're older and fatter, and then there's the beard. But you're still the same pretentious little fop." She held the bloody-edged blade up to his face and slowly drew a red line down his cheek. "There's a special place in hell reserved for those who harm the innocent and defenseless, and you're going there momentarily." She flicked off her sunglasses with the tip of the blade and leaned in eye-to-eye. "Do you remember me now?"

"You!" he gasped.

"You," she hissed back. "You left me there."

The terror was apparent on Oxford's face. His mouth worked, but no sound came out. Finally he breathed, "It can't be you. You were killed by his guards."

"No," she said with a feral smile. "But the guards died. Peter Laurent shot them, right before he carried me out of there." She was maliciously using one blade to nick and slice tiny precise cuts on his face.

Oxford didn't seem to be registering the pain. "But then… You don't know. And here you are in London with no idea..." His expression altered from shock to rapid calculation.

Shade leaned on the blade still at his throat, and a rivulet of blood trickled down his neck, staining his white collar. "Why don't you enlighten me?" She held the point of the other blade poised over his eye for a fatal thrust.

They all heard a gunshot, and a bullet clipped Shade's left shoulder, knocking her into Friend's arms. They heard a distant cry, and no second bullet followed.

Oxford kicked the chair backwards, and clutching his leg, bolted towards the unfinished building. A high-powered rifle shot rang out from high above them, knocking Oxford into a spin. He staggered, regained his balance, and pelted awkwardly towards the building again. The bullet had only winged him, sending up a puff of dust as it hit the ground.

"The watch was a duress alarm," Shade spat. She struggled free and propelled herself forward, running flat out. Friend saw dark shapes moving at the edges of the construction site and heard more shots as two opposing forces targeted one another. He raced after Shade.

She was already far ahead of him and moving like a machine, weaving through the building supports hunting Oxford. Shots impacted against the girders and ricocheted off of them. The metal pinging noise seemed to be coming from all around him.

A blond shadow materialized out of the mist near Shade's slowing form and the two joined up and moved out together, slowly stalking. Friend wove towards them as other shapes appeared and contested with one another. It was impossible to tell the two sides apart in the darkness. He nearly stumbled over a body and then saw another; Bas had been busy while Shade was talking to Oxford.

An armed man edged past a girder in front of him. Lashing out with a kick, he took out the man's knee, knocked the gun out of his hand as he fell forward, caught him in a headlock and snapped his neck. Dropping him, he ran after Shade and Bas.

They had reached the rear of the construction site before Friend caught up with them. Shade was crouched behind a pile of girders, miming directional signals to Bas. Bas circled left around the dirt pile next to him and disappeared. She locked eyes with Friend and pointed to the ground at her feet, telling him to occupy her position. In a crouching run, she took off to the right. Friend knew they were corralling Oxford.

He peeked over the pile of metal beams for a quick look at the landscape. Bas stepped silently out from behind a backhoe and almost negligently broke a man's neck before fading away again. Friend saw a flash of silver, and a dagger flew from Bas' location to impale another creeping man. In the direction Shade had gone, another man was down. Friend had neither seen nor heard her.

He heard a scuffing noise behind him and threw himself to the ground, rolled onto his back, and fired one round into the man training his gun on Friend. He put two more into the man who emerged behind him. He hoped he'd shot the correct side. He vaulted over the end of the girder pile and crept forward in a straight line until he reached a pile of rubble and began easing around it.

He heard the crack of the rifle again, and saw a small shape bolt out from behind a truck. Oxford was running with a limp and a hand clutched to a bleeding shoulder, weaving around obstacles. Shade streaked out from a location behind him, rapidly gaining on the fleeing man. She was a blurred shadow except for the pale skin of her face. Ahead, in Oxford's path, Bas stood up behind a pallet stacked with bags of concrete. Leveraging himself with one arm, he leaped over them as lightly as a cat. His legs moved like pistons as he ran to intercept Oxford. The little man veered, and might have ducked away, but Bas stopped on a dime and reached out with one hand, yanking Oxford back by his collar and tossing him forcefully to the ground. He skidded several feet, sending up a plume of dust. Shade would be upon him in a few more strides. Keeping his gun trained on Oxford, Bas was smiling as he stalked towards the stunned man.

Friend saw movement behind Bas and opened fire. As fire was returned, Shade and Bas both dropped where they were and dove for cover. Bas emptied one clip, ejected it, and loaded another without breaking his rhythm. Friend made for Shade's position. A man had climbed over the pile of girders shielding Shade, and she rose up, grabbed the front of his shirt, and flung him over her head to the ground behind her. When the man jumped to his feet she was already on him, both blades singing out in a flashing blur. She snarled at him as she ran him through and then searched for Oxford again, wearing a desperate expression.

In the confusion and the dark, the small man had vanished again.

By the time Friend reached her location, Shade was moving again in the direction Oxford had been headed, tenaciously refusing to give up pursuit. Bas vaulted over the pallet again and joined up with her. They didn't get far before incoming fire forced them to duck behind another pile of rock. Shade continued trying to creep around the side.

A barrage of supporting fire from the wings drove the incoming group back, but it was too late. They heard the sound of a helicopter from the adjacent lot and saw the lights as the chopper lifted. It was clear to all of them that there was no conflict left on the grounds; all of Oxford's support had either retreated or been taken into custody.

As Friend walked towards them, Shade hurried to Bas and checked him for injuries. She appeared to be favoring one leg again. Peter loped into the area carrying the rifle. Jack watched as, one by one, their support force appeared from concealed locations and began checking for any further gunmen.

"Let me see those," Shade demanded when Friend reached her.

In all the confusion, he'd forgotten he still had the envelopes inside his jacket. He pulled them out and handed them to her. Opening the first one, she pulled out a glossy photograph.

Reaching into her jacket, she produced a small penlight and clicked it on.

Looking over Shade's shoulder with Bas, Peter exclaimed, "Ann!"

Shade looked up at Peter, and then all three of them looked at Friend.

Peter said to Friend, "Damn, she lied to me. She's running you."

Shade handed the photo to Friend and then slid a sheet of paper out of the envelope. "Here's your incriminating evidence," she said in a bitter tone. "I don't imagine your boss will be too happy when she finds out she was his target. You might want to tell her to stay away from that spa for a while. And to move whatever she has in her house."

"Right, I'd almost forgotten. He didn't want a crime scene investigation mucking up his access to her house, you think? That's why she was to be killed elsewhere."

Another man approached them, and Shade revolved in place. The man's eyes lingered on her back before he said to Friend, "I'm to inform you we have a recording. We'd a directional microphone going from the moment we arrived. He won't get out of this one lightly."

"I expect he'll be running for a while, really. Only he'll know what's in store for him if she catches him up." Friend jerked his head towards Shade. He gave the man a nod of dismissal.

Bas was gripping Shade's shoulders from behind as she shuffled through the contents of the second envelope.

In a voice that grew increasingly irate, she said, "School transcripts, medical records, family ancestry…but no names. They've all been carefully redacted. Damn him. Her parents have a right to know what happened to her."

Peter said, "That might be enough to track them down, sweetheart. We can have Curtis work on it."

Gripping the pages, she said, "That man knows. That's why he was so interested in what I look like. Not to compare it to a photograph of a six-year-old, but because he knows what her parents look like. Just like he knows who my parents were." Her voice cracked, and she bowed her head against Bas' chest. He wrapped his arms around her, wearing a dark look.

Chapter 23

Curtis was slumped in an armchair watching his three subdued houseguests. A news broadcast was blaring on the television. Peter kept flipping through the news channels to hear the latest political resignations. Peter had called to let him know that the three of them would be staying with him for a day or two since Al Brandon had passed word that they no longer had to lay low—or at least not any more so than they usually did. Peter had given Curtis a rundown on recent events, but once they'd arrived none of them had been very talkative.

The newspapers had been filled with various step-downs and retirements, including Congressman Richard Harrison. They all gave plausible excuses for their actions, citing ill-health, family issues, or other carefully contrived cover stories.

Commenting on a newspaper article about the murder of a high-ranking member of the French intelligence service, Peter said, "Jacques was right about that guy. Had me fooled. I thought he was one of the good ones."

Sitting on the couch beside Shade, Bas was leaning over the coffee table typing on his laptop. "They were warned."

Shade was nestled into the couch cushions under a blanket. "And look at that, the world goes on turning."

Crawling out from under the blanket, Shade went into the kitchen to start dinner. Peter seemed out-of-sorts and lost in his own thoughts, Shade listless and gloomy, and Bas restless with unspent energy, but Curtis had missed them and wasn't looking forward to their departures. Peter was still engrossed in the newspaper, so when Bas finally took his agitation out of the house, Curtis went in to help Shade.

Curtis was setting the table when Bas finally let himself in through the kitchen door. He was wearing a pair of shorts and had his shirt thrown over one shoulder. Slick with sweat and still breathing hard, he looked like an anatomical study in human musculature. He went straight to the refrigerator and dug for a bottle of water.

"Logging a few hours power-lifting?" Shade asked in a snarky tone. She was standing in front of the stove tasting a simmering sauce.

"Nah, went for a jog." Bas winked at Curtis.

Shade flashed him a surprised look. "How many cars wrecked while you were out there?"

Bas mopped a grin off his sweaty face with the shirt. "None, but there was one woman who drove up onto the sidewalk and followed me for a while."

Shade narrowed her eyes. "Was her name Judy?"

"No, but she did look a lot like Judy's coworker...Patrice, I think it was?"

Shade had opened her mouth to retort when Peter said from the doorway, "Good lord--go get a shower. I should not have to look at all those muscles at my advanced age."

Curtis shot Peter a dirty look. "They were just getting started."

Peter said, "I have been listening to this shit since they were eight years old. It lost its novelty a long time ago."

"Spoilsport." Curtis felt strangely content.

After dinner, Curtis tailed Shade into the kitchen with the dirty plates. She was loading the dishwasher, so Curtis started scrubbing the pans that had been soaking in the sink. "I don't know if you care about this anymore, since it sounds like you're all on pretty good terms with him, but I had those two things about Jack Friend on my to-do list. Since I had some downtime while you all were in London, I followed up."

She paused for a moment, trying to remember. "Sure, why not?"

Curtis grinned. "Well, I got nothing from the piece of paper with all the numbers. I ran them through every cryptography and ciphering program I could think of and got nowhere. It might be just his personal code."

Shade made a thoughtful sound.

"The phone number though..." Curtis shook his head.

"What?" she asked.

"It's a message for you."

"What do you mean?"

"I mean when you call that number, he's got a pre-recorded message for you."

She shut the dishwasher door, and her face broke into a startled smile.

"He called me right back after I dialed it. Thank god I used a throwaway phone." He smacked a wet hand over his face. "I'm spending too much time with you people---the paranoia is contagious. It's really starting to freak me out."

She was drying the last of the pans, lost in thought. "Clever," she said. "He planted that there knowing I'd find it. What a little shit. What does the message say?" She offered Curtis the damp towel.

"Oh, uh, just to call that number if you ever need to speak to him."

"What is it, Curtis?"

He blushed. "It's kind of a sleezy message. You should probably hear it for yourself."

She lifted an eyebrow. "I can imagine. What the hell? I could use a good laugh. Go get me a phone." She made a shooing motion and put the last pan away.

Curtis shrugged and hustled out of the kitchen.

"What's funny?" Peter asked, passing him in the doorway.

"Our friend, Mr. Friend." She herded Peter out of the kitchen and back to the living room.

"I forgot to tell you," Peter said. "I called Ann earlier and had a few words with her about him." He frowned. "I chewed her out about that stunt she pulled, but she's still insisting he's a free operative. She said she uses him from time to time for 'discreet services'—her words—but that the rest of his reputation is genuine. He went out on his own a while back, according to her."

"No, you don't," Shade said, noticing the acquisitive gleam in Peter's eye. "Don't you dare try to pull him in with us. Besides, I'm still not inclined to trust that woman. That was very sneaky, what she did. Her whole monologue was aimed at me— to generate my interest. It was a set-up that he was supposed to capitalize on with his little seduction. And I still don't believe we got the whole story out of her—or him."

Bas was draped across the couch with one arm thrown over the back. "Who?" he asked.

Curtis trotted in, cell phone in hand. "Jack Friend."

Bas sat up and leveled an annoyed look at Shade. "I thought we had wrapped that up?"

Shade shrugged and in an enigmatic cadence, said, "Oh, the rogue, the red, red rogue, he cooked good omelets and stews."

Bas blinked and settled back down on the couch, trying to hide a smile. "If it's any consolation, her plan short-circuited."

Peter and Shade looked at him, puzzled.

"I think he got a load of you at that party and lost his nerve. All that delay when he was casing us, and the fact he didn't try to contact Peter or us again after the initial attempt went wrong? It was because he was spooked. He wanted you bad. So, he kept playing the asshole with all that egotistical crap to keep himself in line. And then you beat him at his own game."

Shade said, "If that's true, Ann threw both of us under the bus. She engineered it so even if he failed to launch, I would. And I think he figured out she'd done it—that would explain why he was so annoyed the first time we talked to him in Fethiye. Based on his wording, I wonder if *she* was the real puppet-master all along. Also, remember that message when Curtis tried to hack SIS? Dad, you'd already put in the call to her."

"I'll be damned," Peter said.

Shade said, "That woman is some piece of work."

"She made one mistake, sweetheart. She underestimated you," Peter said.

Shade scowled. "Oxford got away."

"And all the agents she sent couldn't stop him. Friend couldn't even get near him."

Bas said, "And now Friend's addicted. And we're stuck with him."

Peter relaxed into an armchair. "I thought after he knocked the snot out of you, you decided you liked the guy?"

Curtis gasped. "Someone beat you?"

A flicker of guilt flashed across Bas' face. "He turned out to be useful. But I didn't figure he'd hang around."

Grinning, Shade pounced onto the sofa and grabbed the front of his shirt. "You *let* him win?"

"Why the hell would he do that?" Peter asked her.

Glaring, Bas struggled out of Shade's grasp. "To make a point."

"What point?" Peter asked.

Bas heaved a sigh. "It seemed like a good idea at the time, to reassure you about Shade."

Shade put a hand over her mouth to hide her smile.

Peter did the mental arithmetic. "You've been winning against your sister all these years by cheating, he beat you, Shade beat him …"

"Two pieces of that statement are still true," Bas muttered.

"Bas cheats?" Curtis looked at Shade for corroboration.

She wiggled her eyebrows, and Curtis high-fived her.

"That's just about enough," Bas grumbled.

Peter said, "That's it. Get him on the phone. Everyone is going back to Australia. I'm locking the three of you in Smith's sheep-shearing pen until there's only one person left standing."

"I miss all the best parts," Curtis said, dejected.

"Back to the original point," Bas said. "Are you seriously considering sending work his way?"

"Seems to me you two have been pretty independent lately. And I have a business to run here. At least he knows how to take orders and keep his mouth shut."

Bas laughed outright. "Oh sure, weren't his exact words to Shade, 'I'll answer any question put to me?'"

Shade examined her nails, preening.

"You seriously compromised his professional credibility with that move, sweetheart."

"He's not a big enough fool to tell anyone," she said. "And he knows if he whispers one word about me, I'll leak that promise to everyone I know. No one would ever trust him again."

"Heartless," Peter repeated.

Shade took the cell phone from Curtis and punched the speakerphone button. "Here you go," she said to Peter. "This is what you'll be dealing with."

Friend's cocksure voice boomed out of the speaker. "I've a piece of work I think you'll be interested in and for which you'll be handsomely remunerated. To sweeten the pot, I'll mention that when they raided Oxford's residence they turned up a bit of useful information. As a result, I've a pretty good idea where he's kited off to—and it ties in nicely with this job. Since you have unfinished business with him, let's chat, shall we love?" He was laughing when the message ended.

"He changed it," Curtis said. "It was a lot worse, before."

"I take back the 'heartless' comment," Peter said.

Bas closed his eyes and shook his head.

At the beep, Shade said, "I do love mixing business and pleasure.